SHE HAD MET THE ENEMY . . .

Cordelia turned her face from the muck. Pain exploded through her head in radiating lines. She forced her eyes to focus on the nearest object, about half a metre to the right of her head.

Heavy black boots, sunk in the mud and topped by camouflage trousers, encased legs spread apart in a patient parade rest. Very gently, she laid her head back in the black ooze and rolled cautiously onto her side for a better view of the Barrayaran officer.

Her stunner! She stared into the little grey rectangle of its business end, held steadily in a broad and heavy hand. The officer was stocky and powerful. Untidy dark hair touched with grey, cold intent grey eyes – in fact, his whole appearance was untidy by the strict Barrayaran military standards. His fatigues were almost as muddy and stained as her own, and he had a raw contusion across his right cheekbone. *Looks like he's had a rotten day too . . .*

Shards of Honour

Lois McMaster Bujold

HEADLINE

First published in Great Britain in 1988
by HEADLINE BOOK PUBLISHING PLC

ISBN 0 7472 3125 7

Printed and bound in Great Britain by
Collins, Glasgow

HEADLINE BOOK PUBLISHING PLC
Headline House
79 Great Titchfield Street
London W1P 7FN

To Pat Wrede
for being a voice in the wilderness

▶ ▶ CHAPTER ONE

A sea of mist drifted through the cloud forest, soft, grey, luminescent. On the high ridges the fog showed brighter as the morning sun began to warm and lift the moisture, although in the ravine a cool, soundless dimness still counterfeited a pre-dawn twilight.

Commander Cordelia Naismith glanced at her team botanist and adjusted the straps of her biological collecting equipment a bit more comfortably before continuing her breathless climb. She pushed a long tendril of fog-dampened copper hair out of her eyes, clawing it impatiently toward the clasp at the nape of her neck. Their next survey area would definitely be at a lower altitude. The gravity of this planet was slightly lower than their home world of Beta Colony, but it did not quite make up for the physiological strain imposed by the thin mountain air.

Denser vegetation marked the upper boundary of the forest patch. Following the splashy path of the ravine's brook, they bent and scrambled through the living tunnel, then broke into the open air.

1

A morning breeze was ribboning away the last of the fog on the golden uplands. They stretched endlessly, rise after rise, culminating at last in the great grey shoulders of a central peak crowned by glittering ice. This world's sun shone in the deep turquoise sky giving an overwhelming richness to the golden grasses, tiny flowers, tussocks of a silvery plant like powdered lace dotted everywhere. The two explorers gazed entranced at the mountain above, enveloped by the silence.

The botanist, Ensign Dubauer, grinned over his shoulder at Cordelia and fell to his knees beside one of the silvery tussocks. She strolled to the nearest rise for a look at the panorama behind them. The patchy forest grew denser down the gentle slopes. Five hundred meters below, banks of clouds stretched like a white sea to the horizon. Far to the west, their mountain's smaller sister just broke through the updraft-curdled tops.

Cordelia was just wishing herself on the plains below, to see the novelty of water falling from the sky, when she was jarred from her reverie. "Now what the devil can Rosemont be burning to make a stink like that?" she murmured.

An oily black column of smoke was rising beyond the next spur of the mountain slope, to be smudged, thinned, and dissipated by the upper breezes. It certainly appeared to be coming from the location of their base camp. She studied it intently.

A distant whining, rising to a howl, pierced the silence. Their planetary shuttle burst from behind the ridge and boomed across the sky above them, leaving a sparkling trail of ionized gases.

"What a takeoff!" cried Dubauer, his attention wrenched skyward.

Cordelia keyed her short-range wrist communicator and spoke into it. "Naismith to Base One. Come in, please."

A small, empty hiss was her sole reply. She called again, twice, with the same result. Ensign Dubauer hovered anxiously at her elbow.

"Try yours," she said. But his luck was no better. "Pack up your stuff, we're going back to camp," she ordered. "Double time."

They struggled toward the next ridge at a gasping jog, and plunged back into the forest. The spindly bearded trees at this altitude were often fallen, tangled. They had seemed artistically wild on the way up; on the way down they made a menacing obstacle course. Cordelia's mind ratcheted over a dozen possible disasters, each more bizarre than the last. So the unknown breeds dragons in map margins, she reflected, and suppressed her panic.

They slid down through the last patch of woods for their first clear view of the large glade selected for their primary base camp. Cordelia gaped, shocked. Reality had surpassed imagination.

Smoke was rising from five slagged and lumpy black mounds, formerly a neat ring of tents. A smouldering scar was burned in the grasses where the shuttle had been parked, opposite the camp from the ravine. Smashed equipment was scattered everywhere. Their bacteriologically sealed sanitary facilities had been just downslope; yes, she saw, even the privy had been torched.

"My God," breathed Ensign Dubauer, and started forward like a sleepwalker. Cordelia collared him.

"Get down and cover me," she ordered, then walked cautiously toward the silent ruins.

The grass all around the camp was trampled and

3

churned. Her stunned mind struggled to account for the carnage. Previously undetected aborigines? No, nothing short of a plasma arc could have melted the fabric of their tents. The long-looked-for but still undiscovered advanced aliens? Perhaps some unexpected disease outbreak, not forestalled by their month-long robotic microbiological survey and immunizations—could it have been an attempt at sterilization? An attack by some other planetary government? Their attackers could scarcely have come through the same wormhole exit they had discovered, still, they had only mapped about ten percent of the volume of space within a light-month of this system. Aliens?

She was miserably conscious of her mind coming full circle, like one of her team zoologist's captive animals racing frantically in an exercise wheel. She poked grimly through the rubbish for some clue.

She found it in the high grass halfway to the ravine. The long body in the baggy tan fatigues of the Betan Astronomical Survey was stretched out full length, arms and legs askew, as though hit while running for the shelter of the forest. Her breath drew inward in pain of recognition. She turned him over gently.

It was the conscientious Lieutenant Rosemont. His eyes were glazed and fixed and somehow worried, as though they still held a mirror to his spirit. She closed them for him.

She searched him for the cause of his death. No blood, no burns, no broken bones—her long white fingers probed his scalp. The skin beneath his blond hair was blistered, the tell-tale signature of a nerve disruptor. That let out aliens. She cradled his head in her lap a moment, stroking his familiar features helplessly, like a blind woman. No time now for mourning.

She returned to the blackened ring on her hands and knees, and began to search through the mess for comm equipment. The attackers had been quite thorough in that department, the twisted lumps of plastic and metal she found testified. Much valuable equipment seemed to be missing altogether.

There was a rustle in the grass. She snapped her stun gun to the aim and froze. The tense face of Ensign Dubauer pushed through the straw-colored vegetation.

"It's me, don't shoot," he called in a strangled tone meant to be a whisper.

"I almost did. Why didn't you stay put?" she hissed back. "Never mind, help me look for a comm unit that can reach the ship. And stay down, they could come back at any time."

"Who could? Who did this?"

"Multiple choice, take your pick—Nuovo Brasilians, Barrayarans, Cetagandans, could be any of that crowd. Reg Rosemont's dead. Nerve disruptor."

Cordelia crawled over to the mound of the specimen tent and considered its lumps carefully. "Hand me that pole over there," she whispered.

She poked tentatively at the most probable hump. The tents had stopped smoking, but waves of heat still rose from them to beat upon her face like the summer sun of home. The tortured fabric flaked away like charred paper. She hooked the pole over a half-melted cabinet and dragged it into the open. The bottom drawer was unmelted, but badly warped and, as she found when she wrapped her shirttail around her hand and pulled, tightly stuck.

A few minutes' more search turned up some dubious substitutes for a hammer and chisel, a flat shard of metal and a heavy lump she recognized sadly as having once been a delicate and very expensive meterological recorder. With these caveman's tools and some brute force from Dubauer, they wrenched the drawer open with a noise like a pistol shot that made them both jump.

"Jackpot!" said Dubauer.

"Let's take it over by the ravine to try out," said Cordelia. "My skin is crawling. Anybody upslope could see us."

Still crouching, they made quickly for cover, past Rosemont's body. Dubauer stared back at it as they scuttled by, ill-at-ease, angry. "Whoever did that is damn well going to pay for it." Cordelia just shook her head.

They knelt down in the bracken-like undergrowth to try the comm link. The machine produced some static and sad whining hoots, went dead, then coughed out the audio half of its signal when tapped and shaken. She found the right frequency and began the blind call.

"Commander Naismith to Survey Ship *Rene Magritte*. Acknowledge, please." After an agony of waiting, the faint, static-scrambled reply wavered in.

"Lieutenant Stuben here. Are you all right, Captain?"

Cordelia breathed again. "All right for now. What's your status? What happened?"

Dr. Ullery's voice came on, senior officer in the survey party after Rosemont. "A Barrayaran military patrol surrounded the camp, demanding surrender. Said they claimed the place by right of prior discovery. Then some trigger-happy loon on their side fired a plasma arc, and all hell broke loose. Reg drew them off with his stunner, and the rest of us made it to the shuttle. There's a Barrayaran ship of the General class up here we're playing hide-and-seek with, if you know what I mean—"

"Remember, you're broadcasting in the clear," Cordelia reminded her sharply.

Dr. Ullery hesitated, then went on. "Right. They're still demanding surrender. Do you know if they captured Reg?"

"Dubauer's with me. Is everybody else accounted for?"

"All but Reg."

"Reg is dead."

A crackle of static hissed across Stuben's swearing.

"Stu, you're in command," Cordelia cut in on him. "Listen closely. Those twitchy militarists are not, repeat not, to be trusted. On no account surrender the ship. I've seen the secret reports on the General cruisers. You're out-gunned, out-armored, and out-manned, but you've got at least twice the legs. So get out of his range and stay there. Retreat all the way back to Beta Colony if you have to, but take no chances with my people. Got that?"

"We can't leave you, Captain!"

"You can't launch a shuttle for a pickup unless you get the Barrayarans off your neck. And if we are captured, the chances are better for getting us home through political channels than through some hare-brained rescue stunt, but *only* if you make it home to complain, is that absolutely clear? Acknowledge!" she demanded.

"Acknowledged," he replied reluctantly. "But Captain—how long do you really think you can keep away from those crazy bastards? They're bound to get you in the end, with 'scopes."

"As long as possible. As for you—get going!" She had occasionally imagined her ship functioning without herself; never without Rosemont. Got to keep Stuben from trying to play soldier, she thought. The Barrayarans aren't amateurs. "There are fifty-six lives depending on you up there. You can count. Fifty-six is more than two. Keep it in mind, all right? Naismith out."

"Cordelia . . . Good luck. Stuben out."

Cordelia sat back and stared at the little communicator. "Whew. What a peculiar business."

Ensign Dubauer snorted. "That's an understatement."

"It's an exact statement. I don't know if you noticed—"

A movement in the mottled shade caught her eye. She started to her feet, hand moving toward her stunner. The tall, hatchet-faced Barrayaran soldier in the green and grey splotched camouflage fatigues moved even faster. Dubauer moved faster still, shoving her blindly behind him. She heard the crackle of a nerve disruptor as she pitched backward into the ravine, stunner and comm link flying from her hands. Forest, earth, stream and sky spun wildly around her, her head struck something with a sickening, starry crack, and darkness swallowed her.

The forest mold pressed against Cordelia's cheek. The damp earthy smell tickled her nostrils. She breathed deeper, filling her mouth and lungs, and then the odor of decay wrung her stomach. She turned her face from the muck. Pain exploded through her head in radiating lines.

She groaned inarticulately. Dark sparkling whorls curtained her vision, then cleared. She forced her

8

eyes to focus on the nearest object, about half a meter to the right of her head.

Heavy black boots, sunk in the mud and topped by green and grey splotched camouflage trousers, encased legs spread apart in a patient parade rest. She suppressed a weary whimper. Very gently she laid her head back in the black ooze, and rolled cautiously onto her side for a better view of the Barrayaran officer.

Her stunner! She stared into the little grey rectangle of its business end, held steadily in a broad and heavy hand. Her eyes searched anxiously for his nerve disruptor. The officer's belt hung heavy with equipment, but the disruptor holster on his right hip was empty, as was the plasma arc holster on his left.

He was barely taller than herself, but stocky and powerful. Untidy dark hair touched with grey, cold intent grey eyes—in fact, his whole appearance was untidy by the strict Barrayaran military standards. His fatigues were almost as rumpled and muddy and stained with plant juices as her own, and he had a raw contusion across his right cheekbone. Looks like he's had a rotten day too, she thought muzzily. Then the sparkly black whirlpools expanded and drowned her again.

When her vision cleared again the boots were gone—no. There he was, seated comfortably on a log. She tried to focus on something other than her rebellious belly, but her belly won control in a wrenching rush.

The enemy captain stirred involuntarily as she vomited, but remained sitting. She crawled the few meters to the little stream at the bottom of the ravine, and washed out her mouth and face in its icy water.

Feeling relatively better, she sat up and croaked, "Well?"

The officer inclined his head in a shadow of courtesy. "I am Captain Aral Vorkosigan, commanding the Barrayaran Imperial war cruiser *General Vorkraft*. Identify yourself, please." His voice was baritone, his speech barely accented.

"Commander Cordelia Naismith. Betan Astronomical Survey. We are a scientific party," she emphasized accusingly. "Non-combatants."

"So I noticed," he said dryly. "What happened to your party?"

Cordelia's eyes narrowed. "Weren't you there? I was up on the mountain, assisting my team botanist." And more urgently, "Have you seen my botanist—my ensign? He pushed me into the ravine when we were ambushed—"

He glanced up to the rim of the gorge at the point where she had toppled in—how long ago? "Was he a brown-haired boy?"

Her heart sank in sick anticipation. "Yes."

"There's nothing you can do for him now."

"That was murder! All he had was a stunner!" Her eyes burned the Barrayaran. "Why were my people attacked?"

He tapped her stunner thoughtfully in his palm. "Your expedition," he said carefully, "was to be interned, preferably peacefully, for violation of Barrayaran space. There was an altercation. I was hit in the back with a stun beam. When I came to, I found your camp as you did."

"Good." Bitter bile soured her mouth. "I'm glad Reg got one of you, before you murdered him too."

"If you are referring to that misguided but admittedly courageous blond boy in the clearing, he couldn't

10

have hit the side of a house. I don't know why you Betans put on soldier's uniforms. You're no better trained than children on a picnic. If your ranks denote anything but pay scale, it's not apparent to me."

"He was a geologist, not a hired killer," she snapped. "As for my 'children,' your soldiers couldn't even capture them."

His brows drew together. Cordelia shut her mouth abruptly. Oh, great, she thought. He hasn't even started to wrench my arms off, and already I'm giving away free intelligence.

"Didn't they now," Vorkosigan mused. He pointed upstream with the stunner to where the comm link lay cracked open in the brook. A little sputtering of steam rose from the ruin. "What orders did you give your ship when they informed you of their escape?"

"I told them to use their initiative," she murmured vaguely, groping for inspiration in a throbbing fog.

He snorted. "A safe order to give a Betan. At least you're sure to be obeyed."

Oh, no. My turn. "Hey. I know why my people left me behind—why did yours leave you? Isn't one's commanding officer, even a Barrayaran one, too important to mislay?" She sat up straighter. "If Reg couldn't hit the side of a house, who shot you?"

That's fetched him, she thought, as the stunner with which he had been absently gesturing was swivelled back to aim on her. But he said only, "That is not your concern. Have you another comm link?"

Oh ho—was this stern Barrayaran commander dealing with a mutiny? Well, confusion to the enemy! "No. Your soldiers trashed everything."

"No matter," muttered Vorkosigan. "I know where to get another. Are you able to walk yet?"

"I'm not sure." She pushed herself to her feet, then pressed her hand to her head to contain the shooting pains.

"It's only a concussion," Vorkosigan said unsympathetically. "A walk will do you good."

"How far?" she gasped.

"About two hundred kilometers."

She fell back to her knees. "Have a nice trip."

"By myself, two days. I suppose you will take longer, being a geologist, or whatever."

"Astrocartographer."

"Get up, please." He unbent so far as to help her with a hand under her elbow. He seemed curiously reluctant to touch her. She was chilled and stiff; she could feel the heat from his hand through the heavy cloth of her sleeve. Vorkosigan pushed her determinedly up the side of the ravine.

"You're stone serious," she said. "What are you going to do with a prisoner on a forced march? Suppose I bash in your head with a rock while you sleep?"

"I'll take my chances."

They cleared the top. Cordelia draped herself around one of the little trees, winded. Vorkosigan wasn't even breathing hard, she noticed enviously. "Well, I'm not going anywhere till I've buried my officers."

He looked irritated. "It's a waste of time and energy."

"I won't leave them to the scavengers like dead animals. Your Barrayaran thugs may know more about killing, but not one of them could have died a more soldierly death."

He stared at her a moment, face unreadable, then shrugged. "Very well."

Cordelia began to make her way along the side of the ravine. "I thought it was here," she said, puzzled. "Did you move him?"

"No. But he can't have crawled far, in his condition."

"You said he was dead!"

"So he is. His body, however, was still animate. The disruptor must have missed his cerebellum."

Cordelia traced the trail of broken vegetation over a small rise, Vorkosigan following silently.

"Dubauer!" She ran to the tan clad figure curled up in the bracken. As she knelt beside him he turned and stretched out stiffly, then began to shake all over in slow waves, his lips drawn back in a strange grin. Cold? she thought wildly, then realized what she was seeing. She yanked her handkerchief from her pocket, folded it, and forced it between his teeth. His mouth was already bloody from a previous convulsion. After about three minutes he sighed and went limp.

She blew out her breath in distress and examined him anxiously. He opened his eyes, and seemed to focus on her face. He clutched ineffectually at her arm and made noises, all moans and clotted vowels. She tried to soothe his animal agitation by gently stroking his head, and wiping the bloody spittle from his mouth; he quieted.

She turned to Vorkosigan, tears of fury and pain blurring her vision. "Not dead! Liar! Only injured. He must have medical help."

"You are being unrealistic, Commander Naismith. One does not recover from disruptor injuries."

"So? You can't tell the extent of the damage your filthy weapon has done from the outside. He can still see and hear and feel—you can't demote him to the status of a corpse for your convenience!"

His face seemed a mask. "If you wish," he said

13

carefully. "I can put him out of his suffering. My combat knife is quite sharp. Used quickly, it would cut his throat almost painlessly. Or should you feel it is your duty as his commander, I'll lend you the knife and you may use it."

"Is that what you'd do for one of your men?"

"Certainly. And they'd do the same for me. No man could wish to live on like that."

She stood and looked at him very steadily. "It must be like living among cannibals, to be a Barrayaran."

A long silence fell between them. Dubauer broke it with a moan. Vorkosigan stirred. "What, then, do you propose to do with him?"

She rubbed her temples tiredly, ransacking for an appeal that would penetrate that expressionless front. Her stomach undulated, her tongue was woolly, her legs trembled with exhaustion, low blood sugar, and reaction to pain. "Just where is it you're planning to go?" she asked finally.

"There is a supply cache located—in a place I know. Hidden. It contains communications equipment, weapons, food—possession of it would put me in a position to, ah, correct the problems in my command."

"Does it have medical supplies?"

"Yes," he admitted reluctantly.

"All right." Here goes nothing. "I will cooperate with you—give you my parole, as a prisoner—assist you in any way I can that does not actually endanger my ship—if I can take Ensign Dubauer with us."

"That's impossible. He can't even walk."

"I think he can, if he's helped."

He stared at her in baffled irritation. "And if I refuse?"

14

"Then you can either leave us both or kill us both." She glanced away from his knife, lifted her chin, and waited.

"I do not kill prisoners."

She was relieved to hear the plural. Dubauer was evidently promoted back to humanity in her strange captor's mind. She knelt down to try to help Dubauer to his feet, praying this Vorkosigan would not decide to end the argument by stunning her and killing her botanist outright.

"Very well," he capitulated, giving her an odd intent look. "Bring him along. But we must travel quickly."

She managed to get the ensign up. With his arm draped heavily over her shoulder, she guided him on a shambling walk. It seemed he could hear, but not decode meaning from the noises of speech. "You see," she defended him desperately, "he can walk. He just needs a little help."

They reached the edge of the glade as the last level light of early evening was striping it with long black shadows, like a tiger's skin. Vorkosigan paused.

"If I were by myself," he said, "I'd travel to the cache on the emergency rations in my belt. With you two along, we'll have to risk scavenging your camp for more food. You can bury your other officer while I'm looking around."

Cordelia nodded. "Look for something to dig with, too. I've got to tend to Dubauer first."

He acknowledged this with a wave of his hand and started toward the wasted ring. Cordelia was able to excavate a couple of half-burned bedrolls from the remains of the women's tent, but no clothes, medicine, soap, or even a bucket to carry or heat water.

15

She finally coaxed the ensign over to the spring and washed him, his wounds, and his trousers as best she could in the plain cold water, dried him with one bedroll, put his undershirt and fatigue jacket back on him, and wrapped the other bedroll around him sarong style. He shivered and moaned, but did not resist her makeshift ministrations.

Vorkosigan in the meanwhile had found two cases of ration packs, with the labels burned off but otherwise scarcely damaged. Cordelia tore open one silvery pouch, added spring water, and found that it was soya-fortified oatmeal.

"That's lucky," she commented. "He's sure to be able to eat that. What's the other case?"

Vorkosigan was conducting his own experiment. He added water to his pouch, mixed it by squeezing, and sniffed the result.

"I'm not really sure," he said, handing it to her. "It smells rather strange. Could it be spoiled?"

It was a white paste with a pungent aroma. "It's all right," Cordelia assured him. "It's artificial blue cheese salad dressing." She sat back and contemplated the menu. "At least it's high in calories," she encouraged herself. "We'll need calories. I don't suppose you have a spoon in that utility belt of yours?"

Vorkosigan unhooked an object from his belt and handed it to her without comment. It turned out to be several small useful utensils folded into a handle, including a spoon.

"Thanks," Cordelia said, absurdly pleased, as if granting her mumbled wish had been a conjuror's trick.

Vorkosigan shrugged and wandered away to continue his search in the gathering darkness, and she

16

began to feed Dubauer. He seemed voraciously hungry, but unable to manage for himself.

Vorkosigan returned to the spring. "I found this." He handed her a small geologist's shovel about a meter long, used for digging soil samples. "It's a poor tool for the purpose, but I've found nothing better yet."

"It was Reg's," Cordelia said, taking it. "It will do."

She led Dubauer to a spot near her next job and settled him. She wondered if some bracken from the forest might provide some insulation for him, and resolved to get some later. She marked out the dimensions of a grave near the place where Rosemont had fallen, and began hacking away at the heavy turf with the little shovel. The sod was tough, wiry, and resistant, and she ran out of breath quickly.

Vorkosigan appeared out of the night. "I found some cold lights." He cracked one pencil-sized tube and laid it on the ground beside the grave, where it gave off an eerie but bright blue-green glow. He watched her critically as she worked.

She stabbed away at the dirt, resentful of his scrutiny. Go away, you, she thought, and let me bury my friend in peace. She grew self-conscious as a new thought struck her—maybe he won't let me finish—I'm taking too long . . . She dug harder.

"At this rate, we'll be here until next week."

If she moved fast enough, she wondered irritably, could she succeed in hitting him with the shovel? Just once . . .

"Go sit down with your botanist." He was holding out his hand; it dawned on her at last that he was volunteering to help dig.

"Oh . . ." She relinquished the tool. He drew his

17

combat knife and cut through the grasses' roots where she had marked her rectangle, and began to dig, far more efficiently than she had.

"What kind of scavengers have you found around here?" he asked between tosses. "How deep does this have to be?"

"I'm not sure," she replied. "We'd only been downside three days. It's a pretty complex ecosystem, though, and most imaginable niches seem to be filled."

"Hm."

"Lieutenant Stuben, my chief zoologist, found a couple of those browser hexapeds killed and pretty well consumed. He caught a glimpse of something he called a fuzzy crab at one of the kills."

"How big were they?" asked Vorkosigan curiously.

"He didn't say. I've seen pictures of crabs from Earth, and they don't seem very large—as big as your hand, perhaps."

"A meter may be enough." He continued the excavation with short powerful bites of the inadequate shovel. The cold light illuminated his face from below, casting shadows upward from heavy jaw, straight broad nose, and thick brows. He had an old faded L-shaped scar, Cordelia noticed, on the left side of his chin. He reminded her of a dwarf king in some northern saga, digging in a fathomless deep.

"There's a pole over by the tents," she offered. "I could fix that light up in the air so it shines on your work."

"That would help."

She returned to the tents, beyond the circle of cold light, and found her pole where she had dropped it that morning. Returning to the gravesite, she spliced the light to the pole with a few tough grass stems and

18

fixed it upright in the dirt, flinging the circle of light wider. She remembered her plan to collect bracken for Dubauer, and turned to make for the forest, then stopped.

"Did you hear that?" she asked Vorkosigan.

"What?" Even he was beginning to breathe heavily. He paused, up to his knees in the hole, and listened with her.

"A sort of scuttling noise, coming from the forest."

He waited a minute, then shook his head and continued his work.

"How many cold lights are there?"

"Six."

So few. She hated to waste them by running two at once. She was about to ask him if he would mind digging in the dark for a while, when she heard the noise again, more distinctly.

"There *is* something out there."

"You know that," said Vorkosigan. "The question is—"

The three creatures made a concerted rush into the ring of light. Cordelia caught a glimpse of fast low bodies, entirely too many hairy black legs, four beady black eyes set in neckless faces, and razor-sharp yellow beaks that clacked and hissed. They were the size of pigs.

Vorkosigan reacted instantly, smashing the nearest accurately across its face with the blade of the shovel. A second one flung itself across Rosemont's body, biting deep into the flesh and cloth of one arm, and attempting to drag it away from the light. Cordelia grabbed her pole and ran full tilt upon it, getting in a hard blow between its eyes. Its beak snapped the end off the aluminum rod. It hissed and retreated before her.

19

By this time Vorkosigan had his combat knife out. He vigorously attacked the third, shouting, stabbing, and kicking with his heavy boots. Blood spattered as claws plowed his leg, but he got in a blow with his knife that sent the creature shrieking and hissing back to the shelter of the forest along with its pack mates. With a moment to breathe, he dug out her stun gun from the bottom of the too-large disruptor holster where, judging from his muttered swearing, it had slipped down and stuck, and peered into the night.

"Fuzzy crabs, huh?" Cordelia panted. "Stuben, I'm going to scrag you." Her voice squeaked upward and she clamped her teeth.

Vorkosigan wiped the dark blood from his blade in the grass and returned it to its sheath. "I think your grave had better be a full two meters," he said seriously. "Maybe a little more."

Cordelia sighed in agreement, and returned the shortened pole to its original position. "How's your leg?"

"I can take care of it. You'd better see to your ensign."

Dubauer, drowsing, had been aroused by the uproar and was attempting to crawl away again. Cordelia tried to soothe him, then found herself having to deal with another seizure, after which, to her relief, he went to sleep.

Vorkosigan, in the meanwhile, had patched his scratch using the small emergency medical kit on his belt, and returned to digging, slowing down only a little. Getting down to shoulder depth, he pressed her into hauling dirt up out of the grave using the emptied-out botanical specimen box as a makeshift bucket. It was near midnight before he called from the dark

20

pit, "That should be the last," and clambered out. "Could have done that in five seconds with a plasma arc," he panted, recovering his wind. He was dirty and sweating in the cold night air. Tendrils of fog writhed up from the ravine and the spring.

Together they dragged Rosemont's body to the lip of the grave. Vorkosigan hesitated.

"Do you want his clothes for your ensign?"

It was an unavoidably practical suggestion. Cordelia loathed the indignity of lowering Rosemont naked into the earth, but wished at the same time she had thought of it earlier, when Dubauer was so cold. She horsed the uniform off over the stiffened limbs with the macabre sensation of undressing a giant doll, and they tipped him into the grave. He landed on his back with a muffled thump.

"Just a minute." She dug out Rosemont's handkerchief from his uniform pocket and jumped down into the grave, slipping on the body. She spread the handkerchief over his face. It was a small, reality-defying gesture, but she felt better for it. Vorkosigan grasped her hand and pulled her up.

"All right." They shoveled and pushed the dirt back into the hole far more quickly than it had been excavated, and packed it down as best they could by walking on it.

"Is there some ceremony you wish to perform?" Vorkosigan asked.

Cordelia shook her head, not feeling up to reciting the vague, official funeral service. But she knelt by the grave for a few minutes making a more serious, less certain inward prayer for her dead. It seemed to fly upward and vanish in the void, echoless as a feather.

Vorkosigan waited patiently until she arose. "It's

21

rather late," he said, "and we have just seen three good reasons not to go stumbling around in the dark. We may as well rest here until dawn. I'll take the first watch. Do you still want to bash my head in with a rock?"

"Not at the moment," she said sincerely.

"Very well. I'll wake you later."

Vorkosigan began his watch with a patrol of the perimeter of the glade, taking the cold light with him. It wavered through the black distance like a captive firefly. Cordelia lay down on her back beside Dubauer. The stars glimmered faintly through the gathering mist. Could one be her ship yet, or Vorkosigan's? Not likely, at the range they undoubtedly were by now.

She felt hollow. Energy, will, desire, slipped through her fingers like shining liquid, sucked away through some infinite sand. She glanced at Dubauer beside her, and jerked her mind from the easy vortex of despair. I'm still a commander, she told herself sharply; I have a command. You serve me still, ensign, although you cannot now serve even yourself . . .

The thought seemed a thread to some great insight, but it melted in her grasp, and she slept.

▶▶ CHAPTER TWO

They divided the meager spoils from the camp in makeshift backpacks and started down the mountain in the grey mist of morning. Cordelia led Dubauer by the hand and helped him when he stumbled. She was not sure how clearly he recognized her, but he clung to her and avoided Vorkosigan.

The forest grew thicker and the trees taller as they went down. Vorkosigan hacked through the undergrowth with his knife for a while, then they took to the stream bed. Splashes of sunlight began to filter through the canopy, picking out fiery green velvet humps of moss, sparkling rills of water, and stones on the stream bed like a layer of bronze coins.

Radial symmetry was popular among the tiny creatures occupying the ecological niches held by insects on Earth. Some aerial varieties like gas-filled jellyfishes floated in iridescent clouds above the stream like flocks of delicate soap bubbles, delighting Cordelia's eye. They seemed to have a mellowing effect on

Vorkosigan, too, for he called for a break from what seemed to her a killing pace.

They drank from the stream and sat a while watching the little radials dart and puff in the spray from a waterfall. Vorkosigan closed his eyes and leaned against a tree. He was running on the ragged edge of exhaustion too, Cordelia realized. Temporarily unwatched, she studied him curiously. He had behaved throughout with curt but dignified military professionalism. Still she was bothered by a subliminal alarm, a persistent sense of something of importance forgotten. It popped out of her memory suddenly, like a ball held under water breaking the surface on release and arcing into the air.

"I know who you are. Vorkosigan, the Butcher of Komarr." She immediately wished she had not spoken, for he opened his eyes and stared at her, a peculiar play of expressions passing across his face.

"What do you know about Komarr?" His tone added, "An ignorant Betan."

"Just what everyone knows. It was a worthless ball of rock your people annexed by military force for command of its wormhole clusters. The ruling senate surrendered on terms, and were murdered immediately after. You commanded the expedition, or . . ." Surely the Vorkosigan of Komarr had been an Admiral. "Was it you? I thought you said you didn't kill prisoners."

"It was."

"Did they demote you for it?" she asked, surprised. She had thought that sort of conduct to be Barrayaran standard.

"Not for that. For the sequel." He seemed reluctant to say more, but he surprised her again by going on. "The sequel was more effectively suppressed. I

24

had given my word—*my* word, as Vorkosigan—they were to be spared. My Political Officer countermanded my order, and had them killed behind my back. I executed him for it."

"Good God."

"I broke his neck with my own hands, on the bridge of my ship. It was a personal matter, you see, touching my honor. I couldn't order a firing squad— they were all afraid of the Ministry of Political Education."

That was the official euphemism for the secret police, Cordelia recalled, of which Political Officers were the military branch. "And you aren't?"

"They're afraid of me." He smiled sourly. "Like those scavengers last night, they'll run from a bold attack. But one must not turn one's back."

"I'm surprised they didn't have you hanged."

"There was a great uproar, behind closed doors," he admitted reminiscently, fingering his collar tabs. "But a Vorkosigan can't be made to disappear in the night, not yet. I did make some powerful enemies."

"I'll bet." This bald story, told without adornment or apology, had the ring of truth to her inner ear, although she had no logical reason to trust him. "Did you, uh, happen to turn your back on one of those enemies yesterday?"

He glanced at her sharply. "Possibly," he said slowly. "There are some problems with that theory, however."

"Like what?"

"I'm still alive. I wouldn't have thought they'd risk starting the job without finishing it. To be sure, they'd be tempted by the opportunity to blame my death on you Betans."

"Whew. And I thought I had command troubles

25

just keeping a bunch of Betan intellectual prima donnas working together for months on end. God keep me from politics."

Vorkosigan smiled slightly. "From what I've heard of Betans, that's no easy task either. I don't think I should care to trade commands. It would irritate me to have every order argued over."

"They don't argue *every* order." She grinned, as his crack ferreted up some particular memories. "You learn how to coax them along."

"Where do you suppose your ship is now?"

Wariness dropped across her amusement like a portcullis. "I suppose that depends on where your ship is."

Vorkosigan shrugged and stood, hitching his pack more securely to his shoulders. "Then perhaps we should waste no more time finding out." He gave her a hand to pull her up, the soldier-mask repossessing his features.

It took all the long day to descend the great mountain to the red-soiled plains. A closer view found them cut and channeled by watercourses running turbid from the recent rains, and confused by outcrops of rocky badlands. They caught glimpses of groups of hexapedal grazers. Cordelia deduced from their wary herd behavior that associated predators must lurk nearby.

Vorkosigan would have pushed on, but Dubauer was seized by a serious and prolonged convulsion followed by lethargy and sleepiness. Cordelia insisted adamantly on a halt for the night. They made camp, if one could so describe stopping and sitting down, in an open gap in the trees perhaps three hundred meters above the levels. They shared their simple supper of oatmeal and blue cheese dressing in a beaten-down silence. Vorkosigan cracked another cold light as the last colors of a gaudy sunset drained from the sky, and seated himself on a large flat boulder. Cordelia lay down and watched the Barrayaran watching until sleep relieved her of her aching legs and head.

He woke her past the middle of the night. Her muscles seemed to screech and creak with lactic acid buildup as she rose stiffly to take her watch. This time Vorkosigan gave her the stunner.

"I haven't seen anything close," he commented, "but something out there makes a hellish racket from time to time." It seemed an adequate explanation for the gesture of trust.

She checked Dubauer, then took her place on the boulder, leaning back and staring up at the dark bulk of the mountain. Up there Rosemont lay in his deep grave, safe from the beaks and bellies of the carrion eaters, but still doomed to slow decomposition. She bent her night-wandering thoughts instead to Vorkosigan, lying nearly invisible in his camouflage fatigues in the border of the blue-green light.

A puzzle within a puzzle, he was. Clearly, he must be one of the Barrayaran warrior aristocrats of the old school, at odds with the rising new men of the bureaucracy. The militarists of both parties maintained a bastard, uneasy alliance that controlled both government policy and the armed forces, but at heart they were natural enemies. The Emperor subtly stabilized the delicate balance of power between them, but there was not much doubt that on the clever old man's death Barrayar was destined for a period of political cannibalism, if not outright civil war, unless his successor showed more strength than was currently expected. She wished she knew more about the matrix of blood relationships and power on Barrayar. She could give the Emperor's family name, Vorbarra, it being associated with the name of the planet, but beyond that she was quite vague.

She fingered the little stunner absently, and tantalized herself; who now was the captive, and who the captor? But it would be nearly impossible to care for Dubauer in this wilderness by herself. She had to have supplies for him, and since Vorkosigan had been careful not to say exactly where his cache lay, she needed the Barrayaran to take her there. Besides, she had given her parole. It was a curious insight into Vorkosigan that he should so automatically accept her bare word as binding; he evidently thought along the same lines himself.

The east began to grow grey at last, then peach, green, and gold in a pastel repeat of last night's spectacular sunset. Vorkosigan stirred and sat up, and helped her take Dubauer down to the stream to wash. They had another breakfast of oatmeal and blue cheese dressing. Vorkosigan tried mixing his together this time, for variety. Cordelia tried alternating bites, to see if that would help. Neither commented aloud on the menu.

Vorkosigan led northwest across the sandy, brick-colored plain. In the dry season it would have been near-desert. Now it was brightly decorated with fresh green and yellow growth, and dozens of varieties of low-growing wildflowers. Dubauer did not seem to notice them, Cordelia saw sadly.

After about three hours at a brisk pace they came to their first check of the day, a steep rocky valley with a coffee-and-cream colored river rushing through it. They walked along the edge of the escarpment looking for a ford.

"That rock down there moved," Cordelia observed suddenly.

Vorkosigan pulled his field scope from his belt and took a closer look. "You're right."

Half a dozen coffee-and-cream colored lumps that looked like rocks on a sandbar proved to be low-slung, thick-limbed hexapeds, basking in the morning sun.

"They seem to be some sort of amphibian. I wonder if they're carnivores?" said Vorkosigan.

"I wish you hadn't interrupted my survey so soon," Cordelia complained. "Then I could have answered all those questions. There go some more of those soap-bubble things—goodness, I wouldn't have thought they could grow so big and still fly."

A flock of a dozen or so large radials, transparent as wineglasses and fully a foot across, came floating like a flight of lost balloons above the river. A few of them drifted over to the hexapeds and settled gently on their backs, flattening over their withers like weird berets. Cordelia borrowed the scope for a closer look.

"Do you suppose they could be like those birds from Earth, that pick the parasites off the cattle? Oh. No, I guess not."

The hexapeds roused themselves with hisses and whistles, humping their bodies in a kind of obese bucking, and slid into the river. The radials, colored now like wineglasses filled with burgundy, inflated themselves and retreated into the air.

"Vampire balloons?" asked Vorkosigan.

"Apparently."

"What appalling creatures."

29

Cordelia almost laughed at his revolted look. "As a carnivore yourself, you can't really condemn them."

"Condemn, no; avoid, yes."

"I'll go along with that."

They continued upstream past a frothing, opaque tan waterfall. After about a kilometer and a half they came to a place where two tributaries joined, and stumbled across at the shallowest place they could find. Crossing the second branch, Dubauer lost his footing as a rock turned under him, and went down with a wordless cry.

Cordelia tightened her grip on his arm convulsively, and perforce went with him, slipping into a deeper area. Terror shook her, that he might be swept downstream beyond her reach—those amphibious hexapeds, sharp rocks—the waterfall! Careless of the water filling her mouth, she grabbed him with both hands. Here they went—no.

Something pulled her bodily with a tremendous counter-surge against the rush of waters. Vorkosigan had grabbed her by the back of the belt, and was hauling them both toward the shallows with the strength and style of a stevedore.

Feeling undignified, but grateful, she scrambled to her feet and pushed the coughing Dubauer up the far bank.

"Thanks," she gasped to Vorkosigan.

"What, did you think I'd let you drown?" he inquired wryly, emptying his boots.

Cordelia shrugged, embarrassed. "Well—at least we wouldn't be delaying you."

"Hm." He cleared his throat, but said no more. They found a rocky place to sit, eat their cereal and salad dressing, and dry awhile before moving on.

Kilometers fell behind them, while their view of

the great mountain to their right scarcely seemed to change. At some point Vorkosigan took a bearing known only to himself, and led them more westerly, with the mountain at their backs and the sun beginning to slant into their eyes.

They crossed another watercourse. Coming up over the lip of its valley, Cordelia nearly stumbled over a red-coated hexaped, lying quite still in a depression and blending perfectly with its background. It was a delicately formed thing, as big as a middle-sized dog, and it rippled over the red plains in graceful bounds.

Cordelia woke up abruptly. "That thing's edible!"

"The stunner, the stunner!" cried Vorkosigan. She pressed it hastily into his hand. He fell to one knee, took aim, and dropped the creature in one burst.

"Oh, good shot!" cried Cordelia ecstatically.

Vorkosigan grinned like a boy over his shoulder at her, and jogged after his prize.

"Oh," she murmured, stunned herself by the effect of the grin. It had lit his face like the sun for that brief instant. Oh, do that again, she thought; then shook off the thought. Duty. Stick to duty.

She followed him to where the animal lay. Vorkosigan had his knife out, puzzling over where to begin. He could not cut its throat, for it had no neck.

"The brain is located right behind the eyes. Maybe you could pith it going in between the first set of shoulderblades," Cordelia suggested.

"That would be quick enough," Vorkosigan agreed, and did so. The creature shivered, sighed, and died. "It's early to make camp, but there's water here, and driftwood from the river for a fire. It will mean extra kilometers tomorrow, though," he warned.

Cordelia eyed the carcass, thinking of roast meat. "That's all right."

Vorkosigan hoisted it to his shoulder, and stood. "Where's your ensign?"

Cordelia looked around. Dubauer was not in sight. "Oh, lord," she inhaled, and ran back to the spot they had been standing when Vorkosigan had shot dinner. No Dubauer. She approached the rim of the watercourse.

Dubauer was standing by the stream, arms hanging by his sides, gazing upward blank and entranced. Floating softly down toward his upturned face was a large transparent radial.

"Dubauer, no!" shrieked Cordelia, and scrambled down the bank toward him. Vorkosigan passed her with a bound, and they raced for the waterside. The radial settled over Dubauer's face and began to flatten, and he flung up his hands with a cry.

Vorkosigan arrived first. He grabbed the half-limp thing with his bare hand and pulled it away from Dubauer's face. A dozen dark, tendril-like appendages were hooked into Dubauer's flesh, and they stretched and snapped as the creature was ripped off its prey. Vorkosigan flung it to the sand and stamped on it as Dubauer fell to the ground and curled up on his side. Cordelia tried to pull his hands away from his face. He was making strange, hoarse noises, and his body shook. Another seizure, she thought—but then realized with a shock that he was weeping.

She held his head on her lap to stop the wild rocking. The spots where the tendrils had penetrated his skin were black in the center, surrounded by rings of red flesh that were beginning to swell alarmingly. There was a particularly nasty one at the corner of one eye. She plucked one of the remaining embedded tendrils out of his skin, and found it burned her fingers acidly. Apparently the creature had been

32

coated all over with a similar poison, for Vorkosigan was kneeling with his hand in the stream. She quickly pulled the rest of them, and called the Barrayaran over to her side.

"Have you got anything in your kit that will help this?"

"Only the antibiotic." He handed her a tube, and she smeared some on Dubauer's face. It was not really a proper burn ointment, but it would have to do. Vorkosigan stared at Dubauer a moment, then reluctantly produced a small white pill.

"This is a powerful analgesic. I have only four. It should carry him through the evening."

Cordelia placed it on the back of Dubauer's tongue. It evidently tasted bitter, for he tried to spit it out, but she caught it and forced him to swallow it. In a few minutes she was able to get him to his feet and take him to the campsite Vorkosigan chose overlooking the sandy channel.

Vorkosigan meanwhile made a handsome collection of driftwood for a fire.

"How are you going to light it?" inquired Cordelia.

"When I was a small boy, I had to learn to start a fire by friction," Vorkosigan reminisced. "Military school summer camp. It wasn't easy. Took all afternoon. Come to think of it, I never did get it started that way. I lit it by dissecting a communicator for the power pack." He was searching through his belt and pockets. "The instructor was furious. I think it must have been his communicator."

"No chemical starters?" Cordelia asked, with a nod to his on-going inventory of his utility belt.

"It's assumed if you want heat, you can fire your plasma arc." He tapped his fingers on the empty holster. "I have another idea. A bit drastic, but I

33

think it will be effective. You'd better go sit with your botanist. This is going to be loud."

He removed a useless plasma arc power cartridge from a row on the back of his belt.

"Uh, oh," said Cordelia, moving away. "Won't that be overkill? And what are you going to do with the crater? It'll be visible from the air for kilometers."

"Do you want to sit there and rub two sticks together? I suppose I had better do something about the crater, though."

He thought a moment, then trotted away over the edge of the little valley. Cordelia sat down beside Dubauer, putting an arm around his shoulders and hunching in anticipation.

Vorkosigan shot back over the rim at a dead run, and hit the ground rolling. There was a brilliant blue-white flash, and a boom that shook the ground. A large column of smoke, dust, and steam rose into the air, and pebbles, dirt, and bits of melted sand began to patter down like rain all around. Vorkosigan disappeared over the edge again, and returned shortly with a fine flaming torch.

Cordelia went for a peek at the damage. Vorkosigan had placed the short-circuited cartridge upstream about a hundred meters, at the outer edge of a bend where the swift little river curved away to the east. The explosion had left a spectacular glass-lined crater some fifteen meters wide and five deep that was still smoking. As she watched, the stream eroded its edge and poured in, billowing steam. In an hour it would be scoured into a natural-looking backwater.

"Not bad," she murmured approvingly.

*   *   *

By the time the fire burned down to a bed of coals they had cubes of dark red meat on sticks ready to broil.

"How do you like yours?" Vorkosigan asked. "Rare? Medium?"

"I think it had better be well done," suggested Cordelia. "We hadn't completed the parasite survey yet."

Vorkosigan glanced at his cube with a new dubiousness. "Ah. Quite," he said faintly.

They cooked it thoroughly, then sat by the fire and tore into the smoking meat with happy savagery. Even Dubauer managed to feed himself with small chunks. It was gamey and tough, burned on the outside and with a bitter undertaste, but no one suggested a side dish of either oatmeal or blue cheese dressing.

Cordelia's humor was touched. Vorkosigan's fatigues were filthy, damp, and splashed with dried blood from hacking up their dinner, as were her own. He had a three-day growth of beard, his face glistened in the firelight with hexaped grease, and he reeked with dried sweat. Barring the beard, she suspected she looked no better, and she knew she smelled no better. She found herself disquietingly aware of his body, muscular, compact, wholly masculine, stirring senses she thought she had suppressed. Best think of something else . . .

"From spaceman to caveman in three days," she meditated aloud. "How we imagine our civilization is in ourselves, when it's really in our things."

Vorkosigan glanced with a twisted smile at the carefully-tended Dubauer. "You seem able to carry your civilization on the inside."

Cordelia flushed uncomfortably, glad for the camou-flaging firelight. "One does one's duty."

"Some people find their duty more elastic. Or—were you in love with him?"

"With Dubauer? Heavens, no! I'm no cradle snatcher. He was a good kid, though. I'd like to get him home to his family."

"Do you have a family?"

"Sure. My mom and brother, back home on Beta Colony. My dad used to be in the Survey too."

"Was he one of those who never came back?"

"No, he died in a shuttleport accident, not ten kilometers from home. He'd been home on leave, and was just reporting back."

"My condolences."

"Oh, that was years and years ago." Getting a little personal, isn't he? she thought. But it was better than trying to deflect military interrogation. She hoped fervently that the subject, say, of the latest Betan equipment would not come up. "How about you? Do you have a family?" It suddenly occurred to her that this phrase was also a polite way of asking, "Are you married?"

"My father lives. He is Count Vorkosigan. My mother was half Betan, you know," he offered hesitantly.

Cordelia decided that if Vorkosigan, full of military curtness, was formidible, Vorkosigan trying to make himself pleasant was truly terrifying. But curiosity overcame the urge to cut the conversation short. "That's unusual. How did that happen?"

"My maternal grandfather was Prince Xav Vorbarra, the diplomat. He held the post of ambassador to Beta Colony for a time, in his youth, before the First

Cetagandan War. I believe my grandmother was in your Bureau for Interstellar Trade."

"Did you know her well?"

"After my mother—died, and Yuri Vorbarra's Civil War was brought to an end, I spent some school vacations at the Prince's home in the capital. He was at odds with my father, though, before and after that war, being of different political parties. Xav was the leading light of the liberals in his day, and of course my father was—is—part of the last stand of the old military aristocracy."

"Was your grandmother happy on Barrayar?" Cordelia estimated Vorkosigan's school days were perhaps thirty years ago.

"I don't think she ever adjusted completely to our society. And of course, Yuri's War . . ." He trailed off, then began again. "Outsiders—you Betans particularly—have this odd vision of Barrayar as some monolith, but we are a fundamentally divided society. My government is always fighting these centrifugal tendencies."

Vorkosigan leaned forward and tossed another piece of wood onto the fire. Sparks cascaded upward like a stream of little orange stars flowing home to the sky. Cordelia felt a sharp longing to fly away with them.

"What party has your allegience?" she asked, hoping to keep the conversation on a less unnervingly personal plane. "Do you stand with your father?"

"While he lives. I always wanted to be a soldier, and avoid all parties. I have an aversion to politics; they've been death on my family. But it's past time someone took on those damned bureaucrats and their pet spies. They imagine they're the wave of the future, but it's only sewage flowing downhill."

"If you express those opinions that forcibly at home,

it's no wonder politics come looking for you." She poked at the fire with a stick, freeing more sparks for their journey.

Dubauer, sedated by the pain killer, fell asleep quickly, but Cordelia lay long awake, replaying the disturbing conversation in her mind. Still, what did she care if this Barrayaran chose to run his head into nooses? No reason for her to get involved. None at all. Surely not. Even if the shape of his square strong hands was a dream of power in form . . .

She awakened deep in the night with a start. But it was only the fire flaring up as Vorkosigan added an unusually large armload of wood. She sat up, and he came over to her.

"I'm glad you're awake. I need you." He pressed his combat knife into her hand. "That carcass seems to be attracting something. I'm going to pitch it into the river. Will you hold a torch?"

"Sure." She stretched, got up, and selected a suitable brand. She followed him down into the watercourse, rubbing her eyes. The flickering orange light made jumpy black shadows that were almost harder to see into than plain starlight. As they reached the water's edge she caught movement out of the corner of her eye, and heard a scrambling among the rocks and a familiar hiss.

"Uh, oh. There's a group of those scavengers just upstream to the left."

"Right." Vorkosigan flung the remains of their dinner to the middle of the river, where they vanished with a dim gurgle. There was an extra splash, a loud one, not an echo. Aha! Cordelia thought—I saw you jump too, Barrayaran. But whatever had splashed didn't show above the surface, and its ripples were lost in the current. There came some more hisses, and a shattering shriek, from downstream. Vorkosigan drew the stunner.

"There's a whole herd of them out there," Cordelia commented nervously. They stood back to back, trying to penetrate the blackness. Vorkosigan rested the stunner across one wrist, and let off a carefully-aimed burst. It buzzed quietly, and one of the dark shapes slumped to the ground. Its comrades sniffed it curiously, and moved in closer.

"I wish your gun had more of a bang." He aimed again and dropped two more, without any effect on the rest. He cleared his throat. "You know, your stunner's almost out of charge."

"Not enough to flatten the rest of them, eh?"

"No."

One of the scavengers, bolder than the rest, darted forward. Vorkosigan met its charge with a shout and a rush of his own. It retreated temporarily. The breed of scavengers that ranged the plains was slightly larger than its mountain cousins, and if possible, uglier. Obviously, it also travelled in larger groups. The ring of beasts closed tighter as they attempted to retreat toward the valley rim.

"Oh, hell," said Vorkosigan. "That does it." A dozen silent, ghostly globes were drifting in from above. "What a foul way to die. Well, let's take as many with us as possible." He glanced at her, seemed about to say more, but then only shook his head and braced for the rush.

Cordelia, heart lurching, gazed up at the descending radials and was illuminated by an idea of awesome brilliance.

"Oh, no," she breathed. "That's not the last straw. That's the home fleet, coming to the rescue. Come, my pretties," she coaxed. "Come to Mama."

39

"Have you lost your mind?" asked Vorkosigan.

"You wanted a bang? I'll give you a bang. What do you think holds those things up?"

"Hadn't thought about it. But of course it would almost have to be—"

"Hydrogen! Bet you anything those darling little chemistry sets are electrolyzing water. Notice how they hang around rivers and streams? Wish I had some gloves."

"Allow me." His grin winked out of the fire-streaked dark at her. He jumped up and hooked a radial out of the air by its writhing maroon tendrils, and flung it to earth before the approaching scavengers. Cordelia, holding her torch like a fencer's foil, thrust toward it at full extension. Sparks scattered as she jabbed two, then three times.

The radial exploded in a ball of blinding flame that singed her eyebrows, with a great bass whoom and an astonishing stench. Orange and green afterimages danced across her retinas. She repeated the trick at Vorkosigan's next snatch. One of the scavenger's fur caught fire, and it led a general retreat, screeching and hissing. She poked again at a radial in the air. It went off with a flash that illuminated the whole reach of the river valley and the humping backs of the fleeing pack of scavengers.

Vorkosigan was patting her on the back frantically; it wasn't until the smell caught her that she realized she'd set her own hair on fire. He got it out. The rest of the radials sailed high into the air and away, except for one Vorkosigan captured and held by standing on its tendrils.

"Ha!" Cordelia war danced around him in triumph, the adrenalin rush giving her a silly urge to giggle. She drew a deep breath. "Is your hand all right?"

40

"It's a little burned," he admitted. He took off his shirt and bundled the radial into it. It pulsated and stank. "We might want this later." He rinsed his hand briefly in the stream, and they jogged quickly back to their campsite. Dubauer lay undisturbed, although a few minutes later one stray scavenger turned up at the edge of the firelight, sniffing and hissing. Vorkosigan put it to flight with torch, knife, and swearing—whispered, so as not to wake the ensign.

"I think we'd better live on field rations for the rest of the trip," he said, returning.

Cordelia nodded heartfelt agreement.

She roused the men at the first grey light of dawn, as anxious now as Vorkosigan to complete the trip to the safety of the supply cache as quickly as possible. The radial held captive in Vorkosigan's shirt had died and deflated during the night, turning into a horrible gelid blob. Vorkosigan of necessity took a few minutes to wash it out in the stream, but the stinks and stains it left made him the unquestioned front-runner in the filth-collection contest Cordelia felt they were having. They had a quick snack of their dull but safe oatmeal and blue cheese dressing, and started on their way as the sun rose, sending their long shadows racing ahead of them across the rusty, flower-strewn levels.

Near their noon halt Vorkosigan took a break and disappeared behind a bush for biological necessity. In a few moments a string of curses came floating around it, followed shortly by the speaker himself, hopping from foot to foot and shaking out the legs of his trousers. Cordelia gave him a look of innocent inquiry.

"You know those light yellow cones of sand we've been seeing?" Vorkosigan said, unbuckling his pants.

"Yes . . ."

"Don't stand on one to piss."

Cordelia failed to strangle a giggle. "What did you find? Or should I say, what found you?"

Vorkosigan turned his trousers inside out and began picking out the little round white creatures running among their folds on ciliated legs. Cordelia appropriated one and held it on the palm of her hand for a closer look. It was yet another model of the radials, an underground form.

"Ow!" She brushed it away hastily.

"Stings, doesn't it?" snarled Vorkosigan.

A burble of laughter welled up within her. But she was saved from a lapse of control when she noticed a more sobering feature of his appearance.

"Hey, that scratch doesn't look too good, does it?"

The claw mark of the scavenger on his right leg that Vorkosigan had collected the night they buried Rosemont was swollen and bluish, with ugly red streaks radiating from it up as far as his knee.

"It's all right," he said firmly, beginning to put on his de-radialed pants.

"It doesn't look all right. Let me see."

"There's nothing you can do about it here," he protested, but submitted to a brief examination. "Satisfied?" he inquired sarcastically, and finished dressing.

"I wish your micro people had been a little more thorough when they concocted that salve," Cordelia shrugged. "But you're right. Nothing to be done now."

They trudged on. Cordelia watched him more closely now. From time to time he would begin to favor the leg, then notice her scrutiny and march

42

forward with a determinedly even stride. But by the end of the day he had abandoned subterfuge and was frankly limping. In spite of it he led on into the sunset, the afterglow of the sunset, and the gathering night, until the cratered mountain toward which they had been angling was a black bulk on the horizon. At last, stumbling in the dark, he gave up and called a halt. She was glad, for Dubauer was flagging, leaning on her heavily and trying to lie down. They slept where they stopped on the red sandy soil. Vorkosigan cracked a cold light and took his usual watch, as Cordelia lay in the dirt and watched the unreachable stars wheel overhead.

Vorkosigan had asked to be waked before dawn, but she let him sleep until full light. She didn't like the way he looked, alternately pale and flushed, or his shallow rapid breathing.

"Think you'd better take one of your pain killers?" she asked him when he rose, for he seemed barely able to put weight on the leg, which was much more swollen.

"Not yet. I have to save some for the end." He cut a long stick instead, and the three of them began the day's task of walking down their shadows.

"How far to the end?" Cordelia asked.

"I estimate a day, day and a half, depending on what kind of time we can make." He grimaced. "Don't worry. You're not going to have to carry me. I'm one of the fittest men in my command." He limped on. "Over forty."

"How many men over forty are there in your command?"

"Four."

Cordelia snorted.

"Anyway, if it becomes necessary, I have a stimu-

43

lant in my medkit that would animate a corpse. But I want to save it for the end too."

"What kind of trouble are you anticipating?"

"It all depends on who picks up my call. I know Radnov—my Political Officer—has at least two agents in my communications section." He pursed his lips, measuring her again. "You see, I don't think it was a general mutiny. I think it was a spur-of-the-moment assassination attempt on the part of Radnov and a very few others. Using you Betans, they thought they could get rid of me without implicating themselves. If I'm right, everyone aboard ship thinks I'm dead. All but one."

"Which one?"

"Wouldn't I like to know. The one who hit me on the head and hid me in the bracken, instead of cutting my throat and dumping me in the nearest hole. Lieutenant Radnov seems to have a ringer in his group. And yet—if this ringer were loyal to me, all he'd have to do is tell Gottyan, my first officer, and he'd have had a loyal patrol down to pick me up before now. Now who in my command is so confused in his thinking as to betray both sides at once? Or am I missing something?"

"Maybe they're all still chasing my ship," suggested Cordelia.

"Where is your ship?"

Honesty should be safely academic by now, Cordelia calculated. "Well on its way back to Beta Colony."

"Unless they've been captured."

"No. They were out of your range when I talked to them. They may not be armed, but they can run rings around your battle cruiser."

"Hm. Well, it's possible."

He doesn't sound surprised, Cordelia noted. I'd

bet his secret reports on our stuff would give our counterintelligence people colonic spasms. "How far will they pursue?"

"That's up to Gottyan. If he judges he can't possibly catch them, he'll return to the picket station. If he thinks he can, he's bound to make maximum effort."

"Why?"

He glanced sidelong at her. "I can't discuss that."

"I don't see why not. I'm not going anywhere but a Barrayaran prison cell, for a while. Funny how one's standards change. After this trek, it will seem like the lap of luxury."

"I'll try to see it doesn't come to that," he smiled.

His eyes bothered her, and his smile. His curtness she could meet and match with her own flippancy, guarding herself as with a fencer's foil. His kindness was like fencing with the sea, her strokes going soft and losing all volition. She flinched from the smile, and his face fell, then became closed and grave again.

▶ ▶ CHAPTER THREE

They walked in silence for a time after breakfast. Vorkosigan broke it first. His fever seemed to be eating away at his original taciturnity.

"Converse with me. It will take my mind off my leg."

"What about?"

"Anything."

She considered, walking. "Do you find commanding a warship very different from ordinary vessels?"

He thought it over. "It's not the ship that's different. It's the men. Leadership is mostly a power over imagination, and never more so than in combat. The bravest man alone can only be an armed lunatic. The real strength lies in the ability to get others to do your work. Don't you find it so even in the fleets of Beta Colony?"

Cordelia smiled. "If anything, even more so. If it ever came down to exerting power by force, it would mean I'd already lost it. I prefer to maintain a light touch. Then I have the advantage, because I find I can always keep my temper, or whatever, just a little longer than the next man." She glanced around at the spring desert. "I think civilization must have been invented for the benefit of women, certainly of mothers. I can't imagine how my cavewoman ancestors cared for families under primitive conditions."

"I suspect they worked together in groups," said Vorkosigan. "I'll wager you could have handled it, had you been born in those days. You have the competence one would look for in a mother of warriors."

Cordelia wondered if Vorkosigan were pulling her leg. He did seem to have a streak of dry humor. "Save me from that! To pour your life into sons for eighteen or twenty years, and then have the government take them away and waste them cleaning up after some failure of politics—no thanks."

"I never really looked at it that way," allowed Vorkosigan. He was quiet for a time, stumping along with his stick. "Suppose they volunteered? Do your people have no ideal of service?"

"Noblesse oblige?" But it was her turn to be silent, a little embarrassed. "I suppose, if they volunteered, it would be different. However, I have no children, so fortunately I won't have to face those decisions."

"Are you glad, or sorry?"

"About children?" She glanced at his face. He seemed to have no awareness of having hit a sore point dead on. "They just haven't come my way, I guess."

The thread of their talk was broken as they negotiated a rocky stretch of badlands, full of sudden clefts opening at their feet. It involved some tricky climbing, and shoving Dubauer through safely took all her

48

attention. On the far side they took a break by un-spoken mutual agreement, sitting leaning against a rock in exhaustion. Vorkosigan rolled up his pants leg and loosened his boot top for a look at the fester-ing wound that was threatening to slow him to a halt.

"You seem a fair nurse. Do you think it would help to open and drain it?" he asked Cordelia.

"I don't know. I'd be afraid messing around with it would just make it dirtier." She deduced the injury must be feeling very much worse for him to have mentioned it, confirmed when he took half a pain killer from his precious and limited store.

They pressed on, and Vorkosigan began to talk again. He told some sardonic anecdotes from his cadet days, and described his father, who had been a general commanding ground forces in his day, and a contemporary and friend of the wily old man who was now Emperor. Cordelia caught a faint, far away impression of a cold father whom a young son could never quite please, even with his best efforts, yet who shared with him a bond of underlying loyalty. She described her mother, a tough-minded medical professional resisting retirement, and her brother, who had just purchased his second child permit.

"Do you remember your mother well?" Cordelia asked. "She died when you were quite young, I gather. An accident, like my father?"

"No accident. Politics." His face became sober, and distant. "Had you not heard of Yuri Vorbarra's Massacre?"

"I—don't know much about Barrayar."

"Ah. Well, Emperor Yuri, in the later days of his madness, became extremely paranoid about his rela-tions. It became a self-fulfilling prophecy, in the end. He sent his death squads out, all in one night.

The squad sent for Prince Xav never got past his liveried men. And for some obscure reason, he didn't send one for my father, presumably because he wasn't a descendant of Emperor Dorca Vorbarra. I can't imagine what old Yuri thought he was about, to kill my mother and leave my father alive. That was when my father threw his corps behind Ezar Vorbarra, in the civil war that followed."

"Oh." Her throat seemed dry and thick in the dusty afternoon. She had evoked a coldness in him, so that the film of sweat on his forehead seemed suddenly like a condensation.

"It's been on my mind . . . You were talking about the peculiar things people do in a panic, earlier, and I remembered it. Hadn't thought of it in years. When Yuri's men blew in the door—"

"My God, you weren't *present*?"

"Oh, yes. I was on the list too, of course. Each assassin was assigned a particular target. The one assigned to my mother—I grabbed this knife, a table knife, by my plate, and struck at him. But right in front of me on the table there had been a good carving knife. If only I had grabbed it instead . . . I might as well have struck him with a spoon. He just picked me up, and threw me across the room—"

"How old were you?"

"Eleven. Small for my age. I was always small for my age. He cornered her against the far wall. He fired a . . ." He sucked his lower lip between his teeth and chewed it, just short of breaking the skin to bleed. "Odd how many details come back when you talk about something. I thought I had forgotten more."

He glanced at her white face, and grew suddenly contrite. "I've disturbed you, with this babble. I'm

50

sorry. It was all very long ago. I don't know why I'm talking so much."

I do, thought Cordelia. He was pale and no longer sweating, in spite of the heat. Half-unconsciously, he fastened the top of his shirt. He feels cold, she thought; fever going up. How far up? Plus whatever effect those pills have. This could get very scary.

An obscure impulse made her say, "I know what you mean, though, about talking bringing it back. First there was the shuttle going up, like a bullet as usual, and my brother waving, which was silly, because he couldn't possibly see us—and then there was this smear of light across the sky, like a second sun, and a rain of fire. And this *stupid* feeling of total comprehension. You wait for the shock to set in, and relieve you—and it never does. Then the blank vision. Not blackness, but this silver-purple glow, for days after. I had almost forgotten about being blinded, till just now."

He stared at her. "That's exactly—I was about to say, he fired a sonic grenade into her stomach. I couldn't hear anything after that for quite some time. As if all sound had gone off the scale of human reception. Total noise, emptier of meaning than silence."

"Yes . . ." How strange, that he should know exactly what I felt—he says it better, though . . .

"I suppose my determination to be a soldier stems from that date. I mean the real thing, not the parades and the uniforms and the glamour, but the logistics, the offensive advantage, the speed and surprise—the power. A better-prepared, stronger, tougher, faster, meaner son-of-a-bitch than any who came through that door. My first combat experience. Not very successful."

He was shivering, now. But then, so was she. They walked on, and she sought to turn the subject.

"I've never been in combat. What's it like?"

He paused thoughtfully. Measuring me again, thought Cordelia. And sweating; fever must be topping out, for the moment, thank heavens.

"At a distance, in space, there's the illusion of a clean and glorious fight. Almost abstract. It might be a simulation, or a game. Reality doesn't break in unless your ship is hit." He gazed at the ground in front of him, as if choosing his path, but the ground was very level there. "Murder—murder is different. That day at Komarr, when I killed my Political Officer—I was angrier that day than the day I—than another time. But close up, feeling the life pass out under your hands, seeing that blank unoccupied corpse, you see your own death in the face of your victim. Yet he had betrayed my honor."

"I'm not sure I quite understand that."

"Yes. Anger seems to make you stronger, not weaker like me. I wish I understood how you do that."

It was another one of his weird unmanageable compliments. She fell silent, looking at her feet, the mountain ahead, the sky, anywhere but his unreadable face. So she was the first to notice the contrail glowing in the westering sun.

"Hey, does that look like a shuttle up there to you?"

"Indeed it does. Let's watch from the shade of that big bush," directed Vorkosigan.

"Don't you want to try and attract their attention?"

"No." He turned his hand palm up in response to her look of inquiry. "My best friends and my deadliest enemies all wear the same uniform. I prefer to make my presence known as selectively as possible."

They could hear the distant roar of the shuttle's engines now as it vanished behind the grey-green wooded mountain to the west.

"They seem to be headed for the cache," commented Vorkosigan. "That complicates things." He compressed his lips. "What are they doing back there, I wonder? Could Gottyan have found the sealed orders?"

"Surely he'd inherit all your orders."

"Yes, but I didn't have my files in the standard location, not wishing to share all my affairs with the Council of Ministers. I don't think Korabik Gottyan could find what eludes Radnov. Radnov's a clever spy."

"Is Radnov a tall, broad-shouldered man with a face like an axeblade?"

"No, that sounds like Sergeant Bothari. Where did you see him?"

"He was the man who shot Dubauer in the woods by the ravine."

"Oh, really?" Vorkosigan's eyes lit, and he smiled wolfishly. "Much becomes clear."

"Not to me," Cordelia prodded.

"Sergeant Bothari is a very strange man. I had to discipline him rather severely last month."

"Severely enough to make him a candidate for Radnov's conspiracy?"

"I'll wager Radnov thought so. I'm not sure I can make you understand about Bothari. Nobody else seems to. He's a superb ground combat soldier. He also hates my guts, as you Betans would phrase it. He *enjoys* hating my guts. It seems to be necessary for his ego, somehow."

"Would he shoot you in the back?"

"Never. Strike me in the face, yes. In fact, it was

53

for decking me that he was disciplined last time."
Vorkosigan rubbed his jaw thoughtfully. "But arming
him to the teeth and leading him into battle at my
back is perfectly safe."

"He sounds like an absolute looney."

"Odd, a number of people have said that. I like
him."

"And you accuse us Betans of running a circus."

Vorkosigan shrugged, amused. "Well, it's useful
for me to have someone to work out with who doesn't
pull his punches. Surviving hand-to-hand combat practice with Bothari gives me a real edge. I prefer to
keep that phase of our relationship confined to the
practice ring, however. I can imagine how Radnov
might be misled into including Bothari without examining his politics too closely. He acts like just the
sort of fellow one might stick with the dirty work—by
God, I'll bet that's just what Radnov did! Good old
Bothari."

Cordelia glanced at Dubauer, standing blankly beside her. "I'm afraid I can't share your enthusiasm.
He nearly killed me."

"I can't pretend he's a moral or intellectual giant.
He's a very complex man with a very limited range
of expression, who's had some very bad experiences.
But in his own twisty way, he's honorable."

The ground rose almost imperceptibly as they approached the mountain's base. The change was marked
by the gradual encroachment of vegetation, thin woods
watered by a multitude of small springs from the
mountain's secret sources. They struck south around
the base of the dusty green cone that rose steeply
some 1500 meters above the more gradually sloping
shoulderland.

Pulling the stumbling Dubauer along, Cordelia

mentally cursed, for what seemed the thousandth time, Vorkosigan's choice of weapons. When the ensign fell, cutting his forehead, her grief and irritation erupted into words.

"Why can't you people use civilized weapons, anyway? I'd as soon give a disruptor to a chimpanzee as a Barrayaran. Trigger-happy goons." Dubauer sat dizzily, and she mopped at the blood with her dirty handkerchief, then sat too.

Vorkosigan lowered himself awkwardly to the ground beside them, bad leg out straight, silently endorsing the break. He gazed at her tense unhappy face, and offered her a serious answer.

"I have an aversion to stunners, in that sort of situation," he said slowly. "Nobody hesitates to rush one, and if there are enough of them they can always get it away from you in the end. I've seen men killed, relying on stunners, who could have walked right through with a disruptor or plasma arc. A disruptor has real authority."

"On the other hand, nobody hesitates to *fire* a stunner," said Cordelia suggestively. "And it gives you a margin for error."

"What, would you hesitate to fire a disruptor?"

"Yes. I might as well not have it at all."

"Ah."

Curiosity prodded her, mulling on his words. "How in the world did they kill him with a stunner, the man you saw?"

"They didn't kill him with the stunner. After they took it away from him they kicked him to death."

"Oh." Cordelia's stomach tightened. "Not—not a friend of yours, I hope."

"As it happens, he was. He shared something of

55

your attitude toward weaponry. Soft." He frowned into the distance.

They struggled up, and trudged on through the woods. The Barrayaran tried to help her more with Dubauer, for a time. But Dubauer recoiled from him, and between the ensign's resistance and his own bad leg, the attempt failed awkwardly.

Vorkosigan withdrew into himself, and became less talkative, after that. All his concentration seemed focused on pushing himself ahead just one more step, but he muttered to himself alarmingly. Cordelia had a nasty vision of collapse and fevered delirium, and no faith at all in her ability to take over his role of identifying and contacting a loyal member of his crew. It was plain that an error in judgement could be lethal, and while she could not say that all Barrayarans looked alike to her, she was forcibly reminded of the old conundrum that starts, "All Cretans are liars."

Near sunset, threading their way through a patch of denser woods, they came suddenly on a little glade of astonishing beauty. A waterfall foamed down over a bed of black rocks that glistened like obsidian, a cascade of lace alive with light. The grass that bordered the streambed was backlit by the sun in a translucent gold glow. The surrounding trees, tall, dark green, and shady, set it like a gem.

Vorkosigan leaned on his stick and gazed at it a while. Cordelia thought she had never seen a tireder looking human being, but then, she had no mirror.

"We have about fifteen kilometers to go," he said. "I don't wish to approach the cache in the dark. We'll stop here tonight, rest, and take it in the morning."

They flopped down in the soft grass and watched

the glorious flaming sunset in silence, like an old married couple too tired to get up and turn it off. At last the failing light forced them into action. They washed hands and faces in the stream, and Vorkosigan shared his Barrayaran field rations at last. Even after four days of oatmeal and blue cheese dressing, they were a disappointment.

"Are you sure this isn't instant boots?" asked Cordelia sadly, for in color, taste, and smell they closely resembled pulverized shoe leather pressed into wafers.

Vorkosigan grinned sardonically. "They're organic, nutritious, and they'll keep for years—in fact, they probably have."

Cordelia smiled around a dry and chewy mouthful. She hand-fed Dubauer his—he was inclined to spit them out—then washed and settled him for the night. He had had no seizures this day, which she hoped might be a sign of partial improvement in his condition.

The earth still breathed a comfortable warmth from the heat of the day, and the stream purled softly in the stillness. She wished she could sleep for a hundred years, like an enchanted princess. Instead she rose and volunteered for the first watch.

"I think you'd better have the extra sleep tonight," she told Vorkosigan. "I've had the short watch two nights out of three. It's your turn."

"There's no need—" he began.

"If you don't make it, I don't make it," she pointed out bluntly. "And neither does he." She jerked her thumb at the quiescent Dubauer. "I intend to see that you make it tomorrow."

Vorkosigan took another half pain killer and lay back where he sat, conceding the argument. Still he remained restless, sleep evading him, and he watched her through the dimness. His eyes seemed to gleam feverishly. He finally propped himself up on one elbow, as she finished a patrol around the edge of the glade and sat down cross-legged on the ground beside him.

"I . . ." he began, and trailed off. "You're not what I expected a female officer to be."

"Oh? Well, you're not what I expected a Barrayaran officer to be, either, so I guess that makes two of us." She added curiously, "What did you expect?"

"I'm—not sure. You're as professional as any officer I've ever served with, without once trying to be an, an imitation man. It's extraordinary."

"There's nothing extraordinary about me," she denied.

"Beta Colony must be a very unusual place, then."

"It's just home. Nothing special. Lousy climate."

"So I've heard." He picked up a twig and dug little furrows into the soil with it, until it snapped. "They don't have arranged marriages on Beta Colony, do they?"

She stared. "Certainly not! What a bizarre concept. Sounds almost like a civil rights violation. Heavens—you don't mean to say they do, on Barrayar?"

"In my caste, almost always."

"Doesn't anybody object?"

"They're not *forced*. Arranged, by the parents usually. It—seems to work. For many people."

"Well, I suppose it's possible."

"How, ah—how do you arrange yourselves? With no go-betweens it must be very awkward. I mean, to refuse someone, to their face."

"I don't know. It's something lovers work out after

58

they've known each other quite a time, usually, and wish to apply for a child permit. This contractual thing you describe must be like marrying a total stranger. Naturally it would be awkward."

"Hm." He found another twig. "In the Time of Isolation, on Barrayar, for a man to take a woman of the soldier caste for a lover was regarded as stealing her honor, and he was supposed to die a thief's death for it. A custom more honored in the breach, I'm sure, although it's a favorite subject for drama. Today we are betwixt and between. The old customs are dead, and we keep trying on new ones, like badly-fitting clothes. It's hard to know what's right, anymore." After a moment he added, "What had you expected?"

"From a Barrayaran? I don't know. Something criminal, I suppose. I wasn't too crazy about being taken prisoner."

His eyes fell. "I've—seen what you're talking about, of course. I can't deny it exists. It's an infection of the imagination, that spreads from man to man. It's worst when it goes from the top down. Bad for discipline, bad for morale . . . I hate most how it affects the younger officers, when they encounter it in the men they should be molding themselves on. They haven't the weight of experience, to fight it in their own minds, nor distinguish when a man is stealing the Emperor's authority to cloak his own appetites. And so they are corrupted almost before they know what's happening." His voice was intense in the darkness.

"I'd actually only thought about it from the prisoner's point of view, myself. I take it I am fortunate in my choice of captors."

"They're the scum of the service. But you must

59

believe, a small minority. Although I've no use for those who pretend not to see, either, and they are not such a minority as . . . But make no mistake. It's not an easy infection to fight off. But you have nothing to fear from me. I promise you."

"I'd—already figured that out."

They sat in silence for a time, until the night crept up out of the low places to drain the last turquoise from the sky, and the waterfall ran pearly in the starlight. She thought he had fallen asleep, but he stirred, and spoke again. She could barely see his face, but for a little glint from the whites of his eyes, and his teeth.

"Your customs seem so free, and calm, to me. As innocent as sunlight. No grief, no pain, no irrevocable mistakes. No boys turned criminal by fear. No stupid jealousy. No honor ever lost."

"That's an illusion. You can still lose your honor. It just doesn't happen in a night. It can take years, to drain away in bits and dribbles." She paused, in the friendly dark. "I knew this woman, once—a very good friend of mine. In Survey. She was rather—socially inept. Everyone around her seemed to be finding their soul-mates, and the older she grew, the more panicky she got about being left out. Quite pathetically anxious.

"She finally fell in with a man with the most astonishing talent for turning gold into lead. She couldn't use a word like love, or trust, or honor in his presence without eliciting clever mockery. Pornography was permitted; poetry, never.

"They were, as it happened, of equal rank when the captaincy of their ship fell open. She'd sweated blood for this command, worked her tail off—well, I'm sure you know what it's like. Commands are few, and everybody wants one. Her lover persuaded her, partly by promise that turned out to be lies, later—children, in fact—to stand down in his favor, and he got the command. Quite the strategist. It ended soon after. Thoroughly dry.

"She had no stomach for another lover, after that. So you see, I think your old Barrayarans may have been on to something, after all. The inept—need rules, for their own protection."

The waterfall whispered in the silence. "I—knew a man once," his voice came out of the darkness. "He was married, at twenty, to a girl of high rank of eighteen. Arranged, of course but he was very happy with it.

"He was away most of the time, on duty. She found herself free, rich, alone in the capital in the society of people—not altogether vicious, but older than herself. Rich parasites, their parasites, users. She was courted, and it went to her head. Not her heart, I think. She took lovers, as those around her did. Looking back, I don't think she felt any more emotion for them than vanity and pride of conquest, but at the time . . . He had built up a false picture of her in his mind, and having it suddenly shattered . . . This boy had a very bad temper. It was his particular curse. He resolved on a duel with her lovers.

"She had two on her string, or her on theirs, I can't say which. He didn't care who survived, or if he were arrested. He imagined he was dishonored, you see. He arranged to have each meet him at a deserted place, about half an hour apart."

He paused for a long time. Cordelia waited, barely breathing, uncertain whether to encourage him to go

61

on or not. He continued eventually, but his voice
went flatter and he spoke in a rush.

"The first was another pig-headed young aristocrat
like himself, and he played out the game by the
rules. He knew the use of the two swords, fought
with flair, and almost killed m—my friend. The last
thing he said was that he'd always wanted to be
killed by a jealous husband, only at age eighty."

By this time, the little slip was no surprise to
Cordelia, and she wondered if her story had been as
transparent to him. It certainly seemed so.

"The second was a high government minister, an
older man. He wouldn't fight, although he knocked
him down and stood him up several times. After—
after the other, who had died with a joke in his
mouth, he could hardly bear it. He finally slew him
outright in the middle of his begging, and left them
there.

"He stopped at his wife's apartment, to tell her
what he'd done, and returned to his ship, to wait for
arrest. This all happened in one afternoon. She was
enraged, full of wounded pride—she would have
dueled with him, if she could—and she killed herself. Shot herself in the head, with his service plasma
arc. I wouldn't have thought it a woman's weapon.
Poison, or cutting the wrists, or something. But she
was true Vor. It burned her face entirely away. She'd
had the most beautiful imaginable face . . .

"Things worked out very strangely. It was assumed
the two lovers had killed each other—I swear, he
never planned it that way—and that she'd killed
herself in despondency. No one ever asked him the
first question about it."

His voice slowed, and intensified. "He went
through that whole afternoon like a sleepwalker, or

an actor, saying the expected lines, going through the expected motions, and at the end his honor was no better for it. Nothing was served, no point was proved. It was all as false as her love affairs, except for the deaths. They were real." He paused. "So you see, you Betans have one advantage. You at least permit each other to learn from your mistakes."

"I'm—grieved, for your friend. Does it seem very long ago?"

"Sometimes. Over twenty years. They say that senile people remember things from their youth more clearly than those of last week. Maybe he's getting senile."

"I see." She took the story in like some strange, spiked gift, too fragile to drop, too painful to hold. He lay back, silent again, and she took another turn around the glade, listening at the wood's edge to a silence so profound the roaring of the blood in her ears seemed to drown it out. When she'd completed the round, Vorkosigan was asleep, restless and shivering in his fever. She filched one of the half-burned bedrolls from Dubauer, and covered him up.

▶▶ CHAPTER FOUR

Vorkosigan woke about three hours before dawn, and made her lie down to snatch a couple hours sleep. In the grey before sun-up he roused her again. He had evidently bathed in the stream, and used the single-application packet of depilitory he had been saving in his belt to wipe away the itchy four-day growth on his face.

"I need some help with this leg. I want to open and drain it and cover it back up. That will hold until this afternoon, and after that it won't matter."

"Right."

Vorkosigan stripped off boot and sock, and Cordelia had him hold his leg under a rushing spout at the edge of the waterfall. She rinsed his combat knife, then laid open the grossly swollen wound in a deep, quick stroke. Vorkosigan went white around the lips, but said nothing. It was Cordelia who winced. The cut squirted blood and pus and odd-smelling clotted matter which the stream washed away. She tried not to think about what new microbes they might be introducing by the procedure. It only needed to be a temporary palliative.

She packed the wound with the last of the tube of his rather ineffective antibiotic, and stripped out the tube of plastic bandage to cover it.

"It feels better." But Vorkosigan stumbled and almost fell when he attempted to walk normally. "Right," he muttered. "The time has come." Ceremoniously, he removed the last pain killer and a small blue pill from his first aid kit, swallowed them, and threw the empty case away. Cordelia somewhat absently picked it up, found herself with no place to put it, and surreptitiously dropped it again.

"These things work great," he told her, "until they give out, when you fall down like a marionette with the strings cut. I'm good for about sixteen hours now."

Indeed, by the time they'd finished the field rations and readied Dubauer for the day's march, he looked not merely normal, but fresh and rested and full of energy. Neither referred to the previous night's conversation.

He led them in a wide arc around the mountain's base, so that by noon they were approaching the cratered side from nearly due west. They made their way through woods and glades to a spur opposite a great bowl that was all that remained of the lower mountainside from the days before an ancient volcanic cataclysm. Vorkosigan crawled out on a treeless promontory, taking care not to show himself above the tall grass. Dubauer, wan and exhausted, curled up on his side in their place of concealment and fell asleep. Cordelia watched him until his breathing was slow and steady, then crept out beside Vorkosigan.

66

The Barrayaran captain had his field scope out, sweeping over the hazy green amphitheater.

"There's the shuttle. They're camped in the cache caves. See that dark streak beside the long waterfall? That's the entrance." He lent her the scope for a closer look.

"Oh, there's somebody coming out. You can see their faces on high magnification."

Vorkosigan took back the scope. "Koudelka. He's all right. But the thin man with him is Darobey, one of Radnov's spies in my communications section. Remember his face—you'll need to know when to keep your head down."

Cordelia wondered if Vorkosigan's air of enjoyment was an artifact of the stimulant, or a primitive anticipation of the clash to come. His eyes seemed to gleam as he watched, counted, and calculated.

He hissed through his teeth, sounding a bit like one of the local carnivores himself. "There's Radnov, by God! Wouldn't I like to get my hands on him. But this time I can take the Ministry men to trial. I'd like to see them try to get one of their pets out from under a bona fide charge of mutiny. The high command and the Council of Counts will be with me this time. No, Radnov, you're going to live—and regret it." He settled on stomach and elbows and devoured the scene.

He stiffened suddenly, and grinned. "It's time my luck changed. There's Gottyan, armed, so he must be in charge. We're nearly home. Come on."

They crept back to the cloaking shelter of the trees. Dubauer was not where they'd left him.

"Oh, lord," breathed Cordelia, turning and peering into the brush in all directions. "Which way did he go?"

"He can't have gone far," reassured Vorkosigan, although he too looked worried. They each made a circle of a hundred meters or so through the woods. Idiot! Cordelia castigated herself furiously in her panic. You just had to go peek . . . They met back at the original spot without seeing any mark made by the wandering ensign.

"Look, we haven't the time to search for him now," said Vorkosigan. "As soon as I've regained command, I'll send a patrol out to look for him. With proper search-scopes, they could find him faster than we can."

Cordelia thought of carnivores, cliffs, deep pools, Barrayaran patrols with twitchy trigger fingers. "We've come so far," she began.

"And if I don't regain command soon, neither of you will survive anyway."

Torn, but obedient to reason, she allowed Vorkosigan to take her by the arm. Only leaning on her slightly, he picked a way down through the woods. As they neared the Barrayaran camp, he put a thick finger to his lips.

"Go as quietly as you can. I haven't come this far to be shot by one of my own pickets. Ah. Lie down here." He placed her in a spot behind some fallen logs and knee-high vegetation overlooking a faint new path beaten through the brush.

"You're not just going to knock on the front door?"

"No."

"Why not, if your Gottyan is all right?"

"Because there's something else wrong. I don't know why this landing party is here." He meditated a moment, then handed her back the stunner. "If you have to use a weapon, it had better be one you can handle. It still has a bit of charge—one or two

68

shots. This path runs between sentry points, and sooner or later someone's going to come down it. Keep your head down until I call you."

He loosed his knife in its sheath and took a concealed position on the other side of the path. They waited a quarter of an hour, then another. The woodland drowsed in the warm, soft, white air.

Then down the path came the sound of boots scuffing through the leaf litter. Cordelia went rigidly still, trying to peer through the weeds without raising her head. A tall form in the wonderfully effective Barrayaran camouflage fatigues resolved itself as a grey-haired officer. As he passed Vorkosigan rose from his hiding place as if resurrected.

"Korabik," he said softly, but with genuine warmth in his voice. He stood grinning, arms folded, waiting.

Gottyan spun about, one hand drawing the nerve disruptor at his hip. After a beat, a look of surprise came over his face. "Aral! The landing party reported the Betans had killed you," and he stepped, not forward as Cordelia had expected from the tone of Vorkosigan's voice, but back. The disruptor was still in his hand as if he had forgotten to put it away, but gripped firmly, not dangling. Cordelia's stomach sank.

Vorkosigan looked faintly puzzled, as if disappointed by the cool, controlled reception. "I'm glad to know you're not superstitious," he joked.

"I should have known better than to think you dead until I'd seen you buried with a stake through your heart," said Gottyan, sadly ironic.

"What's wrong, Korabik?" asked Vorkosigan quietly. "You're no Minister's lickspittle."

At these words Gottyan brought the disruptor up to undisguised aim. Vorkosigan stood very still.

"No," he answered frankly. "I thought the story

Radnov told about you and the Betans smelled. And I was going to make damn sure it went through a board of inquiry when we got home." He paused. "But then—I would have been in command. After being acting captain for six months, I'd be sure to be confirmed. What do you think the chances of command are at my age? Five percent? Two? Zero?"

"They're not as bad as you think," said Vorkosigan, still quietly. "There are some things coming up that very few people have heard about. More ships, more openings."

"The usual rumors," Gottyan dismissed this.

"So you didn't believe I was dead?" probed Vorkosigan.

"I was sure you were. I took over—where did you put the sealed orders, by the way? We turned your cabin inside out looking for them."

Vorkosigan smiled dryly and shook his head. "I shall not increase your temptations."

"No matter." Gottyan's aim did not waver. "Then day before yesterday that psychopathic idiot Bothari came to see me in my cabin. He gave me the real story of what happened at the Betans' camp. Surprised the hell out of me—I'd have thought he'd be delighted at a chance to slit your throat. So we came back here to practice ground training. I was sure you'd turn up sooner or later—I expected you before this."

"I was delayed." Vorkosigan shifted position slightly, away from Cordelia's line of fire toward Gottyan. "Where's Bothari now?"

"Solitary confinement."

Vorkosigan winced. "That's very bad for him. I take it you didn't spread the news of my narrow escape?"

70

"Not even Radnov knows. He still thinks Bothari gutted you."

"Smug, is he?"

"Smug as a cat. I'd have taken great pleasure in wiping his face at the board, if only you'd had the good grace to meet with an accident on your hike."

Vorkosigan grimaced wryly. "It seems to me you haven't quite made up your mind what you really want to do. May I suggest it is not too late, even now, to change course?"

"You could never overlook this," stated Gottyan uncertainly.

"In my younger and more stiff-necked days, perhaps not. But to tell you the truth, I'm getting a little tired of slaying my enemies to teach them a lesson." Vorkosigan raised his chin and held Gottyan's eyes. "If you like, you can have my word. You know the worth of it."

The disruptor trembled slightly in Gottyan's hand, as he wavered on the edge of his decision. Cordelia, barely breathing, saw water standing in his eyes. One does not weep for the living, she thought, but for the dead; in that moment, while Vorkosigan still doubted, she knew he intended to fire.

She brought her stunner up, took careful aim, and squeezed off a burst. It buzzed weakly, but it was enough to bring Gottyan, head turning at the sudden movement, to his knees. Vorkosigan pounced on the disruptor, then relieved him of his plasma arc and knocked him to the ground.

"Damn you," croaked Gottyan, half-paralyzed. "Haven't you ever been out-maneuvered?"

"If I had I wouldn't be here," shrugged Vorkosigan. He subjected Gottyan to a rapid search, confiscating his knife and a number of other objects. "Who do you have posted as pickets?"

"Sens to the north, Koudelka to the south."

Vorkosigan removed Gottyan's belt and bound his hands behind his back. "You really did have trouble making up your mind, didn't you?" In an aside to Cordelia he explained, "Sens is one of Radnov's. Koudelka's mine. Rather like flipping a coin."

"And this was your friend?" Cordelia raised her eyebrows. "Seems to me the only difference between your friends and your enemies is how long they stand around chatting before they shoot you."

"Yes," Vorkosigan agreed, "I could take over the universe with this army if I could ever get all their weapons pointed in the same direction. Since your pants will stay up without it, Commander Naismith, may I please borrow your belt?" He finished securing Gottyan's legs with it, gagged him, then stood a moment looking up, then down the path.

"All Cretans are liars," murmured Cordelia, then more loudly, "North or south?"

"An interesting question. How would you answer it?"

"I had a teacher who used to reflect back my questions that way. I thought it was the Socratic method, and it impressed me immensely, until I found out he used it whenever he didn't know the answer." Cordelia stared at Gottyan, whom they had placed in the spot that had so effectively concealed her, wondering whether his directions marked a return to loyalty or a last-ditch effort to complete Vorkosigan's botched assassination. He stared back in puzzlement and hostility.

"North," she said reluctantly at last. She and

72

Vorkosigan exchanged a look of understanding, and he nodded briefly.

"Come on then."

They started quietly up the path, over a rise and through a hollow dense with grey-green thickets. "Have you known Gottyan long?"

"We served together for the last four years, since my demotion. He was a good career officer, I thought. Apolitical, thorough. He has a family."

"Do you think you could—get him back, later?"

"Forgive and forget? I gave him a chance at that. He turned me down. Twice, if you're right in your choice of directions." They were climbing another slope. "The sentry post is at the top. Whoever's there will be able to scope us in a moment. Drop back here and cover me. If you hear firing—" he paused, "use your initiative."

Cordelia smothered a short laugh. Vorkosigan loosed his disruptor in its holster and walked openly up the path, making plenty of noise.

"Sentry, report," she heard his voice call firmly.

"Nothing new since—good God, it's the *Captain*!" followed by the most honestly delighted laugh she felt she'd heard in centuries. She leaned against a tree, suddenly weak. And just when was it, she asked herself, that you stopped being afraid of him and started being afraid for him? And why is this new fear so much more gut-wrenching than the first? You don't seem to have come out ahead on the trade, have you?

"You can come out now, Commander Naismith," Vorkosigan's voice carried back to her. She rounded the last stand of underbrush and climbed a grassy knoll. Camped upon it were two young men looking very neat and military in their clean fatigues. One,

73

taller than Vorkosigan by a head, with a boy's face on a man's body, she recognized from her view through the scope as Koudelka. He was shaking his Captain's hand with unabashed enthusiasm, assuring himself of its unghostly reality. The other man's hand went to his disruptor when he saw her uniform.

"We were told the Betans killed you, sir," he said suspiciously.

"Yes, it's a rumor I've had difficulty living down," said Vorkosigan. "As you can see, it's not true."

"Your funeral was splendid," said Koudelka. "You should have been there."

"Next time, perhaps," Vorkosigan grinned.

"Oh. You know I didn't mean it that way, sir. Lieutenant Radnov made the best speech."

"I'm sure. He'd probably been working on it for months."

Koudelka, a little quicker on the uptake than his companion, said "Oh." His fellow merely looked puzzled.

Vorkosigan went on. "Permit me to introduce Commander Cordelia Naismith, of the Betan Astronomical Survey. She is . . ." he paused, and Cordelia waited interestedly to hear what status she was to be assigned, "—ah . . ."

"Sounds like?" she murmured helpfully.

Vorkosigan closed his lips firmly, pressing a smile out straight. "My prisoner," he chose finally. "On parole. Except for access to classified areas, she is to be extended every courtesy."

The two young men looked impressed, and wildly curious. "She's armed," Koudelka's companion pointed out.

"And a good thing, too." Vorkosigan did not enlarge on this, but went on to more urgent affairs. "Who is in the landing party?"

Koudelka rattled off a list of names, his memory jogged occasionally by his cohort.

"All right," Vorkosigan sighed. "Radnov, Darobey, Sens, and Tafas are to be disarmed, as quietly and cleanly as possible, and placed under arrest on a charge of mutiny. There will be some others later. I don't want any communication with the *General Vorkraft* until they're under lock and key. Do you know where Lieutenant Buffa is?"

"In the caverns. Sir?" Koudelka was starting to look a little miserable, as he began to deduce what was happening.

"Yes?"

"Are you sure about Tafas?"

"Nearly." Vorkosigan gentled his voice. "They'll be tried. That's the purpose of a trial, to separate the guilty from the innocent."

"Yes, sir." Koudelka accepted this limited guarantee for the welfare of a man Cordelia guessed must be his friend with a little bow of his head.

"Do you begin to see why I said the statistics about civil war conceal the most reality?" said Vorkosigan.

"Yes, sir." Koudelka met his eye squarely, and Vorkosigan nodded, sure of his man.

"All right. You two come with me."

They started off, Vorkosigan taking her arm again and scarcely limping, neatly concealing how much weight he was putting on her. They followed another path through the woodlands, up and down uneven ground, coming out within sight of the camouflaged door to the cache caverns.

The waterfall that spun down beside it ended in a

little pool, spilling over into a pretty stream that ran off into the woods. A strange group was assembled beside it. Cordelia could not at first make out what they were doing. Two Barrayarans stood watching while two more knelt by the water. As they approached the two kneelers stood, hauling a dripping, tan-clad figure, hands tied behind his back, from a prone position to his feet. He coughed, struggling for breath in sobbing gasps.

"It's Dubauer!" cried Cordelia. "What are they doing to him?"

Vorkosigan, who seemed to know instantly just what they were doing to him, muttered "Oh, hell," and started forward at a jerky jog. "That's my prisoner!" he roared out as they neared the group. "Hands off him!"

The Barrayarans braced so fast it looked like a spinal reflex. Dubauer, released, fell to his knees, still drawing breath in long sobs. Cordelia, running past them to Dubauer, thought she had never seen a more astonished-looking array of men. Dubauer's hair, swollen face, scanty new beard, and collar were soaking wet, his eyes were red, and he continued to cough and sneeze. Horrified, she finally realized the Barrayarans had been holding his head under water by way of torture.

"What is this, Lieutenant Buffa?" Vorkosigan pinned the senior of the group with a thunderous frown.

"I thought the Betans killed you, sir!" said Buffa.

"They didn't," Vorkosigan said shortly. "What are you doing with this Betan?"

"Tafas captured him in the woods, sir. We've been trying to question him—find out if there's any more around—" he glanced at Cordelia, "but he refuses to

76

talk. Hasn't said a word. And I always thought Betans were soft."

Vorkosigan rubbed his hand over his face for a moment, as if praying for strength.

"Buffa," he said patiently, "this man was hit by disruptor fire five days ago. He can't talk, and if he could he wouldn't know anything anyway."

"Barbarians!" cried Cordelia, kneeling on the ground. Dubauer had recognized her, and was clutching her. "You Barrayarans are nothing but barbarians, scoundrels, and assassins!"

"And fools. Don't leave out fools." Vorkosigan withered Buffa with a glare. A couple of the men had the good grace to look rather ill, as well as ill-at-ease. Vorkosigan let out his breath with a sigh. "Is he all right?"

"Seems to be," she admitted reluctantly. "But he's pretty shaken up." She was shaking herself in her outrage.

"Commander Naismith, I apologize for my men," said Vorkosigan formally, and loudly, so that no one there could mistake that their Captain humbled himself before his prisoner because of them.

"Don't click your heels at me," muttered Cordelia savagely, for his ear alone. At his bleak look she relented a little, and said more loudly, "It was an error in interpretation." Her eye fell on Lieutenant Buffa, attempting to make his considerable height appear to melt into the ground. "Any blind man could have made it. Oh, hell," she added, for Dubauer's terror and distress were triggering another convulsion. Most of the Barrayarans looked away, variously embarrassed. Vorkosigan, who was getting practiced, knelt to give her what aid she needed. When the seizure subsided he stood.

"Tafas, give your weapons to Koudelka," he ordered. Tafas hesitated, glancing around, then slowly complied.

"I didn't want any part of it, sir," he said desperately. "But Lieutenant Radnov said it was too late."

"You'll get a chance to speak for yourself later on," said Vorkosigan wearily.

"What's going on?" asked the bewildered Buffa. "Have you seen Commander Gottyan, sir?"

"I've given Commander Gottyan—separate orders. Buffa, you are now in charge of the landing party." Vorkosigan repeated his orders for the arrest of his short list, and detached a group to carry out the task.

"Ensign Koudelka, take *my* prisoners to the cave, and see that they're given proper food, and whatever else Commander Naismith requires. Then see that the shuttle is ready to go. We'll be leaving for the ship as soon as the—other prisoners are secured." He avoided the word "mutineers," as though it were too strong, like blasphemy.

"Where are you going?" asked Cordelia.

"I'm going to have a talk with Commander Gottyan. Alone."

"Hm. Well, don't make me regret my own advice." Which was as close as she could come at the moment to saying, "Be careful."

Vorkosigan acknowledged all her meanings with a wave of his hand, and turned back for the woods. He was limping more noticeably now.

She helped Dubauer to his feet, and Koudelka led them to the cave's mouth. The young man seemed so much like Dubauer's opposite number, she found it hard to maintain her hostility.

78

"What happened to the old man's leg?" Koudelka asked her, glancing back over his shoulder.

"He's got an infected scratch," she understated, inclined to endorse his evident policy of keeping up a good show for the benefit of his unreliable crew. "It should get some high grade medical attention, as soon as you can get him to slow down for it."

"That's the old man for you. I've never seen anybody that age with that much energy."

"That age?" Cordelia raised an eyebrow.

"Well, of course he wouldn't seem old to you," Koudelka allowed, and looked puzzled when she burst out laughing. "Energy isn't quite what I wanted to say, though."

"How about power," she suggested, curiously glad that Vorkosigan had at least one admirer. "Energy applied to work."

"That's very good," he applauded, gratified. Cordelia decided not to mention the little blue pill, either.

"He seems an interesting person," she said, angling for another view of Vorkosigan. "How did he ever get in this fix?"

"You mean, Radnov?"

She nodded.

"Well, I don't want to criticize the old man, but—I don't know of anyone else who'd tell a *Political* Officer when he came on board to stay out of his sight if he wanted to live to the end of the voyage." Koudelka was hushed in his awe.

Cordelia, making the second turning behind him in the halls of the cave, was jerked alert by her surroundings. *Most* peculiar, she thought. Vorkosigan misled me. The labyrinthine series of caverns was partly natural but mostly carved out by plasma arc, cool, moist, and dimly lit. The huge spaces were stuffed with supplies. This was no cache; it was a full-scale fleet depot. She pursed her lips soundlessly, staring around, suddenly awake to a whole new range of unpleasant possibilities.

In one corner of the caverns stood a standard Barrayaran field shelter, a semicircular ribbed vault covered with a fabric like the Betans' tents. This one was given over to a field kitchen and mess hall, crude and bleak. A lone yeoman was cleaning up after lunch.

"The old man just turned up, alive!" Koudelka greeted him.

"Huh! I thought the Betans had cut his throat," said the yeoman, surprised. "And we did the funeral dinner up so nice."

"These two are the old man's *personal* prisoners," Koudelka introduced them to the cook, whom Cordelia suspected was more combat soldier than gourmet chef, "and you know what he's like on that subject. The guy's got disruptor damage. He said they're to have proper food, so don't try to poison them with the usual swill."

"Everyone's a critic," muttered the yeoman-cook, as Koudelka vanished about his other chores. "What'll you have?"

"Anything. Anything but oatmeal or blue cheese," she amended hastily.

The yeoman disappeared into the back room, and returned a few minutes later with two steaming bowls of a stew-like substance, and real bread with genuine vegetable oil spread. Cordelia fell to it wolfishly.

"How is it?" asked the yeoman tonelessly, hunching down into his shoulders.

"S'delishoush," she said around a large mouthful. "S'wonderful."

"Really?" He straightened up. "You really like it?"

"Really." She stopped to shove a few spoonfuls into the dazed Dubauer. The taste of the warm food cut across his post-seizure sleepiness, and he chewed away with something like her enthusiasm.

"Here—can I help you feed him?" the yeoman offered.

Cordelia beamed upon him like the sun. "You certainly may."

In less than an hour she had learned that the yeoman's name was Nilesa, heard most of his life's history, and been offered the complete, if severely limited, range of dainties a Barrayaran field kitchen had to offer. The yeoman was evidently as starved for praise as his fellows were for home cooking, for he followed her around racking his brain for small personal services to offer her.

Vorkosigan came in by himself, and sat wearily down beside Cordelia.

"Welcome back, sir," the yeoman greeted him. "We thought the Betans had killed you."

"Yes, I know," Vorkosigan waved away this by-now-familiar greeting. "How about some food?"

"What'll you have, sir?"

"Anything but oatmeal."

He too was served with bread and stew, which he ate without Cordelia's appetite, for the fever and stimulant combined to kill it.

"How did things work out with Commander Gottyan?" Cordelia asked him quietly.

"Not bad. He's back on the job."

"How did you do it?"

"Untied him, and gave him my plasma arc. I told him I couldn't work with a man who made my shoulderblades itch, and this was the last chance I was going to give him for instant promotion. Then I sat down with my back to him. Sat there for about ten minutes. We didn't say a word. Then he gave the arc back, and we walked back to camp."

"I wondered if something like that might work. Although I'm not sure I could have done it, if I were you."

"I don't think I could have done it either, if I wasn't so damn tired. It felt good to sit down." His tone became slightly more animated. "As soon as they get the arrests made, we'll lift off for the *General*. It's a fine ship. I'm assigning you the visiting officer's cabin—Admiral's Quarters, they call it, although it's no different from the others." Vorkosigan pushed the last bites of stew around in the bottom of his dish. "How was your food?"

"Wonderful."

"That's not what most people say."

"Yeoman Nilesa has been most kind and thoughtful."

"Are we talking about the same man?"

"I think he just needs a little appreciation for his work. You might try it."

Vorkosigan, elbows on the table, propped his chin on his hands and smiled. "I'll take it under advisement."

They both sat silent, tired and digesting, at the simple metal table. Vorkosigan leaned back in his chair with his eyes closed. Cordelia leaned on the table with her head pillowed on one arm. In about half an hour Koudelka entered.

"We've got Sens, sir," he reported. "But we had— are having—a little trouble with Radnov and Darobey. They tumbled on to it, somehow, and escaped into the woods. I have a patrol out searching now."

Vorkosigan looked like he wanted to swear. "Should

82

have gone myself," he muttered. "Did they have any weapons?"

"They both had their disruptors. We got their plasma arcs."

"All right. I don't want to waste any more time down here. Recall your patrol and seal all the cavern entrances. They can find out how they like spending a few nights in the woods." His eyes glinted at the vision. "We can pick them up later. They've nowhere to go."

Cordelia pushed Dubauer ahead of her into the shuttle, a bare and rather decrepit troop transport, and settled him in a free seat. With the arrival of the last patrol the shuttle seemed crammed with Barrayarans, including the huddled and subdued prisoners, hapless subordinates of the escaped ringleaders, bound in back. They all seemed such large and muscular young men. Indeed, Vorkosigan was the shortest one she'd seen so far.

They stared at her curiously, and she caught snatches of conversation in two or three languages. It wasn't hard to guess their content, and she smiled a bit grimly. Youth, it appeared, was full of illusions as to how much sexual energy two people might have to spare while hiking forty or so kilometers a day, concussed, stunned, diseased, on poor food and little sleep, alternating caring for a wounded man with avoiding becoming dinner for every carnivore within range—and with a coup to plan for at the end. Old folks, too, of thirty-three and forty plus. She laughed to herself, and closed her eyes, shutting them out.

Vorkosigan returned from the forward pilot's compartment, and slid in beside her. "Are you doing all right?"

She gave him a nod. "Yes. Rather overwhelmed by all these herds of boys. I think you Barrayarans are the only ones who don't carry mixed crews. Why is that, I wonder?"

"Partly tradition, partly to maintain an aggressive outlook. They haven't been annoying you?"

"No, amusing me only. I wonder if they realize how they are used?"

"Not a bit. They think they are the emperors of creation."

"Poor lambs."

"That's not how I'd describe them."

"I was thinking of animal sacrifice."

"Ah. That's closer."

The shuttle's engines began to whine, and they rose into the air. They circled the cratered mountain once, then struck east and upward to the sky. Cordelia watched out the window as the land they had so painfully traversed on foot swept under them in as many minutes as they had taken days. They soared over the great mountain where Rosemont lay rotting, close enough to see the snowcap and glaciers gleaming orange in the setting sun. They passed on east through nightrise, and dead of night, the horizon curved away, and they broke into the perpetual day of space.

As they approached the *General Vorkraft's* parking orbit Vorkosigan left her again to go forward and supervise. He seemed to be receding from her, absorbed back into the matrix of men and duty from which he had been torn. Well, surely they would have some quiet times together in the months ahead. Quite a few months, by what Gottyan had said. Pretend you're an anthropologist, she told herself, studying the savage Barrayarans. Think of it as a vacation—you wanted a long vacation after this Survey tour anyway. Well, here it is. Her fingers were picking loose threads from the seat, and she stilled them with a slight frown.

They made their docking very cleanly, and the mob of hulking soldiers rose, gathered their equipment, and clattered out. Koudelka appeared at her elbow, and informed her he was assigned as her guide. Guard, more likely—or babysitter—she did not feel very dangerous this moment. She gathered Dubauer and followed him aboard Vorkosigan's ship.

It smelled different from her Survey ship, colder, full of bare unpainted metal and cost-effective shortcuts taken out of comfort and decor, like the difference between a living room and a locker room. Their first destination was sickbay, to drop off Dubauer. It was a clean, austere series of rooms, much larger even proportionally than her Survey ship's, prepared to handle plenty of company. It was nearly deserted now, but for the chief surgeon and a couple of corpsmen whiling away their duty hours doing inventory, and a lone soldier with a broken arm kicking his heels and kibitzing. Dubauer was examined by the doctor, whom Cordelia suspected was more expert at disruptor injuries than her own surgeon, and turned over to the corpsmen to be washed and bedded down.

"You're going to have another customer shortly," Cordelia told the surgeon, who was one of Vorkosigan's four men over forty. "Your captain has a really filthy infection going on his shin. It's gone systemic. Also, I don't know what those little blue pills you fellows have in your medkits are, but by what he said the one he took this morning ought to be running out just about now."

85

"That damned poison," the doctor bitched. "Sure, it's effective, but they could find something less wearing. Not to mention the trouble we have hanging on to them."

Cordelia suspected this last was the crux of the matter. The doctor busied himself setting up the antibiotic synthesizer and preparing it for programming. Cordelia watched the expressionless Dubauer put to bed, the start, she saw, of an endless series of hospital days as straight and same as a tunnel to the end of his life. The cold whispering doubt of whether she had done him a service would be forever added to her inventory of night thoughts. She dawdled around him for a while, covertly waiting for the arrival of her other ex-charge.

Vorkosigan came in at last, accompanied, in fact supported, by a couple of other officers she had not yet met, and giving orders. He had obviously cut his timing too fine, for he looked frighteningly bad. He was white, sweating, and trembling, and Cordelia thought she could see where the lines on his face would be when he was seventy.

"Haven't you been taken care of yet?" he asked when he saw her. "Where's Koudelka? I thought I told him—oh, there you are. She's to have the Admiral's cabin. Did I say that? And stop by stores and get her some clothes. And dinner. And a new charge for her stunner."

"I'm fine. Hadn't you better lie down yourself?" said Cordelia anxiously.

Vorkosigan, still on his feet, was wandering around in circles like a wind-up toy with a damaged mainspring. "Got to let Bothari out," he muttered. "He'll be hallucinating by now."

"You just did that, sir," reminded one of the officers. The surgeon caught his eye, and jerked his head toward the examining table meaningfully. Together they intercepted Vorkosigan in his orbit, propelled him semi-forcibly to it, and made him lie down.

"It's those damned pills," the surgeon explained to Cordelia, taking pity on her alarmed look. "He'll be all right in the morning, except for lethargy and a hell of a headache."

The surgeon turned back to his task, to cut the taut trouser away from the swollen leg, and swear under his breath at what he found beneath. Koudelka glanced over the surgeon's shoulder, and turned back to Cordelia with a false smile pinned over a green face.

Cordelia nodded and reluctantly withdrew, leaving Vorkosigan in the hands of his professionals. Koudelka, seeming to enjoy his role as courier even though it had caused him to miss the show of his captain's return on board, led her off to stores for clothing, disappeared with her stunner, and dutifully returned it fully charged. It seemed to go against his grain.

"There's not a whole lot I could do with it anyway," she said at the dubious look on his face.

"No, no, the old man said you were to have it. I'm not going to argue with him about prisoners. It's a sensitive subject with him."

"So I understand. I might point out, if it will help your perspective, that our two governments are not at war as far as I know, and that I am being unlawfully detained."

Koudelka puzzled over this attempted readjustment of his point of view, then let it bounce harmlessly off his impermeable habits of thought. Carrying her new kit, he led her to her quarters.

87

> > **CHAPTER FIVE**

Stepping out of her cabin door next morning she found a guard posted. The top of her head was level with his broad shoulders, and his face reminded her of an overbred borzoi, narrow, hook-nosed, with his eyes too close together. She realized at once where she had seen him before, at a distance in a dappled wood, and had a moment of residual fear.

"Sergeant Bothari?" she hazarded.

He saluted her, the first Barrayaran to have done so. "Ma'am," he said, and fell silent.

"I want to go to sickbay," she said uncertainly.

"Yes, ma'am." His voice was a deep bass, monotonous in its cadence. He executed a neat turn and led off. Guessing that he had relieved Koudelka as her guide and keeper, she pattered after him. She was not quite ready to attempt light conversation with him, so asked him no questions en route. He offered her only silence. Watching him, it occurred to her that a guard on her door might be as much to keep others out as her in. Her stunner seemed suddenly heavy on her hip.

At sickbay she found Dubauer sitting up and dressed in insignialess black fatigues like the ones she had been issued. His hair had been cut and he had been shaved. There was certainly nothing wrong with the physical care he was receiving. She spoke to him a while, until her own voice began to sound inane in her ears. He looked at her, but gave little other reaction.

She caught a glimpse of Vorkosigan in a private chamber off the main ward, and he motioned her to enter. He was dressed in plain green pajamas of the standard design, and was sitting up in bed stabbing away with a light pen at a computer interface swung over it. Curiously, although he was clothed almost civilian style, bootless and weaponless, her impression of him was unchanged. He seemed a man who could carry on stark naked, and only make those around him feel overdressed. She smiled a little at this private image, and greeted him with a sketchy wave. One of the officers who had escorted him to sickbay last night was standing by the bed.

"Commander Naismith, this is Lieutenant Commander Vorkalloner, my second officer. Excuse me a moment; captains may come and captains may go, but the administration goes on forever."

"Amen."

Vorkalloner looked very much the professional Barrayaran soldier; he might have stepped out of a recruiting advertisement. Yet there was a certain underlying humor in his expression that made her think him a tolerable preview of Ensign Koudelka in ten or twelve years time.

"Captain Vorkosigan speaks highly of you," said

Vorkalloner, making small talk. A slight frown from his captain at this opening escaped his notice. "I guess if we could only catch one Betan, you were the best choice."

Vorkosigan winced. Cordelia gave him a slight shake of her head, signalling to let the gaffe pass. He shrugged, and began tapping out something on his keyboard.

"As long as all my people are safely on their way home, I'll take it as a fair trade. Almost all of them, anyway." Rosemont's ghost breathed coldly in her ear, and Vorkalloner seemed suddenly less amusing. "Why were you all so anxious to put us in a bottle, anyway?"

"Why, orders," said Vorkalloner simply, like an ancient fundamentalist who answers every question with the tautology, "Because God made it that way." Then a little agnostic doubt began to creep over his face. "Actually, I thought we might have been sent out here on guard duty as some kind of punishment," he joked.

The remark caught Vorkosigan's humor. "For your sins? Your cosmology is too egocentric, Aristede." Leaving Vorkalloner to unravel that, he went on to Cordelia, "Your detention was intended to be free of bloodshed. It would have been, too, but for that other little matter cropping up in the middle of it. It is a worthless apology for some," and she knew he shared the memory of Rosemont's burial in the cold black fog, "but it is the only truth I can offer you. The responsibility is no less mine for that. As I am sure someone in the high command will point out when this arrives." He smiled sourly and continued typing.

"Well, I can't say I'm sorry to have messed up

their invasion plans," she said daringly. There, let's see what that stirs up . . .

"What invasion?" asked Vorkalloner, waking up.

"I was afraid you'd figure that out, once you saw the cache caverns," said Vorkosigan to her. "It was still being hotly debated when we left, and the expansionists were waving the advantage of surprise as a big stick to beat the peace party. Speaking as a private person—well, I have not that right while in uniform. Let it go."

"What invasion?" probed Vorkalloner hopefully.

"With luck, none," answered Vorkosigan, allowing himself to be persuaded to partial frankness. "One of those was enough for a lifetime." He seemed to look inward on private, unpleasant memories.

Vorkalloner plainly found this a baffling attitude from the Hero of Komarr. "It was a great victory, sir. With very little loss of life."

"On our side." Vorkosigan finished typing his report and signed it off, then entered a request for another form and began fencing at it with the light pen.

"That's the idea, isn't it?"

"It depends on whether you mean to stay or are just passing through. A very messy political legacy was left at Komarr. Not the sort of thing I care to leave in trust for the next generation. How did we get onto this subject?" He finished the last form.

"Who were they thinking of invading?" asked Cordelia doggedly.

"Why haven't I heard anything about it?" asked Vorkalloner.

"In order, that is classified information, and it is not being discussed below the level of the General Staff, the central committee of the two Councils, and the Emperor. That means this conversation is to go no farther, Aristede."

Vorkalloner glanced at Cordelia pointedly. "*She's* not on the General Staff. Come to think of it—"

"Neither am I, any more," Vorkosigan conceded. "As for our guest, I've told her nothing she couldn't deduce for herself. As for myself, my opinion was requested on—certain aspects. They didn't like it, once they'd got it, but they did ask for it." His smile was not at all nice.

"Is that why you were shipped out of town?" asked Cordelia perceptively, feeling she was beginning to get the hang of how things were done on Barrayar. "So Lieutenant Commander Vorkalloner was right about pulling guard duty. Was your opinion requested by, uh, a certain old friend of your father's?"

"It certainly wasn't requested by the Council of Ministers," said Vorkosigan, but refused to be drawn any further, and changed the subject firmly. "Have my men been treating you properly?"

"Quite well, yes."

"My surgeon swears he will release me this afternoon, if I am good and stay in bed this morning. May I stop by your cabin to speak with you privately later? There are some things I need to make clear."

"Sure," she responded, thinking the request was phrased rather ominously.

The surgeon came in, aggrieved. "You're supposed to be resting, sir." He glared pointedly at Cordelia and Vorkalloner.

"Oh, very well. Send these off with the next courier, Aristede," he pointed to the screen, "along with the verbals and the formal charges."

The doctor herded them out, as Vorkosigan began typing again.

*　　*　　*

She wandered around the ship for the rest of the morning, exploring the limits of her parole. Vorkosigan's ship was a confusing warren of corridors, sealable levels, tubes, and narrow doors designed, she realized at last, to be defensible from boarding parties in hand-to-hand combat. Sergeant Bothari kept pace with slow strides, looming silently as the shadow of death at her shoulder, except when she would begin to make a turn into some forbidden door or corridor, when he would halt abruptly and say, "No, ma'am." She was not permitted to touch anything, though, as she found when she ran a hand casually over a control panel, eliciting another monotonous "No, ma'am," from Bothari. It made her feel like a two-year-old being taken on a toddle.

She made one attempt to draw him out.

"Have you served Captain Vorkosigan long?" she inquired brightly.

"Yes, ma'am."

Silence. She tried again. "Do you like him?"

"No, ma'am."

Silence.

"Why not?" This at least could not have a yes-or-no answer. For a while she thought he wasn't going to answer at all, but he finally came up with, "He's a Vor."

"Class conflict?" she hazarded.

"I don't like Vors."

"I'm not a Vor," she suggested.

He stared through her glumly. "You're like a Vor. Ma'am."

Unnerved, she gave up.

*　　*　　*

94

That afternoon she made herself comfortable on her narrow bunk and began to explore the menu the library computer had to offer her. She picked out a vid with the unalarming grade school title of "People and Places of Barrayar" and punched it up.

Its narration was as banal as the title had promised, but the pictures were utterly fascinating. It seemed a green, delicious, sunlit world to her Betan eyes. People went about without nose filters or rebreathers, or heat shields in the summer. The climate and terrain were immensely varied, and it had real oceans, with moon-raised tides, in contrast to the flat saline puddles that passed for lakes at home.

A knock sounded at her door. "Enter," she called, and Vorkosigan appeared around it, greeting her with a nod. Odd hour of the day for him to be in dress uniform, she thought—but my word, he cleans up good. Nice, very nice. Sergeant Bothari accompanied him; he remained standing stolidly outside the half-opened door. Vorkosigan walked around the room for a moment as if searching for something. He finally emptied her lunch tray and used it to prop the door open a narrow crack. Cordelia raised her eyebrows at this.

"Is that really necessary?"

"I think so. At the current rate of gossip I'm bound to encounter some joke soon about the privileges of rank that I can't pretend not to hear, and I'll have to quash the unlucky, er, humorist. I have an aversion to closed doors anyway. You never know what's on the other side."

Cordelia laughed outright. "It reminds me of that old joke, where the girl says, 'Let's not, and tell everybody we have.'"

95

Vorkosigan grimaced agreement and seated himself on the bolted-down swivel chair by the metal desk built into the wall, and swung to face her. He leaned back with his legs stretched out before him, and his face became serious. Cordelia cocked her head, half-smiling. He began obliquely, nodding toward the screen swung over her bed. "What have you been viewing?"

"Barrayaran geography. It's a beautiful place. Have you ever been to the oceans?"

"When I was a small boy, my mother used to take me to Bonsanklar every summer. It was a sort of upper-class resort town with a lot of virgin forest backing up to the mountains behind it. My father was away mostly, at the capital or with his corps. Midsummer's Day was the old Emperor's birthday, and they used to have the most fantastic fireworks—at least, they seemed so to me at the time—out over the ocean. The whole town would turn out on the esplanade, nobody even armed. No duels were permitted on the Emperor's birthday, and I was allowed to run all over the place freely." He looked at the floor, beyond the toes of his boots. "I haven't been back there for years. I should like to take you there someday, for the Midsummer's festival, should the opportunity present itself."

"I'd like that very much. Will your ship be returning to Barrayar soon?"

"Not for some time, I'm afraid. You're in for a long period as a prisoner. But when we return, in view of the escape of your ship, there should be no reason to continue your internment. You should be freed to present yourself at the Betan embassy, and go home. If you wish."

"If I wish!" She laughed a little, uncertainly, and

96

sat back against her hard pillow. He was watching her face intently. His posture was a fair simulation of a man at his ease, but one boot was tapping unconsciously. His eye fell on it, he frowned, and it stopped. "Why shouldn't I wish?"

"I thought, perhaps, when we arrive on Barrayar, and you are free, you might consider staying."

"To visit—where you said, Bonsanklar, and so on? I don't know how much leave I'll have, but—sure, I like to see new places. I'd like to see your planet."

"Not a visit. Permanently. As—as Lady Vorkosigan." His face brightened with a wry smile. "I'm making a hash of this. I promise, I'll never think of Betans as cowards again. I swear your customs take more bravery than the most suicidal of our boys' contests of skill."

She let her breath trickle out through pursed lips. "You don't—deal in small change, do you?" She wondered where the phrase about hearts leaping up came from. It felt far more like the bottom dropping out of her stomach. Her consciousness of her own body shot up with a lurch; she was already overwhelmingly conscious of his.

He shook his head. "That's not what I want, for you, with you. You should have the best. I'm hardly that, you must know by now. But at least I can offer you the best that I have. Dear C—Commander, am I too sudden, by Betan standards? I've been waiting for days, for the right opportunity, but there never seemed to be one."

"Days! How long have you been thinking along these lines?"

"It first occurred to me when I saw you in the ravine."

"What, throwing up in the mud?"

He grinned at that. "With great composure. By the time we finished burying your officer, I knew."

She rubbed her lips. "Anybody ever tell you you're a lunatic?"

"Not in this context."

"I—you've confused me."

"Not offended you?"

"No, of course not."

He relaxed just slightly. "You needn't say yes or no right now, of course. It will be months before we're home. But I didn't want you to think—it makes things awkward, your being a prisoner. I didn't want you to think I was offering you an insult."

"Not at all," she said faintly.

"There are some other things I should tell you," he went on, his attention seemingly caught by his boots again. "It wouldn't be an easy life. I have been thinking, since I met you, that a career cleaning up after the failures of politics, as you phrased it, might not be the highest honor after all. Maybe I should be trying to prevent the failures at their source. It would be more dangerous than soldiering—chances of betrayal, false charges, assassination, maybe exile, poverty, death. Evil compromises with bad men for a little good result, and that not guaranteed. Not a good life, but if one had children—better me than them."

"You sure know how to show a girl a good time," she said helplessly, rubbing her chin and smiling.

Vorkosigan looked up, uncertain of his hope.

"How does one set about a political career, on Barrayar?" she asked, feeling her way. "I presume you're thinking of following in your grandfather Prince Xav's steps, but without the advantage of being an Imperial prince, how do you get an office?"

"Three ways. Imperial appointment, inheritance, and rising through the ranks. The Council of Ministers gets its best men through the last method. It's their great strength, but closed to me. The Council of Counts, by inheritance. That's my surest route, but it waits on my father's death. It can just go on waiting. It's a moribund body anyway, afflicted with the narrowest conservatism, and stuffed with old relics only concerned with protecting their privileges. I'm not sure anything can be done with the Counts in the long run. Perhaps they should finally be allowed to dodder over the brink of extinction. Don't quote that," he added as an afterthought.

"It's the weirdest design for a government."

"It wasn't designed. It grew."

"Maybe what you need is a constitutional convention."

"Spoken like a true Betan. Well, perhaps we do, although it sounds like a prescription for civil war, in our context. That leaves Imperial appointment. It's quick, but my fall could be as sudden and spectacular as my rise, if I should offend the old man, or he dies." The light of battle was in his eyes as he spoke, planning. "My one advantage with him is that he enjoys plain speaking. I don't know how he acquired the taste for it, because he doesn't get much of it."

"Do you know, I think you'd like politics, at least on Barrayar. Maybe because it's so similar to what we call war, elsewhere."

"There is a more immediate political problem, though, with respect to your ship, and some other things . . ." he paused, losing momentum. "Maybe—maybe an insoluble one. It really may be premature for me to be discussing marriage until I know which way it's going to fall out. But I couldn't let you go on thinking—what *were* you thinking, anyway?"

She shook her head. "I don't think I want to say, just now. I'll tell you someday. It's nothing you'll dislike, I don't think."

He accepted that with a little hopeful nod, and went on. "Your ship—"

She frowned uneasily. "You won't be getting into any trouble over my ship getting away, will you?"

"It *was* just the situation we were on our way out here to prevent. The fact that I was unconscious at the time should be a mitigating factor. Balancing that are the views I aired at the Emperor's council. There's bound to be suspicion I let it escape on purpose, to sabotage an adventure I deeply disapprove."

"Another demotion?"

He laughed. "I was the youngest admiral in the history of our fleet—I might end up the oldest ensign, too. But no," he sobered, "There will almost certainly be a charge of treason laid, by the war party in the Ministries. Until that's settled, one way or another," he met her eyes, "it may be difficult to settle any personal affairs either."

"Is treason a capital crime on Barrayar?" she asked, morbidly curious.

"Oh, yes. Public exposure and death by starvation." He raised a quizzical eyebrow at her appalled look. "If it's any consolation, high-born traitors always seem to be smuggled some neat means to private suicide, before the event. It saves stirring up any unnecessary public sympathy. I think I should not give them the satisfaction, though. Let it be public, and messy, and tedious, and embarrassing as all hell." He looked alarmingly fey.

"Would you sabotage the invasion, if you could?"

He shook his head, eyes going distant. "No. I am a man under authority. That's what the syllable in front of my name means. While the question is still being debated, I'll continue to argue my case. But if the Emperor puts his word to the order, I'll go without question. The alternative is civil chaos, and we've had enough of that."

"What's different about this invasion? You must have favored Komarr, or they wouldn't put you in charge of it."

"Komarr was a unique opportunity, almost a textbook case. When I was designing the strategy for its conquest, I made maximum use of those chances." He ticked the points off on his thick fingers. "A small population, all concentrated in climate-controlled cities. No place for guerillas to fall back and regroup. No allies—we weren't the only ones whose trade was being strangled by their greedy tariffs. All I had to do was let it leak out that we were going to drop their twenty-five percent cut of everything that passed through their nexus points to fifteen, and the neighbors that should have supported them fell into our pockets. No heavy industry. Fat and lazy from living off unearned income—they didn't even want to do their own fighting, until those scraggly mercenaries they'd hired found out what they were up against, and turned tail. If I'd had a free hand, and a little more time, I think it could have been taken without a shot being fired. A perfect war, it should have been, if the Council of Ministers hadn't been so impatient." Remembered frustrations played themselves out before his eyes, and he frowned into the past. "This other plan—well, I think you'll understand if I tell you it's Escobar."

Cordelia sat up, shocked. "You found a jump

through here to Escobar?" No wonder, then, the Barrayarans had not announced their discovery of this place. Of all the possibilities she had revolved in her mind, that was the last. Escobar was one of the major planetary hubs in the network of wormhole exits that strung scattered humanity together. Large, old, rich, temperate, it counted among its many neighbors Beta Colony itself. "They're out of their minds!"

"Do you know, that's almost exactly what I said, before the Minister of the West started shouting, and Count Vortala threatened—well, became very rude to him. Vortala can be more obnoxious without actually swearing than any man I know."

"Beta Colony would be drawn in for sure. Why, half our interstellar trade passes through Escobar. And Tau Ceti Five. And Jackson's Whole."

"At the very least, I should think," Vorkosigan nodded agreement. "The idea was to make it a quick operation, and present the potential allies with a fait accompli. Being intimately familiar with everything that went wrong with my 'perfect' plan for Komarr, I told them they were dreaming, or words to that effect." He shook his head. "I wish I'd kept my temper better. I could still be back there, arguing against it. Instead, for all I know, the fleet is being readied even now. And the further preparations go, the harder they will be to stop." He sighed.

"War," Cordelia mused, immensely disturbed. "You realize, if your fleet goes—if Barrayar goes to war with Escobar—they'll be wanting navigators at home. Even if Beta Colony doesn't get directly involved in the fight, we're sure to be selling them weapons, technical assistance, shiploads of supplies—"

Vorkosigan started to speak, then stopped himself.

102

"I suppose you would," he said bleakly. "And we would be trying to blockade you."

She could feel the blood beating in her ears in the silence that followed. The little noises and vibrations of Vorkosigan's ship still drifted through the walls, Bothari stirred in the corridor, and footsteps passed by.

She shook her head. "I'm going to have to think about this. It's not as easy as it looked, at first."

"No, it's not." He turned his hand palm-outward, a gesture of completion, and rose stiffly, his leg still bothering him. "That's all I wanted to say. You need not say anything."

She nodded, grateful for the release, and he withdrew, collecting Bothari and shutting the door firmly behind him. She sighed distress and deep uncertainty, and lay back staring at the ceiling until Yeoman Nilesa brought dinner.

▶▶ CHAPTER SIX

Next morning, ship time, she remained quietly in her cabin reading. She wanted time to assimilate yesterday's conversation before she saw Vorkosigan again. She was as unsettled as if all her star maps had been randomized, leaving her lost; but at least knowing she was lost. A step backwards toward truth, she supposed, better than mistaken certainties. She hungered forlornly for certainties, even as they receded beyond reach.

The ship's library offered a wide range of Barrayaran material. A gentleman named Abell had produced a turgid general history, full of names, dates, and detailed descriptions of forgotten battles all of whose participants were irrelevantly dead by now. A scholar named Aczith had done better, with a vivid biography of Emperor Dorca Vorbarra the Just, the ambiguous figure whom Cordelia calculated was Vorkosigan's great-grandfather, and whose reign had straddled the end of the Time of Isolation. Deeply involved in the multitude of personalities and convoluted politics of his day, she did not even look up at the knock on her door, but called, "Enter."

A pair of soldiers wearing green-and-grey planetside camouflage fatigues fell through the door and shut it hastily behind them. What a ratty-looking pair, she thought; finally, a Barrayaran soldier shorter than Vorkosigan. It was only on the third thought that she recognized them, as from the corridor outside, muffled by the door, an alarm klaxon began to hoot rhythmically. *Looks like I'm not going to make it to the B's . . .*

"Captain!" cried Lieutenant Stuben. "Are you all right?"

All the crushing weight of old responsibility descended on her at the sight of his face. His shoulder-length brown hair had been sacrificed to an imitation Barrayaran military burr that looked as though it had been grazed over by some herbivore, and his head looked small, naked, and strange without it. Lieutenant Lai, beside him, slight and thin with a scholarly stoop, made an even less likely-looking warrior, the too-large uniform he wore folded up at the wrists and ankles, with one ankle coming unfolded and getting under the heel of his boot.

She opened her mouth once to speak, closed it, then finally ripped out, "Why aren't you on your way home? I gave you an order, Lieutenant!"

Stuben, anticipating a warmer reception, was momentarily nonplussed. "We took a vote," he said simply, as though it explained everything.

Cordelia shook her head helplessly. "You would. A vote. Right." She buried her face in her hands a moment, and sobbed a laugh. "Why?" she asked through her fingers.

"We identified the Barrayaran ship as the *General*

106

Vorkraft—looked it up and found out who was in command. We just couldn't leave you in the hands of the Butcher of Komarr. It was unanimous."

She was momentarily diverted. "How the devil did you get a unanimous vote out of—no, never mind," she cut him off as he began to answer, a self-satisfied gleam starting in his eye. I shall beat my head against the wall—no. Got to have more information. And so does he.

"Do you realize," she said carefully, "that the Barrayarans were planning to bring an invasion fleet through here, to attack Escobar by surprise? If you had reached home and reported this planet's existence, their chance of surprise would have been destroyed. Now all bets are off. Where is the *Rene Magritte* now, and how did you *ever* get in here?"

Lieutenant Stuben looked astonished. "How did you find all that out?"

"Time, time," Lieutenant Lai reminded him anxiously, tapping his wrist chronometer.

Stuben went on. "Let me tell you on the way to the shuttle. Do you know where Dubauer is? He wasn't in the brig."

"Yes, what shuttle? No—begin at the beginning. I've got to know everything before we set foot in the corridor. I take it they know you're aboard?" The beat of the klaxon still sounded outside, and she cringed in expectation of her door bursting inward at any moment.

"No, they don't. That's the beauty of it," said Stuben proudly. "We had the greatest piece of luck."

"They pursued us for two days when we first ran off. I didn't put on full power—just enough to stay out of their range and keep them trailing us. I thought we might still get a chance to circle back and pick you up, somehow. Then all of a sudden they stopped, turned around, and started back here.

"We waited until they were well away, then turned around ourselves. We hoped you were still hiding in the woods."

"No, I was captured the first night. Go on."

"We got everything lined up, put on max boost, then cut everything we could think of that made electromagnetic noise. The projector worked fine as a muffler, by the way, just like Ross's simulation last month. We waltzed right past 'em and they never blinked—"

"For God's sake, Stu, stick to the point," muttered Lai. "We haven't got all day." He bounced on his heels in impatience.

"If that projector falls into Barrayaran hands—" began Cordelia in rising tones.

"It won't, I tell you. Anyway, the *Rene Magritte's* making a parabola around the sun—as soon as they get close enough to be masked by its noise, they're supposed to brake and boost, then shoot back through here for a pickup. We'll have a two-hour time window to match velocities starting—well, starting about ten minutes ago."

"Too chancey," critized Cordelia, all the possible disasters inherent in this scenario parading through her imagination.

"It worked," defended Stuben. "—at least, it's going to work. Then we struck it lucky. We found these two Barrayarans wandering in the woods while we were looking for you and Dubauer—"

Cordelia's stomach tightened. "Radnov and Darobey, by chance?"

Stuben stared. "How did you know?"

"Go on, just go on."

"They were the ringleaders of a conspiracy to unseat that homicidal maniac Vorkosigan. Vorkosigan was after them, so they were glad to see us."

"I'll bet. Just like manna from heaven."

"A Barrayaran patrol shuttled down after them. We set up an ambush—stunned them all, except for one Radnov shot with a nerve disruptor. Those guys really play for keeps."

"Do you happen to know which—no, never mind. Go on." Her stomach churned.

"We took their uniforms, took their shuttle, and slid on up to the *General* as neat as you please. Radnov and Darobey between 'em knew all the countersigns. We made it to the brig—that was easy, it was where they were expecting their patrol to go anyway—we thought you and Dubauer would be there. Radnov and Darobey let all their buddies out, and went to take over the engine room. They can cut off any system from there, weapons, life support, anything. They're supposed to cut weapons when we make our break with the shuttle."

"I wouldn't count on that," Cordelia warned.

"No matter," said Stuben cheerfully. "The Barrayarans will be so busy fighting each other we can walk right through. Think of the splendid irony! The Butcher of Komarr, shot by his own men! Now I know how judo is supposed to work."

"Splendid," she echoed hollowly. His head, she thought—I'm going to beat his head against the wall, not mine. "How many of us are aboard?"

"Six. Two at the shuttle, two looking for Dubauer, and we two to get you."

"Nobody left planetside?"

"No."

"All right." She rubbed her face tensely, ravenous

for inspiration that would not come. "What a mess. Dubauer's in sickbay, by the way. Disruptor damage." She decided not to detail his condition just then.

"Filthy killers," said Lai. "I hope they choke each other."

She turned to the library interface by her bed, and dialed up the crude schematic map of the *General Vorkraft*, minus technical data, that the library was programmed to allow her. "Study this, and figure out your route to sickbay and the shuttle hatch. I'm going to find something out. Stay here and don't answer the door. Who are the other two wandering around out there?"

"McIntyre and Big Pete."

"Well, at least they have a better chance of passing for Barrayarans close up than you two do."

"Captain, where are you going? Why can't we just go?"

"I'll explain it when I have a week to spare. This time follow your damned orders. Stay here!"

She slipped out the door and dog-trotted toward the bridge. Her nerves screamed to run, but it would draw too much attention. She passed a group of four Barrayarans hurrying somewhere; they barely spared her a glance. She had never been more glad to be a wallflower.

She found Vorkosigan on the bridge with his officers, clustered intently around the intercom from engineering. Bothari was there too, looming like Vorkosigan's sad shadow.

"Who's that guy on the comm?" she whispered to Vorkalloner. "Radnov?"

"Yes. Sh."

The face was speaking. "Vorkosigan, Gottyan, and

110

Vorkalloner, one by one, at two-minute intervals. Unarmed, or all life support systems will be cut off throughout the ship. You have fifteen minutes before we start letting in the vacuum. Ah. Have you patched it in? Good. Better not waste time, *Captain*." His inflection made the rank a deadly insult.

The face vanished, but the voice returned ghost-like over the loudspeaker system. "Soldiers of Barrayar," it blared. "Your Captain has betrayed the Emperor and the Council of Ministers. Don't let him betray you too. Turn him over to the proper authority, your Political Officer, or we will be forced to slay the innocent with the guilty. In fifteen minutes we will cut life support—"

"Cut that off," said Vorkosigan irritably.

"Can't sir," said a technician. Bothari, more direct, unslung his plasma arc and with a negligent gesture fired from the hip. The speaker exploded off the wall and several men ducked the molten fragments.

"Hey, we might need that ourselves," began Vorkalloner indignantly.

"Never mind," Vorkosigan waved him down. "Thank you, Sergeant." A distant echo of the voice continued from loudspeakers all over the ship.

"There's no time for anything more elaborate, I'm afraid," Vorkosigan said, apparently winding up a planning session. "Go ahead with your engineering idea, Lieutenant Saint Simon; if you can get it in place in time, so much the better. I'm sure we'd all rather be clever than brave."

The lieutenant nodded and hurried out.

"If he can't, I'm afraid we'll have to rush them," Vorkosigan went on. "They are perfectly capable of killing everyone aboard and re-recording the log to

111

prove anything they please. Between Darobey and Tafas they have the technical know-how. I want volunteers. Myself and Bothari, of course."

A unanimous chorus put themselves forward.

"Gottyan and Vorkalloner are both out. I need somebody who can explain things, afterward. Now the battle order. First me, then Bothari, then Siegel's patrol, then Kush's. Stunners only, I don't want stray shots smashing up engineering." A number of men glanced at the hole in the wall where the speaker had been.

"Sir," said Vorkalloner desperately, "I question that battle order. They'll be using disruptors for sure. The first men through the door haven't got a chance."

Vorkosigan took a few seconds and stared him down. He dropped his eyes miserably. "Yes, sir."

"Lieutenant Commander Vorkalloner is right, sir," an unexpected bass voice put in. Cordelia realized with a start it was Bothari. "The first place is mine, by right. I've earned it." He faced his captain, narrow jaw working. "It's mine."

Their eyes met in a weird understanding. "Very well, Sergeant," conceded Vorkosigan. "You first, then me, then the rest as ordered. Let's go."

Vorkosigan paused before her as they herded out. "I'm afraid I'm not going to make that walk on the esplanade in the summer, after all."

Cordelia shook her head helplessly, the glimmer of a terrifying idea beginning in the back of her brain. "I—I—I have to withdraw my parole now."

Vorkosigan looked puzzled, then waved it aside for a more immediate concern. "If I should chance to end up like your Ensign Dubauer—remember my preferences. If you can bring yourself to it, I would

112

like it to be by your hand. I'll tell Vorkalloner. Can I have your word?"

"Yes."

"You'd better stay in your cabin until this is over."

He reached out to her shoulder, to touch one curl of red hair resting there, then turned away. Cordelia fled down the corridor, Radnov's propaganda droning senselessly in her ears. Her plan blossomed furiously in her mind. Her reason yammered protest, like a rider on a runaway horse; you have no duty to these Barrayarans, your duty is to Beta Colony, to Stuben, to the *Rene Magritte*—your duty is to escape, and warn . . .

She swung into her cabin. Wonder of wonders, Stuben and Lai were still there. They looked up, alarmed by her wild appearance.

"Go to sickbay now. Pick up Dubauer and take him to the shuttle. When were Pete and Mac supposed to report back there if they couldn't find him?"

"In—" Lai checked his time, "ten minutes."

"Thank God. When you get to sickbay, tell the surgeon that Captain Vorkosigan ordered you to bring Dubauer to me. Lai, you wait in the corridor. You'd never fool the surgeon. Dubauer can't talk. Don't act surprised by his condition. When you get to the shuttle, wait—let me see your chrono, Lai—till 0620 our ship time, then take off. If I'm not back by then I'm not coming. Full power and don't look back. Exactly how many men did Radnov and Darobey have with them?"

"Ten or eleven, I guess," Stuben said.

"All right. Give me your stunner. Go. Go. Go."

"Captain, we came here to rescue you!" cried Stuben, bewildered.

113

Words failed her utterly. She put a hand on his shoulder instead. "I know. Thank you." She ran.

Approaching engineering from one deck above, she came to an intersection of two corridors. Down the larger was a group of men assembling and checking weapons. Down the smaller were two men covering an entry port to the next deck, a last checkpoint before territory covered by Radnov's fire. One of them was Yeoman Nilesa. She pounced on him.

"Captain Vorkosigan sent me down," she lied. "He wants me to try one last effort at negotiation, as a neutral in the affair."

"That's a waste of time," observed Nilesa.

"So he hopes," she improvised. "It'll keep them tied up while he's getting ready. Can you get me in without alarming anybody?"

"I can try, I guess." Nilesa went forward and undogged a circular hatch in the floor at the end of the corridor.

"How many guards on this entrance?" she whispered.

"Two or three, I think."

The hatch swung up, revealing a man-width access tube with a ladder up one side and a pole down the middle.

"Hey, Wentz!" he shouted down it.

"Who's that?" a voice floated up.

"Me, Nilesa. Captain Vorkosigan wants to send that Betan frill down to talk to Radnov."

"What for?"

"How the hell should I know? You're the ones who're supposed to have comm pickups in everybody's bunks. Maybe she's not such a good lay after all." Nilesa shrugged an apology toward her, and she accepted it with a nod.

114

There was a whispered debate below.

"Is she armed?"

Cordelia, readying both stunners, shook her head.

"Would you give a weapon to a Betan frill?" Nilesa called back rhetorically, watching her preparations in puzzlement.

"All right. Put her in, dog the hatch, and let her drop. If you don't close the hatch before she drops, we'll shoot her. Got that?"

"Yo."

"What'll I be looking at when I get to the bottom?" she quizzed Nilesa.

"Nasty spot. You'll be standing in a sort of niche in the storeroom off the main control room. You can only get one man at a time through it, and you're pinned in there like a target, with the wall on three sides. It's designed that way on purpose."

"No way to rush them through it? I mean, you're not planning to?"

"No way in hell."

"Good. Thanks."

Cordelia climbed down into the tube, and Nilesa closed the hatch over her with a sound like the lid of a coffin.

"All right," came the voice from below, "drop."

"It's a long way down," she called back, having no trouble sounding tremulous. "I'm afraid."

"Screw it. I'll catch you."

"All right." She wrapped her legs and one arm around the pole. Her hand shook as she jammed the second stunner into her holster. Her stomach pumped sour bile into the back of her throat. She swallowed, took a deep breath to keep it there, held her stunner pointed ready, and dropped.

She landed face to face with the man below, his

115

nerve disruptor held casually at the level of her waist. His eyes widened as he saw her stunner. Here the Barrayaran custom of all-male crews on warships paid her, for he hesitated just a fraction of a second to shoot a woman. In that fraction she fired first. He slumped heavily over her, head lolling on her shoulder. Bracing, she held him as a shield before her.

Her second shot laid out the next guard as he was bringing his disruptor to aim. The third guard got off a hasty burst that was absorbed by the back of the man she held, although the nimbus of it seared the outer edge of her left thigh. The pain of it flared screamingly, but no sound escaped her clenched teeth. With a wild berserker accuracy that seemed no part of herself, she felled him too, then looked frantically around for a place of concealment.

Some conduits ran overhead; people entering a room usually look down and around before thinking to look up. She stuck the stunner in her belt, and with a leap she could never have duplicated in cold blood, pulled herself up between the conduits and the armored ceiling. Breathing silently through her open mouth, she drew her stunner again and prepared for whatever might come through the oval door to the main engineering bay.

"What was that noise? What's going on in there?"

"Throw in a grenade and seal the door."

"We can't, our men are in there."

"Wentz, report!"

Silence.

"You go in, Tafas."

"Why me?"

"Because I order you."

Tafas crept cautiously around the door, stepping over the threshold almost on tiptoe. He turned around

116

and around, staring. Afraid that they would close and lock the door at another firing, she waited until he at last looked up.

She smiled winningly at him, and gave a little wave of her fingers. "Close the door," she mouthed silently, pointing.

He stared at her with a very odd expression on his face, baffled, hopeful, and angry all at once. The bell of his disruptor seemed large as a searchlight, pointed quite accurately at her head. It was like looking into the eye of judgement. A standoff, of sorts. Vorkosigan is right, she thought; a disruptor *does* have real authority . . .

Then Tafas called, "I think there may be some kind of gas leak or something. Better close the door a second while I check." It swung closed obediently behind him.

Cordelia smiled down from the ceiling, eyes narrowed. "Hi. Want to get out of this mess?"

"What are you doing here—Betan?"

Excellent question, she thought ruefully. "Trying to save a few lives. Don't worry—your friends over there are only stunned." I won't mention the one hit by friendly fire—dead, perhaps, because of a moment's mercy for me . . . "Come on over to our side," she coaxed, madly echoing a child's game. "Captain Vorkosigan will forgive you—expunge the record. Give you a medal," she promised recklessly.

"What medal?"

"How should I know? Any medal you want. You don't even have to kill anybody. I have another stunner."

"What guarantee do I have?"

Desperation made her daring. "Vorkosigan's word. You tell him I pledged it to you."

"Who are you to pledge his word?"

"Lady Vorkosigan, if we both live." A lie? Truth? Hopeless fantasy?

Tafas gave a whistle, staring up at her. Belief began to illuminate his face.

"You really want to be responsible for letting a hundred fifty of your friends breathe vacuum just to save that Ministerial spy's career?" she added cogently.

"No," he said firmly at last. "Give me the stunner."

Now shall trust be tested. . . . She dropped it down to him. "Three down and seven to go. What's the best approach?"

"I can lure a couple more in here. The others are at the main entrance. We can rush them from behind, if we're lucky."

"Go ahead."

Tafas opened the door. "It was a gas leak," he coughed convincingly. "Help me drag these guys out and we'll seal the door."

"I could swear I heard a stunner go off a while ago," said his companion, entering.

"Maybe they were trying to attract attention."

The mutineer's face flared with suspicion as the stupidity of this suggestion sank in. "They didn't have stunners," he began. Fortunately, the second man entered at this point. Cordelia and Tafas fired in unison.

"Five down, five to go," Cordelia said, dropping to the floor. Her left leg buckled; it wasn't moving quite right. "Odds are getting better all the time."

"It had better be quick, if it's going to work at all," warned Tafas.

"Suits me."

They slid out the door and ran lightly across the engineering bay, which continued its automatic tasks, indifferent to its masters' identity. Some black-uniformed bodies were piled carelessly to one side. Tafas held up his hand for caution as they rounded the corner, jabbing a finger significantly. Cordelia nodded. Tafas walked around the corner quietly, and Cordelia pinned herself to its very edge, waiting. As Tafas raised his stunner she oozed around, searching for a target. The chamber narrowed in this L, ending in the main entrance to the deck above. Five men stood with their attention riveted to the clanks and hisses penetrating dimly through a hatch at the top of some metal stairs.

"They're getting ready to storm," said one. "It's time to let their air out."

Famous last words, she thought, and fired, once and twice. Tafas fired too, rapidly fanning the group, and it was over. And I will never, she pledged silently, call one of Stuben's stunts hare-brained again. She wanted to throw down her stunner and howl and roll in reaction, but her own job was not finished.

"Tafas," she called. "I've got to do one more thing."

He came to her side, looking shaky himself.

"I've gotten you out of this, and I need a favor in return. How can I cut control to the long-range plasma weapons so you can't get it back for an hour and a half?"

"Why do you want to do that? Did the Captain order it?"

"No," she said honestly. "The Captain didn't order any of this, but he'll like it when he sees it, don't you think?"

Tafas, confused, agreed. "If you short this panel," he suggested, "it should slow things down quite a bit."

"Give me your plasma arc."

119

Need I? she wondered, looking over the section. Yes. He would fire on us, just as surely as I'm cutting for home. Trust is one thing; treason another. I have no wish to test him to destruction.

Now, if Tafas isn't fooling me by pointing out the controls to the toilets or something . . . She blasted the panel, and stared with a moment's primitive fascination as it popped and sparked.

"Now," she said, handing the plasma arc back, "I want a couple of minutes head start. Then you can open the door and be a hero. I suggest you call first and warn them; Sergeant Bothari's in front."

"Right. Thanks."

She glanced up at the main entry hatch. About three meters away, he is now, she thought. An uncrossable gulf. So in the physics of the heart, distance is relative; it's time that's absolute. The seconds spun like spiders down her spine.

She chewed her lip, eyes devouring Tafas. Last chance to leave a message for Vorkosigan—no. The absurdity of transmitting the words, "I love you" through Tafas's mouth shook her with painful inward laughter. "My compliments" sounded rather swelled-headed, under the circumstances: "my regards," too cold; as for the simplest of all, "yes". . . .

She shook her head silently and smiled at the puzzled soldier, then ran back to the storeroom and scrambled back up the ladder. She beat a rhythmic tattoo upon the hatch. In a moment it opened. She found herself nose to nose with a plasma arc held by Yeoman Nilesa.

"I've got some new terms to carry back to your Captain," she said glibly. "They're a little screwy, but I think he'll like them."

Nilesa, surprised, let her out and resealed the

hatch. She walked away from him, glancing down the main corridor as she passed. Several dozen men were assembled in it. A technical team had half the panels off the walls; sparks flared from a tool. She could just see Sergeant Bothari's head on the far side of the crowd, and knew him to be standing next to Vorkosigan. She reached the ladder at the end of the corridor, ascended it, and began to run, threading her way level by level through the maze of the ship.

Laughing, crying, out of breath and shaking violently, she arrived at the shuttle hatch corridor. Dr. McIntyre stood guard, trying to look grim and Barrayaran.

"Is everybody here?"

He nodded, looking at her with delight.

"Pile in, let's go."

They sealed the doors behind them and fell into their seats as the shuttle pulled away at maximum acceleration with a crunch and a jerk. Pete Lightner was piloting manually, for his Betan pilot's neurological implant would not interface to the Barrayaran control system without an interpreter coupler, and Cordelia braced herself for a terrifying ride.

She lay back in her seat, still gasping, lungs raw from her mad dash. Stuben joined her, seething, and staring worriedly at her uncontrollable trembling.

"It's a crime what they did to Dubauer," he said. "I wish we could blow up their whole damn ship. Is Radnov still covering us, do you know?"

"Their long range weapons will be out for a while," she reported, not volunteering details. Could she ever make him understand? "Oh. I meant to ask— who was the Barrayaran hit by disruptor fire, planet-side?"

"I don't know. Doc Mac got his uniform. Hey, Mac—what's the name on your pocket?"

"Uh, let me see if I can sound out their alphabet." His lips moved silently. "Kou—Koudelka."

Cordelia bowed her head. "Was he killed?"

"He wasn't dead when we left, but he sure didn't look very healthy."

"What were you doing all that time aboard the *General*?" asked Stuben.

"Paying off a debt. Of honor."

"All right, be like that. I'll get the story later." He was silent, then added with a short nod, "I hope you got the bastard good, whoever he was."

"Look, Stu—I appreciate all you've done. But I've really got to be alone for a few minutes."

"Sure, Captain." He gave her a look of concern, and moved off muttering, "Damned monsters," under his breath.

Cordelia leaned her forehead against the cold window, and wept silently for her enemies.

▶ ▶ CHAPTER SEVEN

Captain Cordelia Naismith, Betan Expeditionary Force, fed the last normal space navigational observations into her ship's computer. Beside her, Pilot Officer Parnell adjusted the leads and cannulae to his headset and settled more comfortably into his padded chair, ready for the neurological control of the upcoming wormhole jump.

Her new command was a slow bulk freighter, unarmed, a steady workhorse of the Beta Colony-Escobar trade run. But there had been no direct communication with Escobar for over sixty days now, since the Barrayaran invasion fleet had plugged the Escobaran side of the exit as effectively as a cork in a bottle. At last word the Barrayaran and Escobaran fleets were still maneuvering in a deadly gavotte for tactical position, with little actual engagement. The Barrayarans were not expected to commit their ground forces until their control of Escobaran space was secure.

Cordelia intercomed engineering. "Naismith here. You about ready down there?"

The face of her engineer, a man she had first met but two days ago, appeared on the screen. He was young, and pulled from Survey like herself. No point in wasting experienced and knowledgeable military personnel on this excursion. Like Cordelia he wore Survey fatigues. The Expeditionary Force uniforms were rumored to be in the works, but no one had seen them yet.

"All set, Captain."

No fear trembled his voice. Well, she reflected, perhaps he was not old enough yet to have really come to believe in death after life. She took one last look around, settled herself, and drew a breath. "Pilot, the ship is yours."

"Ship accepted, ma'am," he replied formally.

A few seconds ticked by. An unpleasant wave of nausea passed over her, and she had the gluey, unsettling sensation of just waking up from a bad dream she could not remember. The jump was over.

"Ship is yours, ma'am," muttered the pilot wearily. The few seconds she had experienced translated to several subjective hours for him.

"Ship accepted, Pilot." She grabbed for the comconsole and began punching up a look at the tactical situation into which they had popped. There had been nothing through this passage for a month; she hoped fervently the Barrayaran crews would be bored and slow on the uptake.

There they were. Six ships, two of them starting to move already. So much for slow on the uptake.

"Right through the middle of 'em, Pilot," she ordered, keying data to him. "It's best if we can draw 'em all off their stations."

The two moving ships neared rapidly, and began firing with leisurely accuracy. They were taking their time, and making every shot count. Just a little target practice, that's all we are, she thought. I'll give you target practice. All non-shield power systems dimmed, and the ship seemed to groan as the plasma fire engulfed it. Then they cut across the tickling limit of the Barrayarans' range.

She called engineering. "Projection ready?"

"Ready and steady."

"Go."

Twelve thousand kilometers behind them, as if just emerged from the wormhole, a Betan dreadnought sprang into being. It accelerated astonishingly for so large a craft; indeed, its speed matched their own. It followed them like an arrow.

"Aha!" She clapped her hands in delight, and cried into the intercom, "We've fetched 'em! They're all moving now. Oh, better and better!"

Their pursuit ships slowed, preparing to turn and attack this much bigger prize. The four ships that had previously remained properly on station began to wheel away also. Minutes sped by as they jockeyed for position. The last Barrayaran ships wasted little fire on them, scarcely more than a salute, their attention all drawn to big brother behind them. The Barrayaran commanders undoubtedly felt themselves to be in a fine tactical position, spread out in a gauntlet and beginning a withering fire. The little ship preceding the warship was on the far side of them from Escobar, with nowhere to go. They could pick it off at their leisure.

Her own shields were down now, and acceleration failing as the ghastly power drain of the projector took its toll. But minute by precious minute the Barrayaran blockaders were being drawn farther from their assigned mousehole.

"We can keep this up for about ten more minutes," the engineer called up.

"All right. Save enough power to slag it when you're done. If we're captured Command doesn't want one molecule left connected to another for the Barrayarans to puzzle back together."

"What a crime. It's such a beautiful machine. I'm dying for a look inside."

You might, too, if the Barrayarans capture us, she thought. She directed all her ship's eyes back along their route. Far, far back at the wormhole exit, the first real Betan freighter winked into existence and began to boost for Escobar, unopposed. It was the newest addition to the merchant fleet, stripped of weapons and shields, rebuilt to do two things only now; carry a heavy payload and go like hell. Then the second, and the third. That was it. They were away, and with a start the Barrayarans could never hope to close.

The Betan dreadnought exploded with a spectacular radioactive light show. Unfortunately, there was no way to fake debris. I wonder how long it will take the Barrayarans to figure out they've been had? she thought. I sincerely hope they have a sense of humor . . .

Her ship drifted dead in space now, its power nearly depleted. She felt light in the head, and realized it wasn't psychosomatic. The artificial gravity was failing.

They rendezvoused with the engineer and his two assistants at the shuttle hatch, travelling with gazelle-like leaps that turned into bird-like swoops as the gravity gave up the ghost. The shuttle which was to be their lifeboat was a stripped-down model, cramped and comfortless. Into it they floated and sealed the

126

hatch. The pilot slid into the control chair and lowered his headset, and the shuttle kicked away from the side of their dying ship.

The engineer floated to her and handed her a little black box. "I thought you ought to do the honors, Captain."

"Ha. I bet you wouldn't kill your own dinner, either," she replied, trying to lighten the mood. They had served their ship together for barely five hours, but it still hurt. "Are we out of range, Parnell?"

"Yes, Captain."

"Gentlemen," she said, and paused, gathering them in by eye, "I thank you all. Look away from the left port, please."

She pulled the lever on the box. There was a soundless flash of brilliant blue light, and a general rush for the tiny port immediately after to see the last red glow as the ship folded into itself, carrying its military secrets to a wandering grave.

They shook hands solemnly all around, some right side up, some upside down, some floating at other angles, then secured themselves. Cordelia pulled herself into the navigation station beside Parnell, strapped in, and ran a quick check of its systems.

"Now comes the tricky part," murmured Parnell. "I'd still be happier with a straight max boost and try to outrun 'em."

"We could get away from those fat battlewagons, maybe," Cordelia conceded. "But their fast couriers would eat us alive. At least we look like a rock," she added, thinking of the artistic, probe-reflective camouflage that encased the lifeboat like a shell.

Several minutes of silence followed, as she concentrated on her work. "All right," she spoke at last, "let's sneak out of this neighborhood. It's going to be overcrowded very soon."

She did not fight the acceleration, but let it press her back into her seat. Tired. She hadn't thought it possible to be more tired than she was afraid. This war nonsense was a great psychological education. That chronometer had to be wrong. Surely it had been a year, and not an hour . . .

A small light blinked on her control panel. Fear washed the weariness back out of her body with a rush.

"Kill everything," she ordered, tapping controls herself, and was instantly plunged into weightless darkness. "Parnell, give us a little realistic tumble." Her inner ear and a greasy queasiness in her belly told her she was obeyed.

Now her sense of time began to be truly disordered. Darkness and silence reigned, but for an occasional whisper of movement, fabric on plastic, as someone stirred in his seat. In her imagination she felt the Barrayaran probes touching her ship, touching her, icy fingers up her back. I am a rock. I am a void. I am a silence . . . In the rear the silence was broken by the noise of someone vomiting, and some muffled swearing. Blast this tumble. Hope he had time to grab a bag . . .

There came a jerk and a pressure of weight at an odd angle. Parnell spat an oath like a sob. "Tractor tow! That's it."

She sighed without relief, and reached out to key the shuttle back to life, wincing at the blinding brightness of the little lights. "Well, let's see what's caught us."

Her hands flicked over the panels. She took a glance at her exterior monitors, and hastily pressed the red button that crashed the lifeboat's computer memory and recognition codes.

"What the hell have we got out there?" asked the engineer anxiously, noting the gesture as he made his way to her shoulder.

"Two cruisers and a fast courier," she informed him. "We appear to be slightly outnumbered."

He snorted unhappily.

A disembodied voice blared from the comm, at too great a volume; she turned it down quickly.

". . . not acknowledge surrender, we will destroy you."

"This is Lifeboat Shuttle A5A," she responded, modulating her voice carefully. "Captain Cordelia Naismith, Betan Expeditionary Force, commanding. We are an unarmed lifeboat."

The comm emitted a surprised "Peh!" and the voice added, "Another damned woman! You people are slow learners."

There was an unintelligible murmur in the background, and the voice returned to its original official tone. "You will be taken in tow. At the first sign of resistance, you will be obliterated. Understood?"

"Acknowledged," Cordelia responded. "We surrender."

Parnell shook his head angrily. She killed the comm and raised an eyebrow.

"I think we should try and make a break," he said.

"No. These guys are professional paranoids. The sanest one I ever met didn't like being in a room with a closed door—claimed you never knew what was on the other side. If they say they'll shoot, you'd better believe 'em."

Parnell and the engineer exchanged a look. "Go ahead, 'Nell," said the engineer. "Tell her."

Parnell cleared his throat, and moistened dry lips. "We wanted to let you know, Captain—that if you think, uh, blowing up the lifeboat might be the best thing for all concerned, we're with you. Nobody else is looking forward to being taken prisoner either."

Cordelia blinked at this offer. "That's—very courageous of you, Pilot Officer, but totally unnecessary. Don't flatter yourself. We were hand-picked for our ignorance, not our knowledge. You all only have guesses about what was aboard that convoy, and even I don't know any technical details. If we cooperate on the surface, we've at least some chance of getting through this alive."

"It—wasn't spilling intelligence we were thinking about, ma'am. It's their other habits."

A sticky silence fell. Cordelia sighed, spiraling in a vortex of grieving doubt. "It's all right," she said at last. "Their reputation is way overblown. Quite decent fellows, some of them." Especially one, her mind mocked. And even assuming he's still alive, do you really think you could find him in all this mess? Or finding him, save him from the gifts you yourself have brought from hell's hardware store without betraying your duty? Or is this a secret suicide pact? Do you even know yourself? Know thyself.

Parnell, watching her face, shook his head grimly. "You sure?"

"I've never killed anybody in my life. I'm not going to start with people on my own side, for pity's sake."

Parnell acknowledged the justice of this with a little quizzical shrug, not quite concealing an underlying relief.

"Anyway, I've got things to live for. This war can't last forever."

"Somebody back home?" he asked, and as her eyes turned to the probe readouts, added wisely, "Or out there?"

"Uh, yeah. Out there somewhere."

He shook his head in sympathy. "That's a tough one." He studied her still profile, and added encouragingly, "But you're right. The big boys will blast those bastards out of the sky sooner or later."

She gave vent to a small, mechanical, "Ha," and massaged her face with her fingertips, trying to rub out the tension. She had a sudden waking vision of a great warship cracked open, spilling its living guts like some monstrous seedpod. Frozen, sterile seeds, adrift on no wind, bloated from decompression and turning forever. Could one recognize a face, after that? she wondered. She turned her chair half away from Parnell, signifying an end to the conversation.

A Barrayaran fast courier took them in tow within an hour.

It was the familiar smell that hit her first, the metal-and-machine oil, ozone-redolent, locker room smell of a Barrayaran warship. The two tall soldiers in black who escorted her, each keeping a hand firmly on her elbow, maneuvered her through one last narrow oval doorway to what she guessed must be the main prison area of the great flagship. She and her four men were stripped ruthlessly, searched in minute and paranoid detail, medically examined, holographed, retinaprinted, identified, and issued shapeless orange pajamas. Her men were led away separately. In spite of her words to Parnell, she was sickened by dread of them being peeled, layer by layer, for information they did not hold. Gently now, reason argued; surely the Barrayarans would save them for prisoner exchange.

The guards snapped to attention. Turning, she saw a high-ranking Barrayaran officer enter the processing chamber. The bright yellow of the collar tabs on his dark green dress uniform marked a rank she had not seen before, and with a shock she identified it as the color for a vice-admiral. Knowing what he was, she knew at once who he was, and studied him with grave interest.

Vorrutyer, that was his name. Co-commander of the Barrayaran armada, along with Crown Prince Serg Vorbarra. She supposed he was the one who did the real work; she'd heard he was slated to be the Barrayarans' next Minister of War. So that was what a rising star looked like.

In a way he was a little like Vorkosigan, a bit taller, about the same weight but less of it in bone and muscle and more of it in fat. He had dark hair too, curlier than Vorkosigan's and with less grey in it, was a similar age, and rather more handsome. His eyes were quite different, a deep velvet brown fringed by long black lashes, by far the most beautiful eyes she had ever seen in a man's face. They triggered a small subliminal wailing deep in her mind, crying, you thought you had faced fear earlier today, but you were mistaken; here is the real thing, fear without exhilaration or hope; which was strange, for they ought to have attracted her. She broke eye contact, telling herself firmly the unease and instant dislike were mere nerves, and waited.

"Identify yourself, Betan," he growled. It gave her a disjointed sense of deja vu.

She fought for equilibrium, giving him a snappy salute and saying smartly, "Captain Cordelia Naismith,

Betan Expeditionary. We are a military party. Combatants." This private joke of course passed by him.

"Hah. Strip her, and turn her about."

He stepped back, watching. The two grinning soldiers guarding her obeyed. *I don't like the way this is starting out . . .* She forced her face to blandness, holding on to all her secret sources of serenity. *Calm. Calm. This one wants to rattle you. You can see it in his eyes, his hungry eyes. Calm.*

"A little old, but she'll do. I'll send for her later."

The guard shoved the pajamas back at her. She dressed slowly, to annoy them, like a striptease in reverse, with precise controlled motions of the sort suitable for a Japanese tea ceremony. One growled, and the other shoved her roughly in the back toward her cell. She smiled sourly at her success, thinking, *well, at least I have that much control over my destiny. Should I award myself points if I can goad them into beating me up?*

They bundled her into a bare metal room, and left her. She continued the ploy, for her own thin amusement, by kneeling gracefully on the floor with the same sort of movements, right toe crossed correctly over the left, hands resting motionless upon her thighs. The touch reminded her of the patch on her left leg that was devoid of all sensation, heat, cold, pain, pressure, legacy of her last encounter with the armies of Barrayar. She half-closed her eyes and let her mind drift, hoping to give her captors an unsettling impression of deep and possibly dangerous psychic meditations. *Pretend aggression was better than nothing.*

After an hour or so of stillness, by which time her unaccustomed muscles were protesting the kneeling position most painfully, the guard returned.

133

"Admiral wants you," he said laconically. "Come along."

She had a guard at each elbow again for the trip through the ship. One grinned and undressed her with his eyes. The other looked at her with pity, far more disturbing. She began to wonder just how much her time with Vorkosigan had led her to discount the risks of capture. They came to officer's country, and stopped before an oval metal door in a row of identical ones. The grinning guard knocked, and was bidden to enter.

This admiral's quarters were very different from her austere cabin aboard the *General Vorkraft*. For one thing, the bulkheads had been knocked out of the two adjoining chambers, giving a triple share of space. It was full of personal furnishings of a most luxurious order. Admiral Vorrutyer rose from a velvet-covered seat as she entered, but she did not mistake it for a gesture of courtesy.

He walked slyly around her as she stood silent, watching her gaze travel around the room. "A step up from that cell, eh?" he probed.

For the guards' benefit she replied, "Looks like a whore's boudoir."

The grinning guard choked, and the other one laughed outright, but cut if off quickly at a glare from Vorrutyer. Didn't think it was *that* funny, she puzzled. Some of the details of the decor began to penetrate, and she realized she'd spoken more truly than she knew. What an extremely odd little statuette in that corner, for instance. Although it had a certain redeeming artistic merit, she supposed. "One with very unusual customers," she added.

"Buckle her in," ordered Vorrutyer, "and return to your posts. I'll call you when I'm done."

She was placed on her back across his wide, non-regulation bed, arms and legs stretched to the four corners and tautly attached by soft bracelets to short chains, attached in turn to the bedframe. Simple, chilling, quite beyond her strength to break.

The guard who pitied whispered to her under his breath as he buckled a wrist strap, hidden almost inaudibly in a sigh, "Sorry."

"It's all right," she breathed back. Their eyes passed over each other, hiding the secret transaction from the watching Vorrutyer.

"Ha. That's what you think now," murmured the other through his grin, fastening the other strap.

"Shut up," muttered the first, and shot him a fierce look. An unclean silence filled the room until the guards withdrew.

"Looks like a permanent installation," she observed to Vorrutyer, horribly fascinated. It was like a sick joke come to life. "What do you do when you can't catch Betans? Call for volunteers?"

A frown appeared between his eyes briefly, then smoothed. "Keep it up," he encouraged. "It amuses me. It will make the ultimate denouement so much more piquant."

He loosened his uniform collar, poured himself a glass of wine from a very non-regulation portable bar in one corner, and seated himself on the bed beside her with the chatty air of a man visiting a sick friend. He looked her over minutely, beautiful brown eyes liquid with anticipation.

She tried to string herself along; maybe he's only a rapist. It might be possible to handle a simple rapist. Such direct, childlike souls, hardly offensive at all. Even vileness has a relative range . . .

135

"I don't know any military secrets worth a thing," she fenced. "This isn't really worth your time."

"I didn't think you did," he replied easily. "Although you will undoubtedly insist on telling me everything you know over the next few weeks. Quite tedious, I'm not in the least interested. If I want your information, my medical staff can have it out of you in a trice." He sipped his wine. "Although it's curious you should bring up the subject—perhaps I will send you to sickbay, later today."

Her stomach knotted. Fool, she shrieked silently at herself, did you just blow a chance of ducking interrogation? But no, it had to be standard operating procedure—he's just working you over. Subtle. Calm . . .

He drank again. "Do you know, I think I shall enjoy having an older woman for a change. The young ones may look pretty, but they're too easy. No sport. I can tell already, you're going to be great sport. A very great fall requires a very great height, to fall from, not so?"

She sighed, and gazed up at the ceiling. "Well, I'm sure it will be educational." She tried to remember how she'd occupied her mind during sex with her old lover, in the bad times before she'd finally shed him. This might well be no worse . . .

Vorrutyer, smiling, put his wine down on a bedside table and took from its drawer a small knife, sharp as an old-fashioned scalpel, with a jewelled handle that glittered before his hand eclipsed it. Rather desultorily, he began slicing away at the orange pajamas, peeling them away from her like the skin of a fruit.

"Isn't that government property?" she inquired, but was sorry she'd spoken, for a tremble made the

136

word "property" squeaky. It was like throwing a tidbit to a hungry dog, likely to make him jump higher.

He chuckled, pleased. "Oops." Deliberately, he let the knife slip. It sliced half an inch into her thigh. He watched her face avidly for her reaction. It was in the area without sensation; she could not even feel the wet trickle of blood that welled from the wound. His eyes narrowed in disappointment. She even kept from glancing down. She wished she'd studied more about trance states.

"I'm not going to rape you today," he offered conversationally, "if that's what you've been thinking."

"It had crossed my mind. I can't imagine what suggested it."

"There's scarcely time," he explained. "Today is but the, as it were, hors d'ouevre of the banquet, or a simple clear soup, very pristine. All the complicated things will be saved for dessert, in a few weeks."

"I never eat dessert. Weight, you know."

He chuckled again. "You are a delight." He put the knife down and took another sip of wine. "You know, officers always delegate their work. Now, I am an aficionado of Earth history. My favorite century is the Eighteenth."

"I'd have guessed the Fourteenth. Or the Twentieth."

"In a day or two, I shall teach you not to interrupt. Where was I? Ah, yes. Well, in my reading, I came upon the loveliest scene, where a certain great lady," he raised the wineglass to her in a toast, "was raped by a diseased servant, on the orders of his master. Very piquant. Venereal disease is, alas, a thing of the past. But I am able to command a diseased servant, although his disease is mental rather than physical. A real, bona fide, paranoid schizophrenic."

"Like master, like man," she shot at random. I

137

cannot keep this up much longer; my heart shall fail me soon . . .

This won a rather sour smile. "He hears voices, you know, like Joan of Arc, except that he tells me they are demons, not saints. He has visual hallucinations, too, on occasion. And he's a very large man. I've used him before, many times. He's not the sort of fellow who finds it easy to, er, attract women."

There was a timely knock on the door, and Vorrutyer went to it. "Ah, come in, Sergeant. I was just talking about you."

"*Bothari*," she breathed. Ducking his head through the door came the tall frame and familiar borzoi face of Vorkosigan's soldier. How, how *could* he have hit on her personal nightmare? A kaleidoscope of images spun through her memory; a dappled wood, the crackle of disruptors, the faces of the dead and the half-dead, a looming shape like the shadow of death.

She focused on the present reality. Would he recognize her? His eyes had not yet touched her; they were fixed on Vorrutyer. Too close together, those eyes, and not quite on the same level. They gave his face an unusual degree of asymmetry that added much to his remarkable ugliness.

Her boiling imagination lurched to his body. His body—it was all wrong, somehow, hunched in his black uniform, not like the straight figure she had last seen demanding pride of place from Vorkosigan. Wrong, wrong, terribly wrong. A head taller than Vorrutyer, yet he seemed almost to creep before his master. His spine was coiled with tension as he glowered down at his—torturer? What, she wondered, might a mind molester like Vorrutyer do with the material presented by Bothari? God, Vorrutyer, do you imagine, in your amoral flashy freakiness, in your monstrous vanity, that you *control* this elemental? And you dare play games with that sullen madness in his eyes? Her thoughts kept time with her racing pulse. There are two victims in this room. There are two victims in this room There are two . . .

"There you go, Sergeant." Vorrutyer hooked a thumb over his shoulder at Cordelia, spread-eagled on the bed. "Rape me this woman." He pulled up a chair and prepared to watch, closely and gleefully. "Go on, go on."

Bothari, face as unreadable as ever, unfastened his trousers and approached the foot of the bed. He looked at her for the first time.

"Any last words, 'Captain' Naismith?" Vorrutyer inquired sarcastically. "Or have you finally run out of words?"

She stared at Bothari, shaken by a pity almost like love. He seemed nearly in a trance, lust without pleasure, anticipation without hope. Poor sod, she thought, what a mess they've made of you. No longer fencing for points, she searched her heart for words not for Vorrutyer but for Bothari. Some healing words—I would not add to his madness . . . The air of the room seemed clammy cold, and she shivered, feeling unutterably weary, resistless, and sad. He crouched over her, heavy and dark as lead, making the bed creak.

"I believe," she said slowly at last, "that the tormented are very close to God. I'm sorry, Sergeant."

He stared at her, his face a foot from hers, for so long she wondered if he'd heard her. His breath was not good, but she did not flinch. Then, to her astonishment, he stood up and refastened his pants, trembling slightly.

"No, sir," he said in his bass monotone.

"What?" Vorrutyer sat up, amazed. "Why not?" he demanded.

The Sergeant groped for words. "She's Commodore Vorkosigan's prisoner. Sir."

Vorrutyer stared, first puzzled, then illuminated. "So *you're* Vorkosigan's Betan!" His cool amusement evaporated at the name, with a hiss like a drop of water on a red-hot coil.

Vorkosigan's Betan? A brief hope flared within her, that Vorkosigan's name might be a password to safety, but it died. The chance of this creature being any kind of a friend of his was surely something well under zero. He was looking now not at her, but through her, like a window on some more wonderful view. *Vorkosigan's Betan?*

"I've got that stiff-necked puritan son-of-a-bitch by the balls now," he breathed fiercely. "This could be even better than the day I told him about his wife." The expression on his face was strange and startling, the mask of suavity seeming to melt, and run off in patches. It was like stumbling suddenly over the center of a caldera. He seemed to remember the mask, and clutched its pieces around him, half-effectually.

"Do you know, you have quite overwhelmed me. The possibilities you present—eighteen years were not too long to wait for so ideal a revenge. A woman soldier. Ha! He probably thought you the ideal solution to our mutual—difficulty. My perfect warrior, my dear hypocrite, Aral. You have much to learn of him, I wager. But do you know, I somehow feel quite certain he hasn't mentioned me to you."

"Not by name," she agreed. "Possibly by category."

"And what category was that?"

"I believe the term he used was 'scum of the service.'"

140

He grinned sourly. "I shouldn't recommend name-calling to a woman in your position."

"Oh, you embrace the category, then?" Her response was automatic, but her heart was shrinking within her, leaving an echoing hollowness. *What is Vorkosigan doing in the center of this one's madness? His eyes look like Bothari's, now . . .*

His smile tightened. "I've embraced a number of things in my time. Not least of which was your puritan lover. Let your imagination dwell on that a while, my dear, my sweet, my pet. You'd scarcely believe it to meet him now, but he was quite a merry widower, before he gave himself over so irritatingly to these random outbreaks of righteousness." He laughed.

"Your skin is very white. Has he touched it—so?" He ran one fingernail up the inside of her arm, and she shuddered. "And your hair. I am quite certain he must be fascinated by that twining hair. So fine, and such an unusual color." He twisted a strand gently between his fingers. "I must think what can be done with that hair. One might remove the scalp entirely, of course, but there must be something more creative yet. Perhaps I'll take a bit with me, and take it out and play with it, quite casually, at the Staff meeting. Let it slip silkily through my fingers— see how long it takes to lock his attention on it. Feed the doubt, and the growing fear, with, oh, one or two casual remarks. I wonder how much it would take to start him scrambling those annoyingly perfect reports of his—ha! Then send him off for about a week of detached duty, still wondering, still in doubt. . . ."

He picked up the jewelled knife and sawed off a thick strand, to coil up and place carefully in his breast pocket, smiling down at her the while. "One must be careful, of course, not to goad him quite into violence—he becomes so tediously unmanageable—" he ran one finger in an L-shaped motion across the left side of his chin in the exact position of Vorkosigan's scar. "Much easier to start than stop. Although he's become remarkably temperate of late. Your influence, my pet? Or is he simply growing old?"

He tossed the knife carelessly back on the bedside table, then rubbed his hands together, laughed out loud, and draped himself beside her to murmur lovingly in her ear. "And after Escobar, when we need no longer regard the Emperor's watchdog, there will be no limit to what I can do. So many choices . . ." He gave vent to a stream of plans for torturing Vorkosigan through her, glistening with obscene detail. He was taut with his vision, his face pale and moist.

"You can't possibly get away with anything like that," she said faintly. There was fear in her face now, and tears, running down from the corners of her eyes in iridescent trails to wet the tendrils of hair around her ears, but he was scarcely interested. She had believed she had fallen into the deepest possible pit of fear, but now that floor opened beneath her and she fell again, endlessly, turning in the air.

Some measure of control seemed to return to him, and he walked around the foot of the bed, looking at her. "Well. How very refreshing. Do you know, I am quite energized. I believe I shall do it myself, after all. You should be glad. I'm much better looking than Bothari."

"Not to me."

He dropped his trousers and prepared to climb on her. "Do you forgive me too, sweetheart?"

She felt cold, and dry, and vanishingly small. "I'm afraid I'll have to leave that to the Infinitely Merciful. You exceed my capacity."

"Later in the week," he promised, mistaking her defeat for flippancy, and clearly excited by what he took for a continued show of resistance.

Sergeant Bothari had been mooning around the room, head moving from side to side and narrow jaw working, as Cordelia had seen it once before, a sign of agitation. Vorrutyer, intent on Cordelia, paid no attention to the movements behind him. So his moment of utter astonishment was very brief when the Sergeant grabbed him by his curly hair, yanked his head back, and drew the jewelled knife most expertly around his neck, slicing through all four of the major vessels in a swift double movement. The blood spurted over Cordelia in a fountain, horribly hot and flowing.

Vorrutyer gave one convulsive twist and lost consciousness as the blood pressure in his brain fell to nothing. Sergeant Bothari let go of the hair, and Vorrutyer dropped between her legs and slithered down out of sight over the end of the bed.

The Sergeant stood hulkingly, breathing heavily, by the end of the bed. Cordelia could not remember if she'd screamed. No matter, odds were no one paid much attention to screams coming out of this room anyway. She felt frozen and bloodless in her hands, face, feet; her heart hammered.

She cleared her throat. "Uh, thank you, Sergeant Bothari. That was a very, uh, knightly deed. Do you suppose you could unbuckle me, too?" Her voice squeaked uncontrollably, and she swallowed, irritated at it.

She regarded Bothari with terrorized fascination.

There was absolutely no way of predicting what he might do next. Muttering to himself, with a look of bewilderment on his face, he fumbled apart the buckle on her left wrist. Swiftly, stiffly, she rolled over and loosed the right wrist, then sat up and undid the ankles. She sat cross-legged a moment in the center of the bed, stark naked and dripping with blood, rubbing ankles and wrists and trying to get her paralyzed brain into motion.

"Clothes. Clothes," she muttered to herself. She peeked over the end of the bed at the crumpled form of the late Admiral Vorrutyer, pants about his ankles and his last look of surprise frozen on his face. The great brown eyes had lost their liquid glow, and were already beginning to film over.

She slipped out of the side of the bed away from Bothari and began searching frantically through the metal drawers and cupboards that lined the room. A couple of the drawers contained his toy collection, and she shut them hastily, nauseated, finally understanding what he'd meant by his last words. The man's taste in perversions had certainly had remarkable scope. Some uniforms, all with too much yellow insignia. At last she found a set of plain black fatigues. She wiped the blood from her body with a soft dressing gown, and flung them on.

Sergeant Bothari meanwhile had sat on the floor, curled up with his head resting on his knees, talking under his breath. She knelt beside him. Was he starting to hallucinate? She had to get him to his feet, and out of here. They could not count on being undiscovered much longer. Yet where could they hide? Or was it adrenalin, not reason, that demanded flight? Was there a better option?

As she hesitated, the door slammed suddenly open. She cried out for the first time. But the man standing white-faced in the aperture with the plasma arc in his hand was Vorkosigan.

›› CHAPTER EIGHT

She sighed shakily at the sight of him, and the paralyzing panic streamed out of her in that long breath. "My God, you almost gave me heart failure," she managed in a small tight voice. "Come in, and close the door."

His lips moved silently around the shape of her name, and he entered, a sudden panic in his face almost matching her own. Then she saw he was followed by another officer, a lieutenant with brown hair and a bland puppy face. So she did not fling herself upon him and shriek into his shoulder, as she passionately wished, but said instead cautiously, "There's been an accident."

"Close the door, Illyan," said Vorkosigan to the lieutenant. His features became tightly controlled as the young man came even with him. "You're going to have to witness this with the greatest attention."

His lips pressed to a white slit, Vorkosigan walked slowly around the room, noting the details, some of which he pointed out silently to his companion. The lieutenant said, "Er, ah," at the first gesture, which was with the plasma arc. Vorkosigan stopped before the body, looked at the weapon in his hand as though seeing it for the first time, and put it in its holster.

"Been reading the Marquis again, have you?" he addressed the corpse with a sigh. He turned it over with the toe of his boot, and a little more blood ran out of the meaty slice in its neck. "A little learning is a dangerous thing." He glanced up at Cordelia. "Which of you should I congratulate?"

She moistened her lips. "I'm not sure. How annoyed is everyone going to be about this?"

The lieutenant was going through Vorrutyer's drawers and cupboards also, using a handkerchief to open them, and from his expression finding that his cosmopolitan education was not so complete as he had supposed. He remained staring for a long time into the drawer that Cordelia had shut so hastily.

"The Emperor, for one, will be delighted," said Vorkosigan. "But—strictly in private."

"In fact, I was tied up at the time. Sergeant Bothari, uh, did the honors."

Vorkosigan glanced at Bothari, still sitting curled up on the floor. "Hm." He gazed around the room one last time. "There's something about this that reminds me forcibly of that remarkable scene when we broke into my engine room. It has your personal signature. My grandmother had a phrase for it— something about late, and a dollar . . ."

"A day late and a dollar short?" suggested Cordelia involuntarily.

"Yes, that was it." He bit an ironic twist from his lips. "A very Betan remark—I begin to see why." His face maintained a mask of cool neutrality, but his eyes searched her in secret agony. "Was I, ah, short?"

148

"Not at all," she reassured him. "You're, um, very timely. I was just dithering around in a panic, wondering what to do next."

He was facing away from Illyan, and a quickly suppressed grin crinkled his eyes briefly. "It seems I am rescuing my fleet from you, then," he murmured between his teeth. "Not exactly what I had in mind when I came up here, but I'm glad to rescue *something*." He raised his voice. "As soon as you're done, Illyan, I suggest we adjourn to my cabin for further discussion."

Vorkosigan knelt by Bothari, studying him. "That bloody bastard has about ruined him again," he growled. "He was almost well, after his time with me. Sergeant Bothari," he said more gently, "can you walk a little way with me?"

Bothari muttered something unintelligible into his knees.

"Come here, Cordelia," said Vorkosigan. It was the first time she had heard her first name in his mouth. "See if you can get him up. I don't think I'd better touch him, just now."

She got down into the line of his sight. "Bothari. Bothari, look at me. You've got to get up, and walk a little way." She took his blood-coated hand, and tried to think of a line of reason, or more likely unreason, that might reach him. She tried a smile. "Look. See? You're washed in blood. Blood washes away sin, right? You're going to be all right now. Uh, the bad man is gone, and in a little while the bad voices will go away too. So you come along with me, and I'll take you where you can rest."

During this speech he gradually focused on her, and at the end he nodded, and stood. Still holding his hand, she followed Vorkosigan out, Illyan bringing up the rear. She hoped her psychological band-aid would hold; an alarm of any sort might touch him off like a bomb.

She was astonished when Vorkosigan's cabin proved to be just one door down, across the corridor.

"Are you captain of this ship?" she asked. His collar tabs, now that she got a better look at them, proclaimed him a commodore now. "Were you here all the time?"

"No, I'm on the Staff. My courier just got in from the front a few hours ago. I've been in conference with Admiral Vorhalas and the Prince ever since. It just broke up. I came up straight away when the guard told me about Vorrutyer's new prisoner. You—in my foulest nightmare, I never dreamed it might be you."

Vorkosigan's cabin seemed tranquil as a monk's cell compared to the carnage they had left across the hall. Everything regulation, a proper soldier's room. Vorkosigan locked the door behind them. He rubbed his face and sighed, drinking her in. "Are you sure you're all right?"

"Just shaken up. I knew I was running risks, when I was selected, but I wasn't expecting anything quite like that man. He was a classic. I'm surprised you served him."

His face became shuttered. "I serve the Emperor."

She became conscious of Illyan, standing silent and watchful. What would she say if Vorkosigan asked her about the convoy? He was a greater danger to her duty than torture. She had begun to think, in the past months, that their separation must eventually diminish her heart-hunger for him, but seeing him live and intense before her made it ravenous. No telling what he felt, though. Right now he looked tired, uncertain, and strained. Wrong, all wrong . . .

"Ah, permit me to introduce Lieutenant Simon Illyan, of the Emperor's personal security staff. He's my spy. Lieutenant Illyan, Commander Naismith."

"It's Captain Naismith now," she put in automatically. The lieutenant shook her hand with a bland calm innocence wholly at odds with the bizarre scene they had just left. He might have been at an embassy reception. Her touch left a streak of blood on his palm. "Who do you spy on?"

"I prefer the term, 'surveillance,' " he said.

"Bureaucratic weaselwording," put in Vorkosigan. He added to Cordelia, "The lieutenant spies on me. He represents a compromise between the Emperor, the Ministry of Political Education, and myself."

"The phrase the Emperor used," said Illyan distantly, "was 'cease-fire.' "

"Yes. Lieutenant Illyan also has an eidetic memory biochip. You may think of him as a recording device with legs, which the Emperor may play back at will."

Cordelia stared covertly at him. "It's too bad we couldn't meet again under more auspicious circumstances," she said carefully to Vorkosigan.

"There are no auspicious circumstances here."

Lieutenant Illyan cleared his throat, glancing at Bothari, who stood twining and untwining his fingers and staring at the wall. "What now, sir?"

"Hm. There is entirely too much physical evidence in that room, not to mention witnesses as to who went in and when, to attempt to monkey with the scenario. Personally, I should prefer for Bothari not to have been there at all. The fact that he is clearly *non compos mentis* will carry no weight with the Prince when he gets wind of this." He stood,

151

thinking furiously. "You will simply have to have escaped, before Illyan and I arrived on the scene. I don't know how long it will be possible to hide Bothari in here—maybe I can get some sedatives for him." His eye fell on Illyan. "How about the Emperor's staff agent in the medical section?"

Illyan looked noncommittal. "It's possible something might be arranged."

"Good man." He turned to Cordelia. "You're going to have to stay in here and keep Bothari under control. Illyan and I must go at once, or there will be too many unaccounted minutes between the time we left Vorhalas and the time we sound the alarm. The Prince's security men will be going over that room thoroughly, and everyone's movements as well."

"Were Vorrutyer and the Prince in the same party?" she asked, feeling for footing in the riptides of Barrayaran politics.

Vorkosigan smiled bitterly. "They were just good friends."

And he was gone, leaving her alone with Bothari and utter confusion.

She had Bothari sit down in Vorkosigan's desk chair, where he fidgeted silently and incessantly. She sat cross-legged on the bed, trying to radiate an air of calm control and good cheer. Not easy, from a spirit filled with panic frenzied for expression.

Bothari stood and began to pace about the room, talking to himself. No, not to himself, she realized. And most certainly not to her. The choppy whispered flow of words made no sense to her at all. Time flowed by slowly, viscous with fear.

Both she and Bothari jumped when the door clicked

open, but it was only Illyan. Bothari fell into a knife-fighter's crouch as he slipped in.

"Servants of the beast are the beast's hands," he said. "He feeds them on the wife's blood. Bad servants."

Illyan eyed him nervously, and pressed some ampules into her hand. "Here. You give it to him. One of these would knock out a charging elephant. Can't stay." He slipped back out again.

"Coward," she muttered after him. But he was probably right. She might well have a better chance that he of getting it into the Sergeant. Bothari's agitation was approaching an explosive level.

She set the bulk of the ampules aside, and approached him with a sunny smile. Its effect was diminished by her eyes, large with fear. Bothari's eyes were flickering slits. "Commodore Vorkosigan wants you to rest now. He sent some medicine to help you."

He backed warily before her, and she stopped, cautious of forcing him into a corner. "It's just a sedative, see?"

"The beast's drugs made the demons drunk. They sang and shouted. Bad medicine."

"No, no. This is good medicine. It will make the demons go to sleep," she promised. This was walking a tightrope in the dark. She tried another tack.

"Come to attention, soldier," she said sharply. "Inspection."

It was a wrong move. He batted the ampule nearly out of her hand as she tried to stick it in his arm, and his hand closed around her wrist like a hot iron band. Her breath hissed inward at the pain, but she just managed to twist her fingers around and press the administrative spray end of the ampule against

153

the inside of his wrist, before he picked her up bodily and flung her across the room.

She landed on her back, skidding across the friction matting with what seemed to her a dreadful amount of noise, fetching up with a bang against the door. Bothari lunged after her. Can he kill me before the stuff cuts in? she wondered wildly, and forced herself to go limp, as if unconscious. Surely unconscious people were very non-threatening.

Evidently not to Bothari, for his hands closed around her neck. One knee pressed into her ribcage, and she felt something go painfully wrong in the region. She popped her eyes open in time to see his eyes roll back. His hands slackened in their twisting, and he rolled off her to his hands and knees, head wagging dizzily, then slumped to the deck.

She sat up, leaning against the wall. "I want to go home," she muttered. "This wasn't in my job description." The feeble joke did nothing to dissolve the clot of hysteria rising in her throat, so she fell back on an older and more serious discipline, whispering its words aloud. By the time she finished self-control had returned.

She could not lift Bothari to the bunk. She raised his heavy head and slipped the pillow under it, and pulled his arms and legs into a more comfortable-looking position. When Vorkosigan and his shadow returned they could have a go at it.

The door opened at last, and Vorkosigan and Illyan entered, closing it quickly and walking carefully around Bothari.

"Well?" said Cordelia. "How did it go?"

"With machine-like precision, like a wormhole jump to hell," Vorkosigan replied. He turned his hand palm upward in a familiar gesture that caught her heart like a hook.

She looked her puzzlement at him. "You're as baffling as Bothari. How did they take the murder?"

"It went just fine. I'm under arrest and confined to quarters, for suspicion of conspiracy. The Prince thinks I put Bothari up to it," he explained. "God knows how."

"Uh, I know I'm very tired," she said, "and not thinking too clearly. But you did say, 'Just fine?' "

"Commodore Vorkosigan, sir," interrupted Illyan. "Keep in mind that I'm going to have to report this conversation."

"What conversation?" said Vorkosigan. "You and I are alone in here, remember? You're not required to observe me when I'm alone, as everyone knows. They'll start wondering why you're lingering in here before long."

Lieutenant Illyan frowned over this jesuitry. "The Emperor's intention—"

"Yes? Tell me all about the Emperor's intention." Vorkosigan looked savage.

"The Emperor's intention, as communicated to *me*, was that you be discouraged from incriminating yourself. I cannot edit my report, you know."

"That was your argument four weeks ago. You saw the result."

Illyan looked perturbed.

Vorkosigan spoke low and controlled. "Everything the Emperor requires of me will be accomplished. He's a great choreographer, and he shall have his dance of dreamers down to the last step." Vorkosigan's hand closed in a fist, and opened again. "I have withheld nothing that is mine from his service. Not my life. Not even my honor. Grant me this." He

155

pointed at Cordelia. "You gave me your word on it then. Do you intend to take it back?"

"Will someone please tell me what you are talking about?" interrupted Cordelia.

"Lieutenant Illyan is having a little conflict at the moment between duty and conscience," said Vorkosigan, folding his arms and staring at the far wall. "It is not solvable without redefining one or the other, and he must now choose which."

"You see, there was another incident," Illyan jerked his thumb in the direction of Vorrutyer's quarters, "like that, with a prisoner, a few weeks ago. Commodore Vorkosigan wanted to, er, do something about it then. I talked him out of it. After—afterwards, I agreed that I would not interfere with any action he chose to take, should the situation come up again."

"Did Vorrutyer kill her?" asked Cordelia morbidly.

"No," said Illyan. He stared moodily at his boots.

"Come on, Illyan," said Vorkosigan wearily. "If they aren't discovered, you can give the Emperor your true report, and let him edit it. If they are found here—the public integrity of your reports is not going to be your most pressing worry, believe me."

"Damn! Captain Negri was right," said Illyan.

"He usually is—what was the instance?"

"He said that permitting private judgements to turn my duty in the smallest matter would be just like getting a little bit pregnant—that the consequences would very soon get beyond me."

Vorkosigan laughed. "Captain Negri is a very experienced man. But I can tell you that—very rarely— even he has been known to make a private judgement."

"But Security is tearing the place apart out there. They're going to arrive back here eventually just by

156

process of elimination. The moment it occurs to someone to suspect my integrity, it's all over."

"In time," agreed Vorkosigan. "How much time, do you estimate?"

"They'll complete the search sweep of the ship in a few hours."

"Then you'll just have to re-direct their efforts. Widen their search area—didn't any ships depart the flag during the time window after Vorrutyer's death and before the Security cordon was started?"

"Yes, two, but . . ."

"Good. Use your Imperial influence there. Volunteer all the assistance that you, as Captain Negri's most trusted aide, can supply. Mention Negri frequently. Suggest. Recommend. Doubt. Better not bribe or threaten, that's too obvious, although it may come to that. Slander their inspection procedures, make records evaporate—whatever is necessary to muddy the waters. Buy me 48 hours, Illyan. That's all I ask."

"All?" choked Illyan.

"Ah. Try to be sure it's you and no one else who brings meals and so on. And try to slip in some extra rations when you do."

Vorkosigan relaxed measurably when he had gone, and turned to her with a sad and awkward smile that was good as a touch. "Well met, lady."

She sketched him a salute, and returned the smile. "I hope I haven't messed things up for you too much. Personally, that is."

"By no means. In fact, you have simplified them enormously."

"East is west, up is down, and being falsely arrested for getting your C.O.'s throat cut is a simplification. I must be on Barrayar. I don't suppose you'd care to explain what's going on around here?"

"No. But at last I understand why there have been so many madmen in Barrayaran history. They are not its cause, they are its effect." He sighed, and spoke so low it was almost a whisper. "Oh, Cordelia. You have no idea how much I need one sane clean person near me. You are water in the desert."

"You look pretty, uh—you look like you've lost weight." He looked, she thought, ten years older than six months ago.

"Oh, me." He ran his hand over his face. "I'm not thinking. You must be exhausted. Do you want to go to sleep, or something?"

"I'm not sure I can, yet. But I'd like to wash up. Didn't think I ought to run the shower when you weren't here, in case it's monitored."

"Good thinking. Go ahead."

She rubbed her hand over her nerveless thigh, black cloth sticky with blood. "Uh, have you got a change of clothes for me? These are messed up. Besides, they were Vorrutyer's. They have a psychic stink."

"Right." His face darkened. "Is that your blood?"

"Yeah, Vorrutyer was playing surgeon. It doesn't hurt. I've got no nerves there."

"Hm." Vorkosigan fingered his scar, and smiled a little. "Yes, I think I have just the thing for you."

He unlocked one of his drawers with an eight-digit number code, sorted down to the bottom layer, and to Cordelia's astonishment pulled out the Survey fatigues she had left behind on the General Vorkraft, now cleaned, mended, pressed, and folded neatly. "I haven't got the boots with me, and the insignia are obsolete, but I rather imagine these will fit," Vorkosigan remarked blandly, handing them over.

"You—saved my clothes?"

"As you see."

"Good heavens. Uh—why?"

His mouth crimped ruefully. "Well—it was all you left. Except for the shuttle your people abandoned downside, which would have made a rather awkward memento."

She ran her hand over the tan cloth, feeling suddenly shy. But just before disappearing into the bathroom with the clothes and a first aid kit, she said abruptly, "I've still got my Barrayaran uniform at home. Wrapped in paper, in a drawer." She gave him a firm nod; his eyes lit.

When she came out again the room was dim and night-quiet, but for a light over the desk where Vorkosigan was studying a disc at his computer interface. She hopped onto his bed and sat cross-legged again, wriggling her bare toes. "What's all that?"

"Homework. It's my official function on Vorrutyer's— the late Admiral Vorrutyer's—Staff." He smiled a little as he corrected himself, like the famous tiger of the limerick when he returned from the ride with the lady inside. "I'm charged with planning and keeping the contingency orders up to date, in case we are forced to fall back. As the Emperor said in the Council meeting, since I was so convinced it was going to be a disaster, I could bloody well do the planning for it. I'm regarded as a bit of a fifth wheel around here at the moment."

"Things going well for your side, are they?" she asked, oppressed.

"We're becoming nicely overextended. Some people regard that as progress." He entered some new data, then shut down the interface.

She sought to turn the subject from the dangerous present. "I take it you didn't get charged with treason after all?" she asked, thinking back to their last conversation, long ago and far away above another world.

"Ah, that turned out something of a draw. I was recalled back to Barrayar after you escaped. Minister Grishnov—he's head of Political Education, and third in real power after the Emperor and Captain Negri—was practically drooling on himself, he was so convinced he'd got me at last. But my case against Radnov was air-tight.

"The Emperor stepped in before we could draw blood, and forced a compromise, or more correctly, an abeyance. I haven't actually been cleared, the charges are still pending in some legal limbo."

"How'd he do it?"

"Sleight of hand. He was giving Grishnov and the whole war party everything they'd asked for, the entire Escobar scheme on a platter, and more. He gave them the Prince. And all the credit. After the conquest of Escobar, Grishnov and the Prince each think they're going to be the de facto ruler of Barrayar.

"He even made Vorrutyer swallow my promotion. Pointed out he'd have me directly under his command. Vorrutyer saw the light at once." Vorkosigan's teeth set at some searing memory, his hand opening and closing once, unconsciously.

"How long have you known him?" she asked cautiously, thinking of the bottomless well of hatred she had fallen down.

His eyes slid away from her. "We were in school, and lieutenants together, back when he was only a common voyeur. He grew worse, I understand, in recent years, since he started associating with Prince Serg, and thinking he could get away with anything. God help us, he was nearly right. Bothari has done a great public service."

You knew him better than that, my breath, thought Cordelia. Was that your infection of the imagination, so hard to fight off? Bothari has done a great private service, too, it seems . . . "Speaking of Bothari—next time, you sedate him. He went wild when I came at him with the ampule."

"Ah. Yes. I think I understand why. It was in one of Captain Negri's reports. Vorrutyer was in the habit of drugging his, uh, players, with a variety of concoctions, when he wanted a better show. I'm fairly certain Bothari was one of his victims that way."

"Vile." She felt sick. Her muscles cramped around the ache in her side. "Who's this Captain Negri you keep talking about?"

"Negri? He does keep a low profile, but he's hardly secret. He heads the Emperor's personal security staff. Illyan's boss. They call him Ezar Vorbarra's familiar.

"If you think of the Ministry of Political Education as the Emperor's right hand, then Negri is his left, the one the right is not permitted to know. He watches internal security on the highest levels—the Ministry heads, the Counts, the Emperor's family—the Prince . . ." Vorkosigan frowned introspectively. "I came to know him rather well during the preparations for this strategist's nightmare. Curious fellow. He could have any rank he wanted. But forms are meaningless to him. He's only intersted in substance."

"Is he a good guy or bad guy?"

"What an absurd question!"

"I just thought he might be the power behind the throne."

"Hardly. If Ezar Vorbarra said, 'You're a frog,' he'd hop and croak. No. There is only one Emperor on Barrayar, and he permits no one to get behind him. He still remembers how he came to power."

She stretched, and winced at the pain in her side.

"Something wrong?" he asked, instantly concerned.

"Oh, Bothari got me with his knee, when we had that go-round about the sedative. I thought for sure they'd hear us. Scared me to death."

"May I see?" His fingers slid gently along her ribs. It was only in her imagination that they left a trail of rainbow light.

"Ow."

"Yes. You have two cracked ribs."

"Thought so. I'm lucky it wasn't my neck." She lay back, and he made shift to tape them with strips of cloth, then sat beside her on his bunk. "Have you ever considered chucking it all, and moving someplace nobody ever bothers with?" Cordelia asked. "Earth, for example."

He smiled. "Often. I even had a little fantasy about emigrating to Beta Colony, and turning up on your doorstep. Do you have a doorstep?"

"Not as such, but go on."

"I can't imagine what I'd do for a living there. I'm a strategist, not a technician or navigator or pilot, so I couldn't go into your merchant fleet. They would scarcely take me in your military, and I can't see myself being elected to office."

Cordelia snorted. "Wouldn't that startle Steady Freddy?"

"Is that what you call your President?"

"I didn't vote for him."

162

"The only employment I can think of would be as a teacher of martial arts, for sport. Would you marry a judo instructor, dear Captain? But no," he sighed. "Barrayar is bred in my bones. I cannot shake it, no matter how far I travel. This struggle, God knows, has no honor in it. But exile, for no other motive than ease—that would be to give up all hope of honor. The last defeat, with no seed of future victory in it."

She thought of the deadly cargo she had convoyed, now safe on Escobar. Compared to all the lives that hung on it, her own and Vorkosigan's weighed less than a feather. He misread the grief in her face, she thought, for fear.

"It isn't exactly like waking from the nightmare, to see your face." He touched it gently, fingertips on the curve of her jaw, thumb laid a moment across her lips, lighter than a kiss. "More like, knowing, while dreaming still, that beyond the dream there is a waking world. I mean to join you in that waking world, someday. You'll see. You'll see." He squeezed her hand and smiled reassuringly.

On the floor Bothari stirred, and groaned.

"I'll take care of him," Vorkosigan said. "Get some sleep, while you can."

▶▶ CHAPTER NINE

She woke to movement, and voices. Vorkosigan was rising from his chair, and Illyan was standing before him taut as a bowstring, saying "Vorhalas and the Prince! Here! Now!"

"Son-of-a . . ." Vorkosigan turned on his heel, eyes raking the little room. "It'll have to be the bathroom. Fold him into the shower."

Swiftly, Vorkosigan took Bothari's shoulders and Illyan his feet, bumping through the narrow door and dumping him pell-mell into the fixture.

"Should he have more sedative?" asked Illyan.

"Maybe he'd better. Cordelia, give him another ampule. It's too early, but it's death for you both if he makes a noise now." He bundled her into the closet-sized room, shoving the drug into her hand and killing the light. "No noise, no movement."

"Door shut?" asked Illyan.

"Part way. Lean on the frame, look casual, and don't let the Prince's bodyguard wander into your psychological space."

Cordelia feeling her way in the dimness, knelt and pressed another shot of sedative into the unconscious Sergeant's arm. Seating herself in the logical spot, she found she could just see a slice of Vorkosigan's cabin in the mirror, reversed and disorienting. She heard the cabin door open, and new voices.

"—unless you mean to officially relieve him of his duties as well, I will continue to follow standard procedure. I saw that room. Your charge is nonsensical."

"We will see," replied the second voice, tight and angry.

"Hello, Aral." The owner of the first voice, an officer of perhaps fifty in dress greens, shook Vorkosigan's hand and presented him with a packet of data disks. "We're off to Escobar within the hour. Courier just brought these—the latest hard-copy updates. I've ordered you to be kept up on events. The Escos are falling back through the whole volume. They've even abandoned that slugging match for the wormhole jump to Tau Ceti. We've got them on the run."

The owner of the second voice also wore dress greens, more heavily encrusted with gilt than any she had ever seen. Jewelled decorations on his breast glinted and winked like lizards' eyes in the light from Vorkosigan's desk lamp. He was about thirty, black haired, with a rectangular tense face, hooded eyes, and thin lips compressed now with annoyance.

"You're not both going, are you?" said Vorkosigan. "The senior officer ought properly to stay with the flag. Now that Vorrutyer is dead, his duties devolve on the Prince. That dog-and-pony show you had planned was based on the assumption that he would still be at his post."

Prince Serg went stiff with outrage. "I *will* lead my troops on Escobar! Let my father and his cronies try to say I am no soldier now!"

"You will," said Vorkosigan wearily, "sit in that fortified palace that half the engineers are going to be tied up constructing, and party in it, and let your men do your dying for you, until you've bought your ground by the sheer weight of the corpses piled on it, because that's the kind of soldiering your mentor has taught you. And then send bulletins home about your great victory. Maybe you can have the casualty lists declared top secret."

"Aral, careful," warned Vorhalas, shocked.

"You go too far," the Prince snarled. "Especially for a man who will get no closer to the fighting than clinging to the wormhole exit for home. If you want to talk of—undue caution." His tone clearly made the phrase a euphemism for an uglier term.

"You can hardly order me confined to quarters and then accuse me of cowardice for not being at the front. Sir. Even Minister Grishnov's propaganda has to simulate logic better than that."

"You'd just love that, wouldn't you, Vorkosigan," hissed the Prince. "Stick me back here, and grab all the glory for yourself and that wrinkled clown Vortala and his phoney liberals. Over my dead body! You're going to sit in here till you grow mold."

Vorkosigan's teeth were clenched, his eyes narrowed and unreadable. His lips curled back on a white smile, but closed again instantly. "I must formally protest. By landing with the ground troops on Escobar you are leaving your proper post."

"Protest away." The Prince approached him closely, leaning into his face and dropping his voice. "But even my father can't live forever. And when that day

167

comes, your father won't be able to protect you any more. You, and Vortala, and all his cronies will be first against the wall, I promise you." He looked up, remembering Illyan leaning silently against the door-jamb. "Or perhaps you'll find yourself back on the Leper Colony, for another five years of patrol duty."

In the bathroom, Bothari stirred uncomfortably in his semi-coma and, to Cordelia's horror, began to snore.

Lieutenant Illyan was seized by a spasmodic cough-ing fit. "Excuse me," he gasped, and retreated into the bathroom, shutting the door firmly.

He hit the light and traded a silent look of panic with Cordelia for an equally silent grimace of de-spair. With difficulty, they turned Bothari's dead weight to one side in the constricted space, until he breathed quietly again. Cordelia gave Illyan the thumbs-up signal, and he nodded and squeezed back out the door.

The Prince had left. Admiral Vorhalas lingered a moment, to exchange a last word with his subordinate.

"—put it in writing. I'll sign it before we go."

"At least don't travel in the same ship," begged Vorkosigan seriously.

Vorhalas sighed. "I appreciate your trying to get him out of my hair. But somebody has to clean his cage for the Emperor, with Vorrutyer out, thank God. He won't have you, so it looks like I'm elected. Why can't you just lose your temper with subordi-nates, like normal men, instead of with superiors, like a lunatic? I thought you were cured of that, after what I saw you take from Vorrutyer."

"That's dead and buried now."

"Aye." Vorhalas made a superstitious sign, automatically, evidently a gestural relic from childhood, empty of belief but full of habit.

"By the by—what's the Leper Colony?" asked Vorkosigan curiously.

"You never heard that? Well—maybe I can see why not. Did you never wonder why you received such a remarkable percentage of screw-ups, incorrigibles, and near-discharges among your crew?"

"I hadn't expected to get the cream of the Service."

"They used to call it Vorkosigan's Leper Colony, at headquarters."

"With myself as leper-in-chief, eh?" Vorkosigan seemed more amused than offended. "Well, if they were the worst the Service has to offer, perhaps we shall not do so badly after all. Take care of yourself. I don't fancy being his second-in-command."

Vorhalas chuckled, and they shook hands. He started for the door, then paused. "Do you think they'll counterattack?"

"My God, of course they'll counterattack. This isn't some trade outpost. These people are fighting for their homes."

"When?"

Vorkosigan hesitated. "Sometime after you've started disembarking ground troops, but well before it's completed. Wouldn't you? Worst time to have to start a retreat. Shuttles not knowing whether to go up or down, their mother ships scattering to hell and gone under fire, supplies needed not landed, supplies landed not needed, the chain of command disrupted—an inexperienced commander in absolute control . . ."

"You give me the shivers."

"Yes, well—try to hold the start for as long as possible. And make sure your troopship commanders have their contingency orders crystal clear."

"The Prince doesn't see it your way."

"Yes, he's itching to lead a parade."

"What do you advise?"

"I'm not your commander this time, Rulf."

"Not my fault. I recommended you to the Emperor."

"I know. I wouldn't take it. I recommended you instead."

"So we ended up with that sodomizing son-of-a-bitch Vorrutyer." Vorhalas shook his head bleakly. "Something wrong there . . ."

Vorkosigan chivvied him gently out the door, blew out his breath with a sigh, and remained standing, caught up in his vision of the future. He looked up, and met Cordelia's eyes with unhappy irony. "Wasn't there some character, when the old Romans held their triumphs, who rode along whispering in the honored party's ear that he was mortal, and death waited for him? The old Romans probably thought he was a pain in the neck, too."

She held her peace.

Vorkosigan and Illyan went to retrieve Sergeant Bothari from his makeshift and uncomfortable hiding place. They were halfway through the door with him when Vorkosigan swore. "He's stopped breathing."

Illyan hissed explosively, and they laid Bothari out quickly on the friction matting on his back. Vorkosigan laid his ear to his chest, and felt his neck for a pulse.

"Son of a bitch." He doubled his fists, and brought them down sharply against the Sergeant's sternum, then listened again. "Nothing."

He rolled back on his heels, looking fierce. "Illyan. Whoever you got that lizard's piss from, go find him and get a shot of the antidote. Quickly. And quietly. Very quietly."

"How did you—what if—shouldn't you—is it

worth—" began Illyan. He threw up his hands help-lessly, and fled out the door.

Vorkosigan looked at Cordelia. "Do you want to push, or blow?"

"Push, I guess."

She knelt by Bothari's side, and Vorkosigan went to his head, tilted it back, and gave him his first breath of air. Cordelia pressed the heels of her hands on his sternum and pushed with all her strength, setting up the rhythm. Push, push, push, blow, over and over, don't stop. After a short time her arms were shaking, and sweat beaded on her hairline. She could feel her own ribs grind with each push, scream-ingly, and her chest muscles knotted spasmodically.

"Got to switch."

"Good. I'm hyperventilating."

They changed places, Vorkosigan taking over the heart massage, Cordelia pinching Bothari's nostrils shut and closing her mouth over his. His mouth was wet from Vorkosigan's saliva. The parody of a kiss was horrible, but to shrink from it beneath con-tempt. They went on, and on.

Lieutenant Illyan returned at last, breathless. He knelt and pressed the new ampule against Bothari's corded neck over the carotid artery. Nothing hap-pened. Vorkosigan kept pumping.

Suddenly, Bothari shuddered, then stiffened, arch-ing his back. He took an irregular, gasping gulp of air, then stopped again.

"Come on," urged Cordelia, half to herself.

With a sharp spasmodic intake he began to breathe again, raggedly, but persistently. Cordelia slumped from her knees to a sitting position on the floor and gazed at him in joyless triumph. "Suffering bastard."

"I thought you saw meaning in that sort of thing," said Vorkosigan.

"In the abstract. Most days it's just stumbling around in the dark with the rest of creation, smashing into things and wondering why it hurts."

Vorkosigan gazed at Bothari too, sweat runneling down his face. Then he jumped to his feet and hurried to his desk.

"The protest. Have to get it written and filed before Vorhalas leaves, or it will be no damned good." He slid into his chair and began keying his console rapidly.

"What's so important about it?" asked Cordelia.

"Sh. Later." He typed furiously for ten minutes, then set it electronically in pursuit of his commander.

Bothari in the meanwhile continued to breathe, although his face retained a deathly greenish pallor.

"What do we do now?" asked Cordelia.

"Wait. Pray that the dosage is right," he glanced irritably at Illyan, "and that it won't send him into some kind of manic state."

"Shouldn't we be thinking of some way to get them both out of here?" protested Illyan.

"Think away." Vorkosigan began plugging the new data disks into his console and viewing the tactical readouts. "But as a hiding place it has two advantages not shared by any other spot on the ship. If you're as good as you claim, it's not monitored by either the Chief Political Officer or the Prince's men—"

"I'm quite sure I got them all. I'd stake my reputation on it."

"Right now you're staking your life on it, so you'd better be correct. Second, there are two armed guards

172

in the corridor to keep everybody out. You could scarcely ask for more. I admit it's a bit crowded."

Illyan rolled his eyes in exasperation. "I've diddled the Security search to the limit I dare. I can't do any more without drawing more attention than I divert."

"Will it hold 24 more hours?"

"Maybe." Illyan frowned at his charge, baffled and bothered. "You have something planned, don't you, sir." It was not a question.

"I?" His fingers worked the keys of his console, and reflections of colored light from the readouts played over his impassive face. "I'm merely waiting in hope of some reasonable opportunity. When the Prince leaves for Escobar most of his own security people will go with him. Patience, Illyan."

He keyed his console again. "Vorkosigan to Tactics Room."

"Commander Venne here, sir."

"Oh, good. Venne, I'd like hourly updates piped down here from the time the Prince and Admiral Vorhalas leave. And let me know immediately, regardless of time, if you start getting anything unusual, anything not in the plans."

"Yes, sir. The Prince and Admiral Vorhalas are leaving now, sir."

"Very good. Carry on. Vorkosigan out."

He sat back and drummed his fingers on the desk. "Now we wait. It will be about twelve hours before the Prince reaches Escobar orbit. They'll be starting landings soon after that. An hour for signals to reach us from Escobar. An hour for signals to return. So much lag. A battle can be over in two hours. We could cut the lag by three-quarters if the Prince would let us move off station."

His casual tone barely masked his tension, in spite

173

of his advice to Illyan. The room in which he sat scarcely seemed to exist for him. His mind moved with the armada wheeling in a tightening constellation around Escobar, fast glittering couriers, grim cruisers, sluggish troop carriers, bellies crammed with men. A light pen turned, forgotten, in his fingers, around and over, around and over.

"Hadn't you better eat, sir?" suggested Illyan.

"What? Oh, yes, I suppose. And you, Cordelia—you must be hungry. Go ahead, Illyan."

Illyan left to forage. Vorkosigan worked at his desk console for a few more minutes before shutting it down with a sigh. "I suppose I'd better think about sleep, too. Last time I slept was on board the *General Vorhartung,* closing on Escobar—a day and a half ago, I guess. About the time you were being captured."

"We were captured a bit before that. We were in tow for almost a day."

"Yes. Congratulations, by the way, on a very successful maneuver. That wasn't a real battle cruiser, I take it?"

"I really can't say."

"Somebody wants to claim it as a kill."

Cordelia suppressed a grin. "Fine by me." She braced herself for more questioning, but, strangely, he turned the subject.

"Poor Bothari. I wish the Emperor might give him a medal. I'm afraid the best I'll be able to do for him is get him properly hospitalized."

"If the Emperor disliked Vorrutyer so, why did he put him in charge?"

"Because he was Grishnov's man, and widely famous as such, and the Prince's favorite. Putting all

174

the bad eggs in one basket, so to speak." He cut himself off with a fist-closing gesture.

"He made me feel like I'd met the ultimate in evil. I don't think anything will really scare me, after him."

"Ges Vorrutyer? He was just a little villain. An old-fashioned craftsman, making crimes one-off. The really unforgivable acts are committed by calm men in beautiful green silk rooms, who deal death wholesale, by the shipload, without lust, or anger, or desire, or any redeeming emotion to excuse them but cold fear of some pretended future. But the crimes they hope to prevent in that future are imaginary. The ones they commit in the present—they are real." His voice fell, as he spoke, so that by the end he was almost whispering.

"Commodore Vorkosigan—Aral—what's eating you? You're so keyed up I expect you to start pacing the ceiling any minute." Hag-ridden, she thought.

He laughed a little. "I feel like it. It's the waiting, I expect. I'm bad at waiting. Not a good thing, in a soldier. I envy your ability to wait in patience. You seem calm as moonlight on the water."

"Is that pretty?"

"Very."

"It sounds nice. We don't have either one at home." She was absurdly pleased by the implied compliment.

Illyan returned with a tray, and she got no more out of Vorkosigan. They ate, and Vorkosigan took a turn at sleeping, or at least lying on the bed with his eyes shut, but getting up every hour to view the new tacticals.

Lieutenant Illyan watched over his shoulder, and Vorkosigan pointed out salient features of the strategy to him as they came up.

"It looks pretty good to me," Illyan commented once. "I don't see why you're so anxious. We really could carry it off, in spite of the Esco's superior command of resources in the long run. Won't do them any good if it's all over in the short run."

Afraid to put Bothari back into a deep coma, they let him return to near-consciousness. He sat in the corner in a miserable knot, drifting in and out of sleep with bad dreams in both states.

Eventually Illyan took himself off to his own cabin to sleep, and Cordelia had another nap herself. She slept a long time, not waking until Illyan returned with another tray of food. She was becoming disoriented with respect to time, locked in this changeless room. Vorkosigan, however, was tracking time by the minute now. After they ate he vanished into the bathroom to wash and shave, and returned in fresh dress greens, as neat as though ready for a conference with the Emperor.

He checked through the last tactical update for the second time.

"Have they started landing troops yet?" Cordelia asked.

He checked his chronometer. "Almost an hour ago. We should be getting the first reports through any minute." He sat now without fidgeting, like a man in deep meditation, face like stone.

That hour's tactical update arrived, and he began sorting through its reports, apparently checking key items. In the middle of it his screen was overridden by the face of Commander Venne.

"Commodore Vorkosigan? We're getting something very strange here. Do you want me to shunt a copy of raw incoming straight down there?"

"Yes, please. Immediately."

Vorkosigan searched through an assortment of chatter of all kinds, and picked out a verbal from a ship commander, a dark and heavy-set man who spoke into his log with a gutteral accent tinged by fear.

Here it comes, moaned Cordelia inwardly.

"—attacking with *shuttles!* They're returning our fire shot by shot. Plasma shields at maximum now—we can't put more power into them and still keep firing. We must either drop shields and try to increase our firepower, or give up the attack . . ." The transmission was interrupted by static. "—don't know how they're doing it. They can't possibly have packed enough engine in those shuttles to generate this . . ." More static. The transmission broke off abruptly.

Vorkosigan selected another. Illyan leaned over his shoulder anxiously. Cordelia sat on the bed, silent, head bowed, listening. The cup of victory; bitter on the tongue, heavy in the stomach, sad as defeat . . .

"—the flagship is under heavy fire," reported another commander. Cordelia recognized the voice with a start, and craned her neck for a view of his face. It was Gottyan; evidently he had his captaincy at last. "I'm going to drop shields altogether and attempt to knock one out with a maximum burst."

"Don't do it, Korabik!" Vorkosigan shouted hopelessly. The decision, whatever it was, had been made an hour ago, its consequences ineradicably fixed in time.

Gottyan turned his head to one side. "Ready, Commander Vorkalloner? We are attempting—" he began, and was drowned by static, then silence.

Vorkosigan struck his fist on the desk, hard. "Damn! How the hell long is it going to take them to figure . . ." He stared into the snow, then reran the transmission, transfixing it with a frightening expression, grief and rage and nausea mixed. He then selected another band, this time a computer graphic of the space around Escobar, and the ships as little colored lights winking and diving through it. It looked tiny, and bright, and simple, like a child's game. He shook his head at it, lips tight and bloodless.

Venne's face interrupted again. He was pale, with peculiar lines of tension running down to the corners of his mouth.

"Sir, I think you'd better come to the Tactics Room."

"I can't, Venne, without breaking arrest. Where's Commodore Helski, or Commodore Couer?"

"Helski went forward with the Prince and Admiral Vorhalas, sir. Commodore Couer is here now. You're the ranking flag officer aboard now."

"The Prince was quite explicit."

"The Prince—I believe the Prince is dead, sir."

Vorkosigan closed his eyes, and a sigh went out of him, joylessly. He opened them again, and leaned forward. "Is that confirmed? Do you have any new orders from Admiral Vorhalas?"

"It's—Admiral Vorhalas was with the Prince, sir. Their ship was hit." Venne turned away to view something over his shoulder, then turned back. "It's," he had to clear his throat, "it's confirmed. The Prince's flagship has been—obliterated. There's nothing left but debris. You're in command now, sir."

Vorkosigan's face was cold and unhappy. "Then transmit Contingency Blue orders at once. All ships cease firing immediately. Put all power into shields. This ship to make course for Escobar now at maximum boost. We've got to cut down on our transmission time lag."

178

"Contingency Blue, sir? That's full retreat!"

"I know, Commander. I wrote it."

"But full retreat . . ."

"Commander Venne, the Escobarans have a new weapon system. It's called a plasma mirror field. It's a new Betan development. It turns the attacker's burst back on itself. Our ships are shooting themselves down with their own firepower."

"My God! What can we do?"

"Not a damn thing, unless we want to start boarding their ships and strangling the bastards by hand, one at a time. Attractive, but impractical. Transmit those orders! And order the Commander of Engineers and the Chief Pilot Officer to the Tactics Room. And get the guard commander down here to relieve his men. I don't care to be stunned on the way out the door."

"Yes, sir!" Venne broke off.

"Got to get those troopships turned around first," muttered Vorkosigan, rising from his swivel chair. He turned to find both Cordelia and Illyan staring at him.

"How did you know—" began Illyan.

"—about the plasma mirrors?" finished Cordelia.

Vorkosigan was quite expressionless. "You told me, Cordelia, in your sleep, while Illyan was out. Under the influence of one of the surgeon's potions, of course. You'll suffer no ill effects from it."

She stood upright, aghast. "That—you miserable— torture would have been more honorable!"

"Oh, smooth, sir!" congratulated Illyan. "I knew you were all right!"

Vorkosigan shot him a look of dislike. "It doesn't

179

matter. The information was confirmed too late to do us any good."

There was a knock on the door.

"Come on, Illyan. It's time to take my soldiers home."

▶▶ CHAPTER TEN

Illyan came back promptly for Bothari, barely an hour later. This was followed for Cordelia by twelve hours alone. She considered escaping the room, as her soldierly duty, and engaging in a little one-woman sabotage. But if Vorkosigan was indeed directing a full retreat, it would hardly do to interfere.

She lay on his bed in a black weariness. He had betrayed her; he was no better than the rest of them. "My perfect warrior, my dear hypocrite"—and it appeared Vorrutyer had known him better than she, after all—no. That was unjust. He had done his duty, in extracting that information; she had done the same, in concealing it for as long as possible. And as one soldier to another, even if an ersatz one—five hours active service, was it?—she had to agree with Illyan, it had been smooth. She could detect no after-effects at all in herself from whatever he had used for the secret invasion of her mind.

Whatever he had used . . . What, indeed, could be have used? Where had he cadged it, and when?

Illyan hadn't brought it to him. He had been as surprised as she when Vorkosigan dropped that bit of intelligence. One must either believe he kept a secret stash of interrogation drugs hidden in his quarters, or . . .

"Dear God," she whispered, not a curse, but a prayer. "What have I stumbled into now?" She paced the room, the connections clicking unstoppably into place.

Heart-certainty. Vorkosigan had never questioned her; he had known about the plasma mirrors in advance.

It appeared, further, that he was the only man in the Barrayaran command who knew. Vorhalas had not. The Prince certainly had not. Nor Illyan.

"Put all the bad eggs in one basket," she muttered. "And—drop the basket? Oh, it couldn't have been his own plan! Surely not . . ."

She had a sudden horrific vision of it, all complete; the most wasteful political assassination plot in Barrayaran history, and the most subtle, the corpses hidden in a mountain of corpses, forever inextricable.

But he must have had the information from somewhere. Somewhere between the time she had left him with no worse troubles than an engine room full of mutineers, and now, struggling to pull a disarmed armada back to safety before the destruction they had unleashed crashed back on them. Somewhere in a quiet, green silk room, where a great choreographer designed a dance of death, and the honor of a man of honor was broken on the wheel of his service.

Vorrutyer of the demonic vanity shrank, and shrank, before the swelling vision, to a mouse, to a flea, to a pinprick.

"My God, I thought Aral seemed twitchy. He

must be half-mad. And the Emperor—the Prince was his *son*. Can this be real? Or have I gone as crazy as Bothari?"

She forced herself to sit, then lie down, but the plots and counterplots still turned in her brain, an orrery of betrayal within betrayal lining up abruptly at one point in space and time to accomplish its end. The blood beat in her brain, thick and sick.

"Maybe it's not true," she consoled herself at last. "I'll ask him, and that's what he'll say. He just questioned me in my sleep. We got the drop on them, and I'm the heroine who saved Escobar. He's just a simple soldier, doing his job." She turned on her side, and stared into the dimness. "Pigs have wings, and I can fly home on one."

Illyan relieved her at last, and took her to the brig.

The atmosphere there was somewhat changed, she noticed. The guards did not look at her in the same way; in fact, they seemed to try to avoid looking at her. The procedures were still stark and efficient, but subdued, very subdued. She recognized a face; the guard who had escorted her to Vorrutyer's quarters, the one who'd pitied her, seemed to be in charge now, a pair of new red lieutenant's tabs pinned hastily and crookedly to his collar. She had donned Vorrutyer's fatigues again for the trip down. This time she was permitted to change into the orange pajamas in physical privacy. She was then escorted to a permanent cell, not a holding area.

The cell had another occupant, a young Escobaran woman of extraordinary beauty who lay on her bunk staring at the wall. She did not look up at Cordelia's entrance, nor respond to her greeting. After a time, a Barrayaran medical team arrived and took her away.

She went wordlessly, but at the door she started to struggle with them. At a sign from the doctor a corpsman sedated her with an ampule Cordelia thought she recognized, and after another moment she was carried out unconscious.

The doctor, who from his age and rank Cordelia guessed might be the chief surgeon, stayed a short time to attend to her ribs. After that she was left alone, with nothing but the periodic delivery of rations to mark the time, and occasional changes in the slight noises and vibrations from the walls around her to base guesses on what was happening outside.

About eight ration packs later, as she was lying on her bunk bored and depressed, the lights dimmed. They came back, but dimmed again almost immediately.

"Awk," she muttered, as the bottom dropped out of her stomach and she began to float upward. She made a hasty grab and held onto her bunk firmly. Her foresight was rewarded a moment later when she was crushed back into it at about three gees. The lights flickered on and off again, and she was weightless once more.

"Plasma attack," she murmured to herself. "Shields must be overloaded."

A tremendous shock rattled the ship. She was flung from her bunk across the cell into total blackness, weightlessness, silence. Direct hit! She ricocheted off the far wall, flailing for a handhold, banging an elbow painfully on—a wall? the floor, the ceiling? She spun in midair, crying out. Friendly fire, she thought hysterically—I'm going to be killed by friendly fire. The perfect end to my military career . . . She clamped her jaw and listened with fierce concentration.

Too much silence. Had they lost air? She had a

nasty vision of herself as the only one left alive, trapped in this black box and doomed to float until either slow suffocation or slow freezing squeezed out her life. The cell would be her coffin, to be unsealed months later by some salvage crew.

And, more horribly; could the hit have been on the bridge? The nerve center where Vorkosigan would surely be, on which the Escobarans would surely concentrate their fire—was he smashed by flying debris, flash frozen in vacuum, burned up in plasma fire, pinned somewhere between crushed decks?

Her fingers found a surface at last, and scrabbled for a hold. A corner; good. She braced herself in it, curled up on the floor, breath firing in and out of her lungs in uneven gasps.

An unknowable time passed in the stygian dark. Her arms and legs trembled with the effort of bracing herself in place. Then the ship groaned about her, and the lights came back on.

Oh hell, she thought, this is the *ceiling*.

The gravity returned and smashed her to the floor. Pain flashed up her left arm, and numbness. She scrambled back to the bunk, taking a white-knuckle grip on its rigid bars with her right hand, sticking one foot through as well, bracing herself again.

Nothing. She waited. There was a wetness soaking her orange shirt. She looked down to see a shard of pinkish-yellow bone poking through the skin of her left forearm, and blood welling around it. She slipped awkwardly out of her smock top, wrapping it around one arm and trying to staunch the flow. The pressure woke the pain. She tried, rather experimentally, calling out for help. Surely the cell was monitored.

No one came. Over the next three hours she varied the experiment with screaming, speaking reasonably, banging on the door and walls endlessly with her good hand, or simply sitting on the bunk crying in pain. The gravity and lights flip-flopped several more times. Finally she had the familiar sensation of being pulled inside-out through a pot of glue, marking a wormhole jump, and the environment steadied.

When the door of the cell opened at last, it startled her so she recoiled into the wall, banging her head. But it was the lieutenant in charge of the brig, with a medical corpsman. The lieutenant had an interesting reddish-purple bruise the size of an egg on his forehead; the corpsman looked harried.

"This is the next worst one," said the lieutenant to the corpsman. "After that you can just go down the row in order."

White-faced and exhausted into silence, she unwrapped her arm for examination and repair. The corpsman was competent, but lacked the delicacy of touch of the chief surgeon. She nearly fainted before the plastic cast was at last applied.

There were no more signs of attack. A clean prisoner's uniform was delivered through a wall slot. Two ration packs later she felt another wormhole jump. Her thought revolved endlessly on the wheel of her fears; her sleep was all dreams and her dreams were all nightmares.

It was Lieutenant Illyan who came to escort her at last, along with an ordinary guard. She nearly kissed him, in her joy at seeing a familiar face. Instead she cleared her throat diffidently, and asked with what she hoped would pass for nonchalance, "Was Commodore Vorkosigan all right, after that attack?"

His eyebrows rose, and he shot her a look of bemused study from beneath them. "Of course."

Of course. Of course. That "of course" even suggested, uninjured. Her eyes puddled with relief, which she attempted to mask with an expression of cool professional interest. "Where are you taking me?" she asked him, as they left the brig and started down the corridor.

"Shuttle. You're to be transferred to the POW camp planetside, until the exchange arrangements are made, and they begin shipping you all home."

"Home! What about the war?"

"It's over."

"Over!" She assimilated that. "Over. That was quick. Why aren't the Escobarans pursuing their advantage?"

"They can't. We've blocked the wormhole exit."

"Blocked? Not blockaded?"

He nodded.

"How the devil do you block a wormhole?"

"In a way, it's a very old idea. Fireships."

"Huh?"

"Send a ship in, set up a major matter-antimatter explosion at a midpoint between nodes. It sets up a resonance—nothing else can get through for weeks, until it dies down."

Cordelia whistled. "Clever—why didn't we think of that? How do you get the pilot out?"

"Maybe that's why you didn't think of it. We don't."

"God—what a death." Her vision of it was clear and instant.

"They were volunteers."

She shook her head numbly. "Only a Barrayaran . . ." She probed for some less horrifying subject. "Did you take many prisoners?"

"Not very. Maybe a thousand in all. We left over eleven thousand ground troops behind on Escobar.

187

It makes you rather valuable, if we have to try to trade you more than ten for one."

The prisoners' shuttle was a windowless craft, and she shared it with only two others, one of her own engineer's assistants, and the dark-haired Escobaran girl who had been in her cell. Her tech was eager to exchange stories, although he didn't have much to trade. He had spent the whole time locked in one cell with his other three shipmates, who had been taken downside yesterday.

The beautiful Escobaran, a young ensign who had been captured when her ship was disabled in the fighting for the wormhole jump to Beta Colony over two months ago, had even less to tell. "I must have lost track of time, somewhere," she said uneasily. "Not hard to do in that cell, seeing no one. Except that I woke up in their sickbay, yesterday, and couldn't remember how I'd come there."

And if that surgeon's as good as he looked, you never will, thought Cordelia. "Do you remember Admiral Vorrutyer?"

"Who?"

"Never mind."

The shuttle landed at last, and the hatch was opened. A shaft of sunlight and a breath of summer-scented air fell through it, sweet green air that made them suddenly realize they had been breathing reek for days.

"Wow, where is this place?" said the technician, awed, as he stepped through the hatch, prodded by the guards. "It's beautiful."

Cordelia followed him, and laughed out loud, although not happily, in instant recognition.

The prison camp was a triple row of Barrayaran field shelters, ugly grey half-cylinders surrounded by a force screen, set at the bottom of a kilometers-wide amphitheater of dry woodland and waterfall, beneath a turquoise sky. It was a hazy, warm, quiet afternoon that made Cordelia feel she had never left.

Yes, there was even the entrance to the underground depot, not camouflaged any more, but widened, with a great paved area for landing and loading gouged out before it, alive with shuttles and activity. The waterfall and pool were gone. She turned about, as they walked, gazing at her planet. Now that she thought about it, it seemed inevitable that they should end up here, quite logical really. She shook her head helplessly.

She and her young Escobaran companion were signed in and directed to a shelter halfway down one row by a neat and expressionless guard. They entered, to find it occupied by eleven women in a space meant for fifty. They had their choice of bunks.

They were pounced upon by the older prisoners, frantic for news. A plump woman of about forty restored order, and introduced herself.

"I'm Lieutenant Marsha Alfredi. I'm ranking officer in this shelter. In so far as there is order in this cess pit. Do you know what the hell is going on?"

"I'm Captain Cordelia Naismith. Betan Expeditionary."

"Thank God. I can dump it on you."

"Oh, my." Cordelia braced herself. "Fill me in."

"It's been hell. The guards are pigs. Then, all of a sudden yesterday afternoon, this bunch of high-ranking Barrayaran officers came trooping through. At first we thought they were shopping for rapees, like the last bunch. But this morning about half the guards had disappeared—the worst of the lot—and been replaced by a crew that look like they're on parade.

189

And the Barrayaran camp commandant—I couldn't believe it. They paraded him out on the shuttle tarmac this morning and *shot* him! In full view of everyone!"

"I see," said Cordelia, rather tonelessly. She cleared her throat. "Uh—have you heard yet? The Barrayarans have been run completely out of Escobaran local space. They're probably sending around the long way for a formal truce and some sort of negotiated settlement by now."

There was a stunned silence, then jubilation. Some laughed, some cried, some hugged each other, and some sat alone. Some broke away to spread the news to neighboring shelters and from there up and down the whole camp. Cordelia was pressed for details. She gave a brief precis of the fighting, leaving out her own exploits and the source of her information. Their joy made her a little happier, for the first time in days.

"Well, that explains why the Barrayarans have straightened up all of a sudden," said Lieutenant Alfredi. "I guess they didn't expect to be held accountable, before."

"They've got a new commander," explained Cordelia. "He's got a thing about prisoners. Win or lose, there'd have been changes with him in charge."

Alfredi didn't look convinced. "Oh? Who is he?"

"A Commodore Vorkosigan," Cordelia said neutrally.

"Vorkosigan, the Butcher of Komarr? My God, we're in for it now." Alfredi looked genuinely afraid.

"I should think you had an adequate pledge of good faith on the shuttle pad this morning."

"I should think it just proves he's a lunatic," said Alfredi. "The commandant didn't even participate in those abuses. He wasn't the worst by a long shot."

"He was the man in charge. If he knew about them, he should have stopped them. If he didn't know, he was incompetent. Either way, he was responsible." Cordelia, hearing herself defending a Barrayaran execution, stopped abruptly. "I don't know." She shook her head. "I'm not Vorkosigan's keeper."

The noise of near-riot penetrated from outside, and their shelter was invaded by a deputation of fellow prisoners, all eager to hear the rumors of peace confirmed. The guards withdrew to the perimeter and let the excitement play itself out. She had to repeat her precis, twice. Her own crew members, led by Parnell, came over from the men's side.

Parnell jumped up on a bunk to address the orange-clad crowd, shouting over the glad babble. "This lady isn't telling you everything. I had the real story from one of the Barrayaran guards. After we were taken aboard the flagship, she escaped and personally assassinated the Barrayaran commander, Admiral Vorrutyer. That's why their advances collapsed. Let's *hear* it for Captain Naismith!"

"That's not the real story," she objected, but was drowned out by shouts and cheers. "I didn't kill Vorrutyer. Here! Put me down!" Her crew, ring-led by Parnell, hoisted her to their shoulders for an impromptu parade around the camp. "It's not true! Stop this! Awk!"

It was like trying to turn back the tide with a teacup. The story had too much innate appeal to the battered prisoners, too much wish-fulfillment come to life. They took it in like balm for their wounded spirits, and made it their own vicarious revenge. The story was passed around, elaborated, built up, sea-changed, until within twenty-four hours it was as

191

rich and unkillable as legend. After a few days she gave up trying.

The truth was too complicated and ambiguous to appeal to them, and she herself, suppressing everything in it that had to do with Vorkosigan, was unable to make it sound convincing. Her duty seemed drained of meaning, dull and discolored. She longed for home, and her sensible mother and brother, and quiet, and one thought that would connect to another without making a chain of secret horror.

> > **CHAPTER ELEVEN**

Camp returned to routine soon, or what routine should always have been. There followed weeks of waiting for the slow negotiations for prisoner exchange to be completed, with everyone honing elaborate plans for what they would do when they got home. Cordelia gradually came to a nearly normal relationship with her shelter mates, although they still tried to give her special privileges and services. She heard nothing from Vorkosigan.

She was lying on her bunk one afternoon, pretending to sleep, when Lieutenant Alfredi roused her.

"There's a Barrayaran officer out here who says he wants to talk to you." Alfredi trailed her to the door, suspicion and hostility in her face. "I don't think we should let them take you away by yourself. We're so close to going home. They've surely got it in for you."

"Oh. It's all right, Marsha."

Vorkosigan stood outside the shelter, in the dress greens worn daily by the Staff, accompanied as usual by Illyan. He seemed tense, deferential, weary, and closed.

"Captain Naismith," he said formally, "may I speak with you?"

"Yes, but—not here." She was acutely conscious of the eyes of her fellows upon her. "Can we take a walk or something?"

He nodded, and they started off in shared silence. He clasped his hands behind his back. She shoved hers into the pockets of her orange smock top. Illyan trailed them, dog-like, impossible to shake. They left the prison compound, and headed into the woods.

"I'm glad you came," said Cordelia. "There are some things I've been meaning to ask you."

"Yes. I wanted to see you sooner, but winding this thing up properly has been keeping me rather busy."

She nodded toward his yellow collar tabs. "Congratulations on your promotion."

"Oh, that." He touched one briefly. "It's meaningless. Just a formality, to expedite the work I'm doing now."

"Which is what?"

"Dismantling the armada, guarding the local space around this planet, shuffling politicians back and forth between Barrayar and Escobar. General housecleaning, now the party's over. Supervising prisoner exchange."

They were following a wide beaten path through the grey-green woods, up the slope out of the crater's bowl.

"I wanted to apologize for questioning you under drugs. I know it offended you deeply. Need drove me. It was a military necessity."

"You have nothing to apologize for." She glanced

194

back at Illyan. I must know . . . "Quite literally nothing, I eventually realized."

He was silent. "I see," he said at last. "You are very acute."

"On the contrary, I am very baffled."

He swung to face Illyan. "Lieutenant, I crave a boon from you. I wish a few minutes alone with this lady to discuss a very personal matter."

"I shouldn't, sir. You know that."

"I once asked her to marry me. She never gave me her answer. If I give you my word that we will discuss nothing but what touches on that, *may* we have a few moments privacy?"

"Oh . . ." Illyan frowned. "Your word, sir?"

"My word. As Vorkosigan."

"Well—I guess it's all right then." Illyan seated himself glumly on a fallen log to wait, and they walked on up the path.

They came out, at the top, on a familiar promontory overlooking the crater, the very spot where Vorkosigan had planned the repossession of his ship, so long ago. They seated themselves on the ground, watching the activity of the camp made silent by distance.

"Time was you would never have done that," Cordelia observed. "Pledged your word falsely."

"Times changed."

"Nor lied to me."

"That is so."

"Nor shot a man out of hand for crimes he didn't participate in."

"It wasn't out of hand. He had a summary court martial first. And it did get things straightened around in a hurry. Anyway, it will satisfy the Interstellar Judiciary's commission. I'll have them on my hands too, come tomorrow. Investigating prisoner abuses."

195

"I think you're getting blood-glutted. Individual lives are losing their meaning for you."

"Yes. There have been so many. It's nearly time to quit." Expression was deadened in his face and words.

"How did the Emperor buy you for that—extraordinary assassination? You of all men. Was it your idea? Or his?"

He did not evade, or deny. "His idea, and Negri's. I am but his agent."

His fingers pulled gently on the grass stems, breaking them off delicately one by one. "He didn't come out with it directly. First he asked me to take command of the Escobar invasion. He started with a bribe—the viceroyalty of this planet, in fact, when it's colonized. I turned him down. Then he tried a threat, said he'd throw me to Grishnov, let him have me up for treason, and no Imperial pardon. I told him to go to hell, not in so many words. That was a bad moment, between us. Then he apologized. Called me Lord Vorkosigan. He called me Captain when he wished to be offensive. Then he called in Captain Negri, with a file that didn't even have a name, and the play-acting stopped.

"Reason. Logic. Argument. Evidence. We sat in that green silk room in the Imperial Residence at Vorbarr Sultana one whole mortal week, the Emperor and Negri and I, going over it, while Illyan kicked his heels in the hall, studying the Emperor's art collection. You are correct in your deduction about Illyan, by the way. He knows nothing about the real purpose of the invasion.

"You saw the Prince, briefly. I may add that you saw him at his best. Vorrutyer may have been his teacher once, but the Prince surpassed him some time ago. But if only he had had some saving notion of political service, I think his father would have forgiven him even his vilest personal habits.

"He was not balanced, and he surrounded himself with men whose interests lay in making him even less balanced. A true nephew of his Uncle Yuri. Grishnov meant to rule Barrayar through him when he came to the throne. On his own—Grishnov would have been willing to wait, I think—the Prince had engineered two assassination attempts on his father in the last eighteen months."

Cordelia whistled soundlessly. "I almost begin to see. But why not just put him out of the way quietly? Surely the Emperor and your Captain Negri could have managed it between them, if anyone could."

"The idea was discussed. God help me, I even volunteered to lend myself to it, as an alternative to this—bloodbath."

He paused. "The Emperor is dying. He has run out of time to wait for the problem to solve itself. It's become an obsession with him, to try to leave his house in order.

"The problem is the Prince's son. He's only four. Sixteen years is a long time for a Regency government. With the Prince dead Grishnov and the whole Ministerial party would just slide right into the power vacuum, if they were left intact.

"It was not enough to kill the Prince. The Emperor felt he had to destroy the whole war party, so effectively that it would not rise again for another generation. So first there was me, bitching about the strategic problems with Escobar. Then the information about the plasma mirrors came through Negri's own intelligence network. Military intelligence didn't have it. Then me again, with the news that surprise had been lost. Do you know, he suppressed part of that, too? It could only be a disaster. And then there was Grishnov, and the war party, and the Prince, all crying for glory. He had only to step aside and let them rush to their doom." Grass was being pulled up in bunches now.

"It all fit so well, there was a hypnotizing fascination to it. But chancey. There was even a possibility, leaving events to themselves, that everyone might be killed *but* the Prince. I was placed where I was to see the script was followed. Goading the Prince, making sure he got to the front lines at the right time. Hence that little scene you witnessed in my cabin. I never lost my temper. I was just putting another nail in the coffin."

"I suppose I can see why the other agent was—the chief surgeon?"

"Quite."

"Lovely."

"Isn't it, though." He lay back on the grass, looking through the turquoise sky. "I couldn't even be an honest assassin. Do you recall me saying I wanted to go into politics? I believe I'm cured of that ambition."

"What about Vorrutyer? Were you supposed to get him killed, too?"

"No. In the original script he was cast as the scapegoat. It would have been his part, after the disaster, to apologize to the Emperor for the mess, in the full old Japanese sense of the phrase, as part of the general collapse of the war party. For all he was the Prince's spiritual advisor, I did not envy him his future. All the while he was riding me, I could see the ground crumbling away beneath his feet. It baffled him. He always used to be able to make me lose my temper. It was great sport for him, when we were younger. He couldn't understand why he'd lost his touch." His eyes remained focused somewhere in the high blue emptiness, not meeting hers.

"For what it's worth to you, his death just then saved a great many lives. He would have tried to continue the fight much longer, to save his political skin. That was the price that bought me, in the end. I thought, if only I were in the right place at the right time, I could do a better job of running the pullout than anyone else on the General Staff."

"So we are, all of us, just Ezar Vorbarra's tools," said Cordelia slowly, belly-sick. "Me and my convoy, you, the Escobarans—even old Vorrutyer. So much for patriotic hoopla and righteous wrath. All a charade."

"That's right."

"It makes me feel very cold. Was the Prince really that bad?"

"There was no doubt of it. I shall not sicken you with the details of Negri's reports . . . But the Emperor said if it wasn't done now, we would all be trying to do it ourselves, five or ten years down the road, and probably botching the job and getting all our friends killed, in a full-scale planet-wide civil war. He's seen two, in his lifetime. That was the nightmare that haunted him. A Caligula, or a Yuri Vorbarra, can rule a long time, while the best men hesitate to do what is necessary to stop him, and the worst ones take advantage.

"The Emperor spares himself nothing. Reads the reports over and over—he had them all nearly word-perfect. This wasn't something undertaken lightly, or casually. Wrongly, perhaps, but not lightly. He didn't want him to die in shame, you see. It was the last gift he could give him."

She sat hugging her knees numbly, memorizing

his profile, as the soft airs of the afternoon rustled in the woods and stirred the golden grasses.

He turned his face toward her. "Was I wrong, Cordelia, to give myself to this thing? If I had not gone, he would simply have had another. I've always tried to walk the path of honor. But what do you do when all choices are evil? Shameful action, shameful inaction, every path leading to a thicket of death."

"You're asking me to judge you?"

"Someone must."

"I'm sorry. I can love you. I can grieve for you, or with you. I can share your pain. But I cannot judge you."

"Ah." He turned on his stomach, and stared down at the camp. "I talk too much to you. If my brain would ever grant me release from reality, I believe I would be the babbling sort of madman."

"You don't talk to anyone else like that, do you?" she asked, alarmed.

"Good God, no. You are—you are—I don't know what you are. But I need it. Will you marry me?"

She sighed, and laid her head upon her knees, twisting a grass stem around her fingers. "I love you. You know that, I hope. But I can't take Barrayar. Barrayar eats its children."

"It isn't all these damnable politics. Some people get through their whole lives practically unconscious of them."

"Yes, but you're not one of them."

He sat up. "I don't know if I could get a visa for Beta Colony."

"Not this year, I suspect. Nor next. All Barrayarans are considered war criminals there at the moment. Politically speaking, we haven't had this much excitement in years. They're all a little drunk on it just now. And then there is Komarr."

"I see. I should have trouble getting a job as a judo instructor, then. And I could hardly write my memoirs, all things considered."

"Right now I should think you'd have trouble avoiding lynch mobs." She looked up at his bleak face. A mistake; it wrenched her heart. "I've—got to go home for a while, anyway. See my family, and think things through in peace and quiet. Maybe we can come up with some alternate solution. We can write, anyway."

"Yes, I suppose." He stood, and helped her up. "Where will you be, after this?" she asked. "You have your rank back."

"Well, I'm going to finish up all this dirty work," a wave of his arm indicated the prison camp, and by implication the whole Escobaran adventure, "—and then I believe I too shall go home. And get drunk. I cannot serve him any more. He's used me up on this. The death of his son, and the five thousand men who escorted him to hell, will always hang between us now. Vorhalas, Gottyan . . ."

"Don't forget the Escobarans. And a few Betans, too."

"I shall remember them." He walked beside her down the path. "Is there anything you need, in camp? I've tried to see that everything was provided generally, within the limits of our supplies, but I may have missed something."

"Camp seems to be all right, now. I don't need anything special. All we really need is to go home. No—come to think of it, I do want a favor."

"Name it," he said eagerly.

"Lieutenant Rosemont's grave. It was never marked.

I may never get back here. While it's still possible to find the remains of our camp, could you have your people mark it? I have all his numbers and dates. I handled his personnel forms often enough, I still have them memorized."

"I'll see to it personally."

"Wait." He paused, and she held out a hand to him. His thick fingers engulfed her tapering ones; his skin was warm and dry, and scorched her. "Before we go pick up poor Lieutenant Illyan again . . ."

He took her in his arms, and they kissed, for the first time, for a long time.

"Oh," she muttered after. "Perhaps that was a mistake. It hurts so much when you stop."

"Well, let me . . ." His hand stroked her hair gently, then desperately wrapped itself in a shimmering coil; they kissed again.

"Uh, sir?" Lieutenant Illyan, coming up the path, cleared his throat noisily. "Had you forgotten the Staff conference?"

Vorkosigan put her from him with a sigh. "No, lieutenant. I haven't forgotten."

"May I congratulate you, sir?" he smiled.

"No, lieutenant."

He unsmiled. "I—don't understand, sir."

"That's quite all right, lieutenant."

They walked on, Cordelia with her hands in her pockets, Vorkosigan with his clasped behind his back.

Most of the Escobaran women had already gone up by shuttle to the ship that had arrived to transport them home, late next afternoon, when a spruce Barrayaran guard appeared at the door of their shelter requesting Captain Naismith.

"Admiral's compliments, ma'am, and he wishes to

know if you'd care to check the data on the marker he had made for your officer. It's in his office."

"Yes, certainly."

"Cordelia, for God's sake," hissed Lieutenant Alfredi, "don't go in there alone."

"It's *all right,*" she murmured back impatiently. "Vorkosigan's all right."

"Oh? So what did he want yesterday?"

"I told you, to arrange for the marker."

"That didn't take two solid hours. Do you realize that's how long you were gone? I saw how he looked at you. And you—you came back looking like death warmed over."

Cordelia waved away her concerned protests irritably, and followed the extremely polite guard to the cache caverns. The planetside administrative offices of the Barrayaran force were set up in one of the side chambers. They had a carefully busy air that suggested the nearby presence of Staff officers, and indeed when they entered Vorkosigan's office, his name and rank emblazoned over the smudge that had been his predecessor's, they found him within.

Illyan, a captain, and a commodore were grouped around a computer interface with him, evidently undergoing some kind of briefing. He broke off to greet her with a careful nod, which she acknowledged in kind. *I wonder if my eyes look as hungry as his,* she thought. *This minuet of manners we go through to conceal our private selves from the mob will be for nothing, if we don't hide our eyes better.*

"It's on the clerk's desk, Cor—Captain Naismith," he directed her with a wave of his hand. "Go ahead and look it over." He returned his attention to his waiting officers.

It was a simple steel tablet, standard Barrayaran

military issue, and the spelling, numbers, and dates were all in order. She fingered it briefly. It certainly looked like it ought to last. Vorkosigan finished his business and came to her side.

"Is it all right?"

"Fine." She gave him a smile. "Could you find the grave?"

"Yes, your camp's still visible from the air at low altitude, although another rainy season will obliterate it—"

The duty guard's voice floated in over a commotion at the door. "So *you* say. For all I know they could be bombs. You can't take that in there," followed by another voice replying, "He has to sign it personally. Those are *my* orders. You guys act like you won the damn war."

The second speaker, a man in the dark red uniform of an Escobaran medical technician, backed through the door followed by a float-pallet on a control lead, looking like some bizarre balloon. It was loaded with large canisters, each about half a meter high, studded with control panels and access apertures. Cordelia recognized them at once, and stiffened, feeling sick. Vorkosigan looked blank.

The technician stared around. "I have a receipt for these that requires Admiral Vorkosigan's personal signature. Is he here?"

Vorkosigan stepped forward. "I'm Vorkosigan. What are these, um . . ."

"Medtech," Cordelia whispered in cue.

"Medtech?" Vorkosigan finished smoothly, although the exasperated glance he gave her suggested that was not the cue he'd wanted.

The medtech smiled sourly. "We're returning these to the senders."

Vorkosigan walked around the pallet. "Yes, but what *are* they?"

"All your bastards," said the medtech.

Cordelia, catching the genuine puzzlement in Vorkosigan's voice, added, "They're uterine replicators, um, Admiral. Self-contained, independently powered—they need servicing, though—"

"Every week," agreed the medtech, viciously cordial. He held up a data disk. "They sent you instructions with them."

Vorkosigan looked appalled. "What the hell am I supposed to do with them?"

"Thought you were going to make our women answer that question, did you?" replied the medtech, taut and sarcastic. "Personally, I'd suggest you hang them around their fathers' necks. The paternal gene complements are marked on each one, so you should have no trouble telling who they belong to. Sign here."

Vorkosigan took the receipt panel, and read it through twice. He walked around the pallet again, counting, looking deeply troubled. He came up beside Cordelia in his circuit, and murmured, "I didn't realize they could do things like that."

"They use them all the time at home, for medical emergencies."

"They must be fantastically complex."

"And expensive, too. I'm surprised—maybe they just didn't want to argue about taking them home with any of the mothers. A couple of them were pretty emotionally divided about abortions. This puts the blood guilt on you." Her words seemed to enter him like bullets, and she wished she'd phrased herself differently.

"They're all alive in there?"

"Sure. See all the green lights? Placentas and all. They float right in their amniotic sacs, just like home."

"Moving?"

"I suppose so."

He rubbed his face, staring hauntedly at the canisters. "Seventeen. God, Cordelia, what do I do with them? Surgeon, of course, but . . ." He turned to the fascinated clerk. "Get the chief surgeon down here, on the double." He turned back to Cordelia, keeping his voice down. "How long will those things keep working?"

"The whole nine months, if necessary."

"May I have my receipt, Admiral?" said the medtech loudly. "I have other duties waiting." He stared curiously at Cordelia in her orange pajamas.

Vorkosigan scribbled his name absently on the bottom of the receipt panel with a light pen, thumbprinted it, and handed it back, still slightly hypnotized by the pallet load of canisters. Cordelia, morbidly curious, walked around them too, inspecting the readouts. "The youngest one seems to be about seven weeks old. The oldest is over four months. Must have been right after the war started."

"But what do *I* do with them?" he muttered again. She had never seen him more at a loss.

"What do you usually do with soldier's by-blows? Surely the situation has come up before, not on this scale, maybe."

"We usually abort bastards. In this case, it seems to have already been done, in a sense. So much trouble—do they expect us to keep them alive? Floating fetuses—babies in cans . . ."

"I don't know." Cordelia sighed thoughtfully. "What a thoroughly rejected little group of humanity they are. Except—but for the grace of God and Sergeant

Bothari, one of those canned kids might have been mine, and Vorrutyer's. Or mine and Bothari's, for that matter."

He looked quite ill at the thought. He lowered his voice almost to a whisper, and began again. "But what do I—what would *you* have me do with them?"

"You're asking me for orders?"

"I've never—Cordelia, please—what honorable. . . ."

It must be quite a shock to suddenly find out you're pregnant, seventeen times over—at your age, too, she thought. She squelched the black humor—he was so clearly out of his depth—and took pity on his real confusion. "Take care of them, I suppose. I have no idea what that will entail, but—you did sign for them."

He sighed. "Quite. Pledged my word, in a sense," he set the problem up in familiar terms, and found his balance therein. "My word as Vorkosigan, in fact. Right. Good. Objective defined, plan of attack proposed—we're in business."

The surgeon entered, and was taken aback at the sight of the float pallet. "What the hell—oh, I know what they are. I never thought I'd see one . . ." he ran his fingers over one canister in a sort of technical lust. "Are they ours?"

"All ours, it seems," replied Vorkosigan. "The Escobarans sent them down."

The surgeon chuckled. "What an obscene gesture. One can see why, I suppose. But why not just flush them?"

"Some unmilitary notion about the value of human life, perhaps," said Cordelia hotly. "Some cultures have it."

The surgeon raised an eyebrow, but was quelled,

207

as much by the total lack of amusement on his commander's face as by her words.

"There are the instructions." Vorkosigan handed him the disk.

"Oh, good. Can I empty one out and take it apart?"

"No, you may not," said Vorkosigan coldly. "I pledged my word—as Vorkosigan—that they would be cared for. All of them."

"How the devil did they maneuver you into that? Oh, well, I'll get one later, maybe . . ." He returned to his examination of the glittering machinery.

"Have you the facilities here to handle any problems that may arise?" asked Vorkosigan.

"Hell, no. Imp Mil would be the only place. And they don't even have an obstetrics department. But I bet Research would love to get hold of these babies . . ."

It took Cordelia a dizzy moment to realize he was referring to the uterine replicators, and not their contents.

"They have to be serviced in a week. Can you do it here?"

"I don't think . . ." The surgeon set the disk into the monitor at the clerk's station, and began flashing through it. "There must be ten written kilometers of instructions—ah. No. We don't have—no. Too bad, Admiral. I'm afraid you'll have to eat your word this time."

Vorkosigan grinned, wolfishly and without humor. "Do you recall what happened to the last man who called me on my word?"

The surgeon's smile faded into uncertainty.

"These are your orders, then," Vorkosigan went on, clipped. "In thirty minutes you, personally, will lift off with these—things, for the fast courier. And it

208

will arrive in Vorbarr Sultana in less than a week.
You will go to the Imperial Military Hospital and
requisition, by whatever means necessary, the men
and equipment needed to—complete the project.
Get an Imperial order if you have to. Directly, not
through channels. I'm sure our friend Negri will put
you in touch. See them set up, serviced, and report
back to me."

"We can't possibly make it in under a week! Not
even in the courier!"

"You'll make it in five days, boosting six points
past emergency max the whole way. If the engineer's
been doing his job, the engines won't blow until you
hit eight. Quite safe." He glanced over his shoulder.
"Couer, scramble the courier crew, please. And get
their captain on the line, I want to give him his
orders personally."

Commodore Couer's eyebrows rose, but he moved
to obey.

The surgeon lowered his voice, glancing at Cordelia.
"Is this Betan sentimentality at work, sir? A little
odd in the Emperor's service, don't you think?"

Vorkosigan smiled, narrow-eyed, and matched his
tone. "Betan insubordination, doctor? You will oblige
me by directing your energies to carrying out your
orders instead of evolving excuses why you can't."

"Hell of a lot easier just to open the stopcocks.
And what are you going to do with them once
they're—completed, born, whatever you call it? Who's
going to take responsibility for them then? I can
sympathize with your wish to impress your girlfriend,
but think ahead, sir!"

Vorkosigan's eyebrows snapped together, and he
growled, down in his throat. The surgeon recoiled.

Vorkosigan buried the growl in a throat-clearing noise, and took a breath.

"That will be my problem. My word. Your responsibility will end there. Twenty-five minutes, doctor. If you're on time I may let you ride up on the inside of the shuttle." He grinned a small white grin, eloquently aggressive. "You can have three days home leave after they're in place at Imp Mil, if you wish."

The surgeon shrugged wry defeat, and vanished to collect his things.

Cordelia looked after him doubtfully. "Will he be all right?"

"Oh, yes, it just takes him a while to turn his thinking around. By the time they get to Vorbarr Sultana, he'll be acting like he invented the project, and the—uterine replicators." Vorkosigan's gaze returned to the float pallet. "Those are the damndest things . . ."

A guard entered. "Pardon me, sir, but the Escobaran shuttle pilot is asking for Captain Naismith. They're ready to lift."

Couer spoke from the communications monitor. "Sir, I have the courier captain on line."

Cordelia gave Vorkosigan a look of helpless frustration, acknowledged by a small shake of his head, and each turned wordlessly to the demands of duty. She left meditating on the doctor's parting shot. *And we thought we were being so careful. We really must do something about our eyes.*

▶ ▶ CHAPTER TWELVE

She travelled home with about 200 others, mostly Escobarans, on a Tau Cetan passenger liner hastily converted for the purpose. There was a lot of time spent exchanging stories and sharing memories among the ex-prisoners, sessions subtly guided, she realized shortly, by the heavy sprinkling of psyche officers the Escobarans had sent with the ship. After a while her silence about her own experiences began to stand out, and she learned to spot the casual-looking roundup techniques for the only-apparently-impromptu group therapy, and make herself scarce.

It wasn't enough. She found herself quietly but implacably pursued by a bright-faced young woman named Irene, whom she deduced must be assigned to her case. She popped up at meals, in the corridors, in the lounges, always with a novel excuse for starting a conversation. Cordelia avoided her when she could, and turned the conversation deftly, or sometimes bluntly, to other topics when she couldn't.

After another week the girl disappeared back into

the mob, but Cordelia returned to her cabin one day to discover her roommate gone and replaced by another, a steady-eyed, easy-going older woman in civilian dress who was not one of the ex-prisoners. Cordelia lay on her bed glumly and watched her unpacking.

"Hi, I'm Joan Sprague," the woman introduced herself sunnily.

Time to get explicit. "Good afternoon, Dr. Sprague. I am correct, I think, in identifying you as Irene's boss?"

Sprague paused. "You're quite right. But I prefer to keep things on a casual basis."

"No, you don't. You prefer to keep things *looking* like they're on a casual basis. I appreciate the difference."

"You are a very interesting person, Captain Naismith."

"Yes, well, there's more of you than there are of me. Suppose I agree to talk to you. Will you call off the rest of your dogs?"

"I'm here for you to talk to—but when you are ready."

"So, ask me what you want to know. Let's get this over with, so we can both relax." I could use a little therapy, at that, Cordelia thought wistfully. I feel so lousy. . . .

Sprague seated herself on the bed, a mild smile on her face and the utmost attention in her eyes. "I want to try and help you remember what happened during the time you were a prisoner aboard the Barrayaran flagship. Getting it into your consciousness, however horrible it was, is your first step to healing."

"Um, I think we may be at cross-purposes. I remember everything that happened during that time with the utmost clarity. I have no trouble getting it into my consciousness. What I would like is to get it out, at least long enough to sleep now and then."

"I see. Go on. Why don't you describe what happened?"

Cordelia gave an account of events, from the time of the wormhole jump from Beta Colony until after the murder of Vorrutyer, but ended it before Vorkosigan's entrance, saying vaguely, "I moved around to different hiding places on the ship for a couple of days, but they caught me in the end and put me back in the brig."

"So. You don't remember being tortured or raped by Admiral Vorrutyer, and you don't remember killing him."

"I *wasn't*. And I *didn't*. I thought I made that clear."

The doctor shook her head sorrowfully. "It's reported you were taken away from camp twice by the Barrayarans. Do you remember what happened during those times?"

"Yes, of course."

"Can you describe it?"

She balked. "No." The secret of the Prince's assassination would be nothing to the Escobarans—they could hardly dislike the Barrayarans any more than they did already—but the mere rumor of the truth could be devastating to civil order on Barrayar. Riots, military mutiny, the downfall of Vorkosigan's Emperor—those were just the beginnings of the possible consequences. If there was a civil war on Barrayar, could Vorkosigan be killed in it? God, please, thought Cordelia wearily, no more death . . .

Sprague looked tremendously interested. Cordelia

felt pounced on. She amended herself. "There was an officer of mine, who was killed during the Betan survey of that planet—you know about that, I hope?" The doctor nodded. "They made arrangements to put a marker on his grave, at my request. That's all."

"I understand," Sprague sighed. "We had another case like yours. The girl had also been raped by Vorrutyer, or some of his men, and had it covered up by the Barrayaran medical people. I suppose they were trying to protect his reputation."

"Oh, I believe I met her, aboard the flagship. She was in my shelter, too, right?"

Sprague's surprised look confirmed it, although she made a little vague gesture indicating professional confidence.

"You're right about her," Cordelia went on. "I'm glad she's getting what she needs. But you're wrong about me. You're wrong about Vorrutyer's reputation, too. The whole reason they put out this stupid story about me was because they thought it would look worse for him to be killed by a weak woman than by one of his own combat soldiers."

"The physical evidence from your medical examination alone is enough to make me question that," said Sprague.

"What physical evidence?" asked Cordelia, momentarily bewildered.

"The evidence of torture," the doctor replied, looking grim, even a little angry. Not angry at her, Cordelia realized.

"What? I was never tortured!"

"Yes. An excellent cover-up. Outrageous—but they couldn't hide the physical traces. Are you aware that you had a broken arm, two broken ribs, numerous contusions on your neck, head, hands, arms—your

214

whole body, in fact? And your biochemistry—evidence of extreme stress, sensory deprivation, considerable weight loss, sleep disorders, adrenal excess—shall I go on?"

"Oh," said Cordelia. "That."

"Oh, that?" echoed the doctor, raising an eyebrow.

"I can explain that," said Cordelia eagerly. She laughed a little. "In a way, I suppose I can blame it on you Escobarans. I was in a cell on the flagship during the retreat. It took a hit—shook everything around like gravel in a can, including me. That's where I got the broken bones and so on."

The doctor made a note. "Very good. Very good indeed. Subtle. But not subtle enough—your bones were broken on two different occasions."

"Oh," said Cordelia. And how am I going to explain Bothari, without mentioning Vorkosigan's cabin? 'A friend tried to strangle me . . .'

"I would like you to think," said Dr. Sprague carefully, "about the possibility of drug therapy. The Barrayarans have done an excellent cover-up on you, even better than the other, and it took very deep probing indeed for her. I think it's going to be even more necessary in your case. But we must have your voluntary cooperation."

"Thank God for that." Cordelia lay back on her bed and pulled her pillow over her face, thinking of drug therapy. It made her blood run cold. She wondered how long she could take deep probing for memories that weren't there before she started manufacturing them to meet the demand. And worse; the very first effect of probing must be to bring up those secret agonies that were uppermost on her mind—Vorkosigan's secret wounds . . . She sighed, removed the pillow from her head and hugged it to her chest, and looked up to find Sprague regarding her with deep concern. "You still here?"

"I'll always be here, Cordelia."

"That's—what I was afraid of."

Sprague got no more from her after that. She was afraid to sleep, now, for fear of talking or even being questioned in her sleep. She took little catnaps, waking with a start whenever there was movement in the cabin, such as her roommate getting up to go to the bathroom in the night. Cordelia did not admire Ezar Vorbarra's secret purposes in the late war, but at least they had been accomplished. The thought of all that pain and death being made vain as smoke haunted her, and she resolved that all Vorkosigan's soldiers, yes, even Vorrutyer and the camp commandant, would not be made to have died for nothing through her.

She ended the trip far more frayed than she had begun it, floating on the edge of real breakdown, plagued by pounding headaches, insomnia, a mysterious left-hand tremula, and the beginnings of a stutter.

The trip from Escobar to Beta Colony was much easier. It only took four days, in a Betan fast courier sent, she was surprised to find, especially for her. She viewed the news reports on her cabin holovid. She was deathly tired of the war, but she caught by chance a mention of Vorkosigan's name, and could not resist following it up to find out what the public view of his part was.

Horrified, she discovered that his work with the Judiciary's investigative commission led the Betan and Escobaran press to blame him for the way the prisoners had been treated, as if he had been in charge of them from the beginning. The old false

Komarr story was dragged out on parade, and his name was reviled everywhere. The injustice of it all made her furious, and she gave up the news in disgust.

At last they orbited Beta Colony, and she haunted Nav and Com for a glimpse of home.

"There's the old sandbox at last." The captain cheerfully keyed her a view. "They're sending a shuttle up for you, but there's a storm over the capital, and it's a bit delayed, till it subsides enough for them to drop screens at the port."

"I may as well wait till I get down to call my mom," Cordelia commented. "She's probably at work now. No point bothering her there. Hospital's not far from the shuttleport. I can get a nice relaxing drink while I wait for her to get off shift and pick me up."

The captain gave her a peculiar look. "Uh, yeah."

The shuttle arrived eventually. Cordelia shook hands all around, thanking the courier crew for the ride, and went aboard. The shuttle stewardess greeted her with a pile of new clothes.

"What's all this? By heavens, the Expeditionary Force uniforms at last! Better late than never, I guess."

"Why don't you go ahead and put them on," urged the stewardess, smiling extraordinarily.

"Why not." She had been wearing the same borrowed Escobaran uniform for quite some time now, and was thoroughly tired of it. She took the sky blue cloth and the shiny black boots, amused. "Why jackboots, in God's name? There's scarcely a horse on Beta Colony, except in the zoos. I admit, they do look wicked."

Finding she was the sole passenger on the shuttle,

she changed on the spot. The stewardess had to help her with the boots.

"Whoever designed these should be forced to wear them to bed," Cordelia muttered. "Or perhaps he does."

The shuttle descended, and she went to the window, eager for the first look at her home town. The ochre haze parted at last, and they spiraled neatly down to the shuttleport and taxied to the docking bay.

"Seems to be a lot of people out there today."

"Yes, the President's going to make a speech," said the stewardess. "It's very exciting. Even if I didn't vote for him."

"Steady Freddy got that many people to show up for one of his speeches? Just as well. I can blend with the crowd. This thing is a bit bright. I think I'd rather be invisible, today."

She could feel the let-down beginning, and wondered how far down it would end. The Escobaran doctor had been right in her principles, if not in her facts; there was an emotional debt yet to be paid, knotted somewhere under her stomach.

The shuttle's engines whined to silence, and she rose to thank the grinning stewardess, uneasy. "There's not going to be a r-reception committee out there for me, is there? I really don't think I could handle it today."

"You'll have some help," the stewardess assured her. "Here he comes now."

A man in a civilian sarong entered the shuttle, smiling broadly. "How do you do, Captain Naismith," he introduced himself. "I'm Philip Gould, the President's Press Secretary." Cordelia was shocked. Press

Secretary was a cabinet-level post. "It's an honor to meet you."

She was tumbling fast. "You're not p-planning some kind of, of d-dog and pony show out there, are you? I r-really just want to go home."

"Well, the President is planning a speech. And he has a little something for you," he said soothingly. "In fact, he was hoping he might make several speeches with you, but we can discuss that later. Now, we hardly expect the Heroine of Escobar to suffer from stage fright, but we have prepared some remarks for you. I'll be with you all the time, and help you with the cues, and the press." He passed her a hand viewer. "Do try and look surprised, when you first step out of the shuttle."

"I am surprised." She scanned the script rapidly. "Th-this is a p-pack of lies!"

He looked worried. "Have you always had that little speech impediment?" he asked cautiously.

"N-no, it's my souvenir from the Escobaran psyche service, and the l-late war. Who came up with this g-garbage, anyway?" The line that particularly caught her eye referred to "the cowardly Admiral Vorkosigan and his pack of ruffians." "Vorkosigan's the bravest man I ever met."

Gould took her firmly by the upper arm, and guided her to the shuttle hatch. "We have to go, now, to make the holovid timing. Maybe you can just leave that line out, all right? Now, smile."

"I want to see my mother."

"She's with the President. Here we go."

They exited the tube from the shuttle hatch into a milling mob of men, women, and equipment. They all began shouting questions at once. Cordelia began to shake, all over, in waves that began in the pit of her stomach and radiated outward. "I don't know any of these people," she hissed to Gould.

"Keep walking," he hissed back through a fixed smile. They mounted a reviewing stand set up on the balcony overlooking the shuttleport concourse. The concourse was packed solidly with a colorful crowd in a holiday mood. They blurred before Cordelia's eyes. She saw a familiar face at last, her mother, smiling and crying, and she fell into her arms, to the delight of the press who recorded it copiously.

"Get me out of this as fast as you can," she whispered fiercely into her mother's ear. "I'm about to lose it."

Her mother held her at arm's length, not understanding, still smiling. Her place was taken by Cordelia's brother, his family clustered nervously and proudly behind him, looking at her, she felt, with eyes that devoured her.

She spotted her crew, also dressed in the new uniforms, standing with some government officials. Parnell gave her a thumbs-up, grinning dementedly. She was bundled over to stand behind a rostrum with the President of Beta Colony.

Steady Freddy seemed larger than life to her confused eyes, big and booming. Perhaps that was why he projected over the holovid so well. He grasped her hand and held it up in his, to the cheers of the crowd. It made her feel like an idiot.

The President gave a fine performance with his speech, not even using the prompter. It was full of the jingoistic patriotism that had so intoxicated the place when she'd left, and not one word in a dozen touched the real truth even from the Betan point of view. He worked up gradually and with perfect showmanship to the medal. Cordelia's heart began to pound lumpishly as she caught the drift of it. She tried desperately to evade the knowledge, turning to the Press Secretary.

"Is this on behalf of m-my crew, for the plasma mirrors?"

"They have theirs already." Was he ever going to stop smiling? "This is your very own."

"I s-see."

The medal, it appeared, was to be awarded for her brave, one-woman assassination of Admiral Vorrutyer. Steady Freddy actually avoided the word assassination, along with blunt terms like murder and killing, favoring more liquid phrases like "freeing the universe of a viper of iniquity."

The speech lumbered to its close, and the glittering medal on its colorful ribbon, Beta Colony's highest honor, was lowered over her head by the President's own hand. Gould positioned her in front of the rostrum, and pointed out the glowing green words of the prompter marching across thin air before her eyes. "Start reading," he whispered.

"Am I on? Oh. Uh . . . People of Beta Colony, my beloved home," that was all right so far, "when I left you to meet the m-menace of Barrayaran tyranny, s-succoring our friend and ally Escobar, it was with no idea that fate was to bring me face-to-face with a n-nobler d-destiny."

It was here she departed from the script, watching herself go helplessly, like a doomed sea ship sinking beneath the waves. "I don't see what's so n-noble about b-butchering that sadistic ass Vorrutyer. And I wouldn't take a medal for m-murdering an unarmed m-man even if I had done it."

She pulled it off over her head. The ribbon caught in her hair, and she yanked it free, painfully, angrily.

"For the last time. I did *not* kill Vorrutyer. One of his own men killed Vorrutyer. He c-caught him from behind and cut his throat from ear to ear. I was *there*, damn it. He bled all over me. The press from both sides are stuffing you with lies about that s-stupid war. D-damn voyeurs! Vorkosigan was *not* in charge of the prison camp when the atrocities took place. As s-soon as he was in charge he stopped them. Sh-sh-shot one of his own officers just to feed your l-lust for vengeance, and it cost him in his honor, too, I can tell you."

The sound going out from the rostrum was cut off suddenly. She turned to Steady Freddy, tears of fury blurring her view of his astonished face, and flung the medal back at him with all the force of her arm. It missed his head and glittered down over the balcony into the crowd.

Her arms were pinned from behind. It triggered some buried reflex, and she kicked out frantically.

If only the President hadn't tried to dodge, he would have been all right. As it was, the toe of her jackboot caught him in the groin with perfect unplanned accuracy. His mouth made a soundless "O" and he went down behind the rostrum.

Cordelia, hyperventilating uncontrollably, began to cry as a dozen more hands grabbed her arms, waist, legs. "*P-please* don't lock me up again! I couldn't take it. I just wanted to go home! Get that goddamn ampule away from me! No! No! No drugs, please, please! I'm *sorry!*"

She was hustled out, and the media event of the year collapsed just like Steady Freddy.

She was taken to a quiet room, one of the shuttle-port's administrative offices, immediately afterwards.

The President's personal physician arrived after a time and took charge, had everyone removed but himself and her mother, and gave her some breathing space to regain her self-control. It took her almost an hour to stop crying, once she had started. The embarrassment and outrage stopped seesawing at last, and she was able to sit up and talk in a voice like a bad cold.

"Please apologize to the President for me. If only someone had warned me, or asked me about it first. I'm—n-not in very good shape right now."

"We should have realized it ourselves," said the physician sorrowfully. "Your ordeal, after all, was much more personal than the usual soldier's experience. It is we who must apologize, for subjecting you to an unnecessary strain."

"We thought it would be a nice surprise," added her mother.

"It was a surprise, all right. I only hope I don't get myself locked in a padded cell. I'm a bit off cells at the moment." The thought tightened her throat, and she breathed carefully to calm back down.

She wondered where Vorkosigan was now, what he was doing. Getting drunk sounded better all the time, and she wished she were with him, doing so. She pressed thumb and forefinger to the bridge of her nose, rubbing out the tension. "May I be permitted to go home now?"

"Is there still a crowd out there?" asked her mother.

"I'm afraid so. We'll try to keep them back."

With the doctor on one side and her mother on the other, she dwelt in Vorkosigan's kiss all during the long walk to her mother's ground car. The crowd still pressed upon her, but in a hushed, respectful, almost frightened way, a great contrast to their ear-

223

lier holiday mood. She felt sorry to have taken away their party.

There was a crowd at her mother's apartment shaft too, in the foyer by the lift tubes, and even in the hallway to her door. Cordelia smiled and waved a little, cautiously, but just shook her head at questions, not trusting herself to speak coherently. They made their way through and closed the door at last.

"Whew! I suppose they meant well, but my Lord—I felt like they wanted to eat me alive."

"There was so much excitement about the war, and the Expeditionary Force—anyone in a blue uniform is getting star treatment. And when the prisoners got home, and your story came out—I'm glad I knew you were safe by then. My poor darling!" Cordelia got another hug, and welcomed it.

"Well, that explains where they got the nonsense. It was the wildest rumor. The Barrayarans started it, and everyone just ate it up. I couldn't stop it."

"What did they do to you?"

"They kept following me around, pestering me with these offers of therapy—they thought the Barrayarans had been messing with my memory . . . Oh, I see. You mean, what did the *Barrayarans* do to me. Nothing much. V-vorrutyer might have liked to, but he met with his accident before he'd got half started." She decided not to disturb her mother with the details. "Something important did happen, though." She hesitated. "I ran into Aral Vorkosigan again."

"That horrible man? I wondered, when I heard the name in the news, if it was the same fellow who killed your Lieutenant Rosemont last year."

224

"No. Yes. I mean, he didn't kill Rosemont, one of his people did. But he's the same one."

"I don't understand why you're so sympathetic to him."

"You ought to appreciate him now. He saved my life. Hid me in his cabin, during those missing two days after Vorrutyer was killed. I'd have been executed for it, if they'd caught me before the change in command."

Her mother looked more disturbed than appreciative. "Did he—do anything to you?"

The question was filled with unanswerable irony. Cordelia dared not tell even her mother about the intolerable burden of truth he had laid on her. Her mother misunderstood the haunted look on her face.

"Oh, dear. I'm so sorry."

"Huh? No, damn it. Vorkosigan's no rapist. He's got this thing about prisoners. Wouldn't touch one with a stick. He asked me . . ." she trailed off, looking into the kind, concerned, and loving wall of her mother's face. "We talked a lot. He's all right."

"He doesn't have a very good reputation."

"Yeah, I've seen some of it. It's all lies."

"He's—not a murderer, then?"

"Well . . ." Cordelia foundered on the truth. "He has k-killed a lot of people, I suppose. He's a soldier, you know. It's his job. It can't help spilling over a bit. I only know about three that weren't in the line of duty, though."

"*Only* three?" repeated her mother faintly. There was a pause. "He's not a, a sex criminal, then?"

"Certainly not! Although I gather he went through a rather strange phase, after his wife committed suicide—I don't think he realizes how much I know about it, not that that maniac Vorrutyer should be

225

trusted as a source of information, even if he was there. I suspect it's partly true, at least about their relationship. Vorrutyer was clearly obsessed with him. And Aral went awfully vague when I asked him about it."

Looking at her mother's appalled face, Cordelia thought, it's a good thing I never wanted to be a defense lawyer. All my clients would be in therapy *forever*. "It all makes a lot more sense if you meet him in person," she offered hopefully.

Cordelia's mother laughed uncertainly. "He certainly seems to have charmed you. What does he have, then? Conversation? Good looks?"

"I'm not sure. He mostly talks Barrayaran politics. He claims to have an aversion to them, but it sounds more like an obsession to me. He can't leave them alone for five minutes. It's like they're in him."

"Is that—a very interesting subject?"

"It's awful," said Cordelia frankly. "His bedtime stories can keep you awake for weeks."

"It can't be his looks," sighed her mother. "I've seen a holovid of him in the news."

"Oh, did you save it?" asked Cordelia, instantly interested. "Where is it?"

"I'm sure there's something in the vid files," her mother allowed, staring. "But really, Cordelia—your Reg Rosemont was ten times better looking."

"I suppose he was," Cordelia agreed, "by any objective standard."

"So what does the man have, anyway?"

"I don't know. The virtues of his vices, perhaps. Courage. Strength. Energy. He could run me into the ground any day. He has power over people. Not leadership, exactly, although there's that too. They either worship him or hate his guts. The strangest man I ever met did both at the same time. But nobody falls asleep when he's around."

"And which category do you fall in, Cordelia?" asked her mother, bemused.

"Well, I don't hate him. Can't say as I worship him, either." She paused a long time, and looked up to meet her mother's eyes squarely. "But when he's cut, I bleed."

"Oh," said her mother, whitely. Her mouth smiled, her eyes flinched, and she busied herself with unnecessary vigor in getting Cordelia's meager belongings settled.

On the fourth afternoon of her leave, Cordelia's commanding officer brought a disturbing visitor.

"Captain Naismith, this is Dr. Mehta, from the Expeditionary Force Medical Service," Commodore Tailor introduced them. Dr. Mehta was a slim, tan-skinned woman about Cordelia's age, with dark hair drawn back, cool and antiseptic in her blue uniform.

"Not another psychiatrist," Cordelia sighed. Her muscles knotted up the back of her neck. More interrogations—more twisting, more evasions, ever-shakier webs of lies to cover the gaps in her story where Vorkosigan's bitter truths dwelt . . .

"Commodore Sprague's reports finally caught up with your file, a little late, it seems." Tailor's lips thinned sympathetically. "Ghastly. I'm sorry. If we'd had them earlier, we might have been able to spare you last week. And everybody else."

Cordelia flushed. "I didn't mean to kick him. He kind of ran into me. It won't happen again."

Commodore Tailor suppressed a smile. "Well, I didn't vote for him. Steady Freddy is not my main concern. Although," he cleared his throat, "he has taken a personal interest in your case. You're a public figure now, like it or not."

"Oh, nonsense."

"It's not nonsense. You have an obligation."

Who are you quoting, Bill? thought Cordelia. That's not your voice. She rubbed the back of her neck. "I thought I'd discharged all my obligations. What more do they want from me?"

Tailor shrugged. "It was thought—I was given to understand—that you could have a future as a spokesman for—for the government. Due to your war experience. Once you're well."

Cordelia snorted. "They've got some awfully strange illusions about my soldierly career. Look—as far as I'm concerned, Steady Freddy can put on falsies and go woo the hermaphrodite vote in Quartz. But I'm n-not going to play the part of a, a propaganda cow, to be milked by any party. I've an aversion to politics, to quote a friend."

"Well . . ." he shrugged, as though he too had discharged a duty, and went on more firmly. "Be that as it may, getting you fit for duty again *is* my concern."

"I'm—I'll be all right, after m-my month's leave. I just need a rest. I want to go back to Survey."

"And so you can. Just as soon as you're medically cleared."

"Oh." The implications of that took a moment to sink in. "Oh, no—wait a minute. I had a little p-problem with Dr. Sprague. Very nice lady, her reasoning was sound, but her premises were wrong."

Commodore Tailor gazed at her sadly. "I think I'd better turn you over to Dr. Mehta, now. She'll explain everything. You will cooperate with her, won't you, Cordelia?"

Cordelia pursed her lips, chilled. "Let me get this straight. What you're saying is, if I can't make your shrink happy, I'll never set foot on a Survey ship again. No c-command—no job, in fact."

"That's—a very harsh way of putting it. But you know yourself, for Survey, with small groups of people isolated together for extended periods of time, the psyche profiles are of the utmost importance."

"Yes, I know . . ." She twitched her mouth into a smile. "I'll c-cooperate. S-sure."

> > **CHAPTER THIRTEEN**

"Now," said Dr. Mehta cheerfully, setting up her box on a table in the Naismiths' apartment next afternoon, "this is a completely non-invasive method of monitoring. You won't feel a thing, it won't do a thing to you, except give me clues as to which subjects are of subconscious importance to you." She paused to swallow a capsule, remarking, "Allergy. Excuse me. Think of it as an emotional dowsing rod, looking for those buried streams of experience."

"Telling you where to drill the well, eh?"

"Exactly. Do you mind if I smoke?"

"Go ahead."

Mehta lit an aromatic cigarette and set it casually in an ashtray she had brought with her. The smoke drifted toward Cordelia; she squinted at its acridity. Odd perversion for a doctor; well, we all have our weaknesses. She eyed the box, suppressing irritation.

"Now for a baseline," said Mehta. "July."

"Am I supposed to say August, or something?"

"No, it's not a free association test—the machine will do the work. But you may, if you wish."

"That's all right."

"Twelve."

Apostles, thought Cordelia. Eggs. Days of Christmas.

"Death."

Birth, thought Cordelia. Those upper-class Barrayarans put everything into their children. Name, property, culture, even their government's continuity. A huge burden, no wonder the children bend and twist under the strain.

"Birth."

Death, thought Cordelia. A man without a son is a walking ghost there, with no part in their future. And when their government fails, they pay the price in their children's lives. Five thousand.

Mehta moved her ashtray a little to the left. It didn't help; made it worse, in fact.

"Sex."

Not likely, with me here and him there . . .

"Seventeen."

Canisters, thought Cordelia. Wonder how those poor desperate little scraps of life are doing?

Dr. Mehta frowned uncertainly at her readouts. "Seventeen?" she repeated.

Eighteen, Cordelia thought firmly. Dr. Mehta made a note.

"Admiral Vorrutyer."

Poor butchered toad. You know, I think you spoke the truth—you must have loved Aral once, to have hated him so. What did he do to you, I wonder? Rejected you, most likely. I could understand that pain. We have some common ground after all, perhaps . . .

Mehta adjusted another dial, frowned again, turned it back. "Admiral Vorkosigan."

Ah love, let us be true to one another . . . Cordelia focused wearily on Mehta's blue uniform. She'll get a geyser if she drills her well there—probably knows it already, she's making another note . . .

Mehta glanced at her chronometer, and leaned forward with increased attention. "Let's talk about Admiral Vorkosigan."

Let's not, thought Cordelia. "What about him?"

"Does he work much in their Intelligence section, do you know?"

"I don't think so. His main line seems to be Staff tactician, when—when he isn't on patrol duty."

"The Butcher of Komarr."

"That's a damned lie," said Cordelia automatically, then wished she hadn't spoken.

"Who told you that?" asked Mehta.

"He did."

"He did. Ah."

I'll get you for that "Ah"—no. Cooperation. Calm. I do feel calm . . . Wish that woman would either finish smoking that thing or put it out. Stings my eyes.

"What proof did he offer you?"

None, Cordelia realized. "His word, I guess. His honor."

"Rather intangible." She made another note. "And you believed him?"

"Yes."

"Why?"

"It—seemed consistent, with what I saw of his character."

"You were his prisoner for six days, were you not, on that Survey mission?"

233

"That's right."

Mehta tapped her light pen and said "hm," absently, looking through her. "You seem quite convinced of this Vorkosigan's veracity. You don't think he ever lied to you, then?"

"Well—yes, but after all, I was an enemy officer."

"Yet you seem to accept his statements unquestioningly."

Cordelia tried to explain. "A man's word is something more to a Barrayaran than a vague promise, at least for the old-fashioned types. Heavens, it's even the basis for their government, oaths of fealty and all that."

Mehta whistled soundlessly. "You approve of their form of government now, do you?"

Cordelia stirred uncomfortably. "Not exactly. I'm just starting to understand it a little, is all. It could be made to work, I suppose."

"So this word of honor business—you believe he never breaks it?"

"Well . . ."

"He does, then."

"I have seen him do so. But the cost was huge."

"He breaks it for a price, then."

"Not for a price. At a cost."

"I fail to see the distinction."

"A price is something you get. A cost is something you lose. He lost—much, at Escobar."

The talk was drifting onto dangerous ground. *Got* to change the subject, Cordelia thought drowsily. Or take a nap . . . Mehta glanced at the time again, and studied Cordelia's face intently.

"Escobar," said Mehta.

"Aral lost his honor at Escobar, you know. He said

he was going to go home and get drunk, afterwards. Escobar broke his heart, I think."

"Aral . . . You call him by his first name?"

"He calls me 'dear Captain.' I always thought that was funny. Very revealing, in a way. He really does think of me as a lady soldier. Vorrutyer was right again—I think I am the solution to a difficulty for him. I'm glad . . ." The room was getting warm. She yawned. The wisps of smoke wound tendril-like about her.

"Soldier."

"He loves his soldiers, you know. He really does. He's stuffed with this peculiar Barrayaran patriotism. All honor to the Emperor. The Emperor hardly seems worthy of it . . ."

"Emperor."

"Poor sod. Tormented as Bothari. May be as mad."

"Bothari? Who is Bothari?"

"He talks to demons. The demons talk back. You'd like Bothari. Aral does. I do. Good guy to have with you on your next trip to hell. He speaks the language."

Mehta frowned, twiddled her dials again, and tapped her readout screen with a long fingernail. She backtracked. "Emperor."

Cordelia could hardly keep her eyes open. Mehta lit another cigarette and set it beside the stub of the first.

"Prince," said Cordelia. Mustn't talk about the Prince . . .

"Prince," repeated Mehta.

"Mustn't talk about the Prince. That mountain of corpses . . ." Cordelia squinted in the smoke. The smoke—the odd, acrid smoke from cigarettes, once lit, never again lifted to the mouth . . .

"You're—drugging—*me* . . ." Her voice broke in a

235

strangled howl, and she staggered to her feet. The air was like glue. Mehta leaned forward, lips parted in concentration. She then jumped from her chair and back in surprise as Cordelia lurched toward her.

Cordelia swept the recorder from the table and fell upon it as it smashed to the floor, beating on it with her good hand, her right hand. "Never talk! No more death! You can't make me! Blew it—you can't get away with it, I'm sorry, watchdog, remembers every word, I'm sorry, shot him, please, talk to me, please, let me out, please let me out pleaseletmeout . . ."

Mehta was trying to lift her from the floor, speaking soothingly. Cordelia caught pieces in the outwash of her own babble. "—not supposed to do that—idiosyncratic reaction—*most* unusual. Please, Captain Naismith, come lie down . . ."

Something glittered at Mehta's fingertips. An ampule.

"No!" screamed Cordelia, rolling on her back and kicking at her. She connected. The ampule arced away to roll under a low table. "No drugs no drugs no no no . . ."

Mehta was pale olive. "All right! All right! But come lie down—that's it, like that . . ." She darted away to turn the air conditioning up full blast, and stub out the second cigarette. The air cleared quickly.

Cordelia lay on the couch, regaining her breath and trembling. So close—she had come so close to betraying him—and this was only the first session. Gradually she began to feel cooler and clearer.

She sat up, her face buried in her hands. "That was a dirty trick," she observed in a flat voice.

Mehta smiled, thin as plastic over an underlying excitement. "Well, it was, a little. But it's been an enormously productive session. Far more than I ever expected."

I'll bet, thought Cordelia. Enjoyed my performance, did you? Mehta was kneeling on the floor, picking up pieces of the recorder.

"Sorry about your machine. Can't imagine what came over me. Did I—destroy your results?"

"Yes, you should have just fallen asleep. Strange. And no," rather triumphantly, she pulled a data cartridge from the wreck, and set it carefully on the table. "You won't have to go through that again. It's all right here. Very good."

"What do you make of it?" asked Cordelia dryly, through her fingers.

Mehta regarded her with professional fascination. "You are without doubt the most challenging case I've ever handled. But this should relieve your mind of any lingering doubts about whether the Barrayarans have, ah, violently rearranged your thinking. Your readouts practically went off the scales." She nodded firmly.

"You know," said Cordelia, "I'm not too crazy about your methods. I have a—particular aversion to being drugged against my will. I thought that sort of thing was illegal."

"But necessary, sometimes. The data are much purer if the subject is not aware of the observation. It's considered sufficiently ethical if permission is obtained post facto."

"Post facto permission, eh?" Cordelia purred. Fear and fury wound a double helix up her spine, coiling tighter and tighter. With an effort, she kept her smile straight, not letting it turn into a snarl. "That's a legal concept I'd never thought of. It sounds—almost Barrayaran. I don't want you on my case," she added abruptly.

Mehta made a note, and looked up, smiling.

"That's not a statement of emotion," Cordelia emphasized. "That's a legal demand. I refuse any further treatment from you."

Mehta nodded understandingly. Was the woman deaf?

"Enormous progress," said Mehta happily. "I wouldn't have expected to uncover the aversion defense for another week yet."

"What?"

"You didn't expect the Barrayarans would put that much work into you and not plant defenses around it, did you? Of course you feel hostile. Just remember, those are not your own feelings. Tomorrow, we will work on them."

"Oh no we won't!" The muscles up her scalp were tense as wire. Her head ached fiercely. "You're fired!"

Mehta looked eager. "Oh, excellent!"

"Did you hear me?" demanded Cordelia. Where did that shrieky whine in my voice come from? Calm, calm . . .

"Captain Naismith, I remind you that we are not civilians. I am not in the ordinary legal physician-patient relationship with you; we are both under military discipline, pursuing, I have reason to believe, a military—never mind. Suffice it to say, you did not hire me and you can't fire me. Tomorrow, then."

Cordelia remained seated for hours after she left, staring at the wall and swinging her leg in absent thumps against the side of the couch, until her mother came home with supper. The next day she left the

238

apartment early in the morning on a random tour of the city, and didn't return until late at night.

That night, in her weariness and loneliness, she sat down to write her first letter to Vorkosigan. She threw away her original attempt halfway through, when she realized his mail was probably read by other eyes, perhaps Illyan's. Her second was more neutrally worded. She made it handwritten, on paper, and being alone kissed it before she sealed it, then smiled wryly at herself for doing so. A paper letter was far more expensive to ship to Barrayar than an electronic one, but he would handle it, as she had. It was as close to a touch as they could come.

The next morning Mehta called early on the comconsole, to tell Cordelia cheerily she could relax; something had come up, and their session that afternoon was cancelled. She did not refer to Cordelia's absence the previous afternoon.

Cordelia was relieved at first, until she began thinking about it. Just to be sure, she absented herself from home again. The day might have been pleasant, but for a dust-up with some journalists lurking around the apartment shaft, and the discovery about mid-afternoon that she was being followed by two men in very inconspicuous civilian sarongs. Sarongs were last year's fashion; this year it was exotic and whimsical body paint, at least for the brave. Cordelia, wearing her old tan Survey fatigues, lost them by trailing them through a pornographic feelie-show. But they turned up again later in the afternoon as she puttered through the Silica Zoo.

*　　*　　*

At Mehta's appointed hour the next afternoon the door chimed. Cordelia slouched reluctantly to answer it. *How am I going to handle her today?* she wondered. *I'm running low on inspiration. So tired . . .*

Her stomach sank. *Now what?* Framed in the doorway were Mehta, Commodore Tailor, and a husky medtech. *That one,* Cordelia thought, staring up at him, *looks like he could handle Bothari.* Backing up a bit, she led them into her mother's living room. Her mother retreated to the kitchen, ostensibly to prepare coffee.

Commodore Tailor seated himself and cleared his throat nervously. "Cordelia, I have something to say that will be a little painful, I'm afraid."

Cordelia perched on the arm of a chair and swung her leg back and forth, baring her teeth in what she hoped was a bland smile. "S-sticking you with the dirty work, eh? One of the joys of command. Go ahead."

"We're going to have to ask you to agree to hospitalization for further therapy."

Dear God, here we go. The muscles of her belly trembled beneath her shirt; it was a loose shirt, maybe they wouldn't notice. "Oh? Why?" she inquired casually.

"We're afraid—we're very much afraid that the Barrayaran mind programming you underwent was a lot more extensive than anyone realized. We think, in fact . . ." he paused, taking a deep breath, "that they've tried to make you an agent."

Is that an editorial or an imperial "we," Bill? "Tried, or succeeded?"

Tailor's gaze wavered. Mehta fixed him with a cold stare. "Our opinion is divided on that—"

Note, class, how sedulously he avoids the "I" of personal responsibility—it suggests the worst "we" of all, the guilty "we"—what the hell are they planning?

"—but that letter you sent day before yesterday to the Barrayaran admiral, Vorkosigan—we thought you should have a chance to explain it, first."

"I s-see." You dared! "Not an official l-letter. How could it be? You know Vorkosigan's retired now. But perhaps," her eye nailed Tailor, "you would care to explain by what right you are intercepting and reading my private mail?"

"Emergency security. For the war."

"War's over."

He looked uncomfortable at that. "But the espionage goes on."

Probably true. She had often wondered how Ezar Vorbarra came by the knowledge of the plasma mirrors, until the war the most closely guarded new weapon in the Betan arsenal. Her foot was tapping nervously. She stilled it. "My letter." My heart, on paper—paper wraps stone . . . She kept her voice cool. "And what did you learn from my letter, Bill?"

"Well, that's a problem. We've had our best cryptographers, our most advanced computer programs, working on it for the better part of two days. Analyzed it right down to the molecular structure of the paper. Frankly," he glanced rather irritably at Mehta, "I'm not convinced they found anything."

No, Cordelia thought, you wouldn't. The secret was in the kiss. Not subject to molecular analysis. She sighed glumly. "Did you send it on, after you were done?"

"Well—I'm afraid there wasn't anything left, by then."

Scissors cut paper . . . "I'm no agent. I g-give you my word."

Mehta looked up alertly.

"I find it hard to believe, myself," Tailor said.

Cordelia tried to hold his eyes; he looked away. You do believe it, she thought. "What happens if I refuse to have myself committed?"

"Then as your commanding officer, I must order you to do so."

I'll see you in hell first—no. Calm. Must stay calm, keep them talking, maybe I can talk my way out of this yet. "Even if it's against your private judgement?"

"This is a serious security matter. I'm afraid it doesn't admit private judgements."

"Oh, come on. Even Captain Negri has been known to make a private judgement, they say."

She'd said something wrong. The temperature in the room seemed to drop suddenly.

"How do you know about Captain Negri?" said Tailor frozenly.

"Everybody knows about Negri." They were staring at her. "Oh, c-come on! If I were an agent of Negri's, you'd never know it. He's not so inept!"

"On the contrary," said Mehta in a clipped tone, "we think he's so good that *you'd* never know it."

"Garbage!" said Cordelia, disgusted. "How *do* you figure that?"

Mehta answered literally. "My hypothesis is that you are being controlled—unconsciously, perhaps—by this rather sinister and enigmatic Admiral Vorkosigan. That your programming began during your first captivity and was completed, probably, during the late war. You were destined to be the linchpin of a new Barrayaran intelligence network here, to replace the

242

one that was just rooted out. A mole, perhaps, put in place and not activated for years, until some critical moment—"

"Sinister?" Cordelia interrupted. "Enigmatic? Aral? I could laugh." I could weep . . .

"He is obviously your control," said Mehta complacently. "You have apparently been programmed to obey him unquestioningly."

"I am not a computer." Thump, thump, went her foot. "And Aral is the one person who has *never* constrained me. A point of honor, I believe."

"You see?" said Mehta. To Tailor; she didn't look at Cordelia. "All the evidence points one way."

"Only if you're s-standing on your head!" cried Cordelia, furious. She glared at Tailor. "That's not an order I have to take. I can resign my commission."

"We need not have your permission," said Mehta calmly, "even as a civilian. If your next of kin will agree to it."

"My mother'd never do that to me!"

"We've already discussed it with her, at length. She's very concerned for you."

"I s-see." Cordelia subsided abruptly, glancing toward the kitchen. "I wondered why that coffee was taking so long. Guilty conscience, eh?" She hummed a snatch of tune under her breath, then stopped. "You people have really done your homework. Covered all the exits."

Tailor summoned up a smile and offered it to her, placatingly. "You don't have anything to be afraid of, Cordelia. You'll have our very best people working for—with—"

On, thought Cordelia.

"—you. And when you're done, you'll be able to

return to your old life as if none of this had ever happened."

Erase me, will you? Erase *him* . . . Analyze me to death, like my poor timid love letter. She smiled back at him, ruefully. "Sorry, Bill. I just have this awful vision of being p-peeled like an onion, looking for the seeds."

He grinned. "Onions don't have seeds, Cordelia."

"I stand corrected," she said dryly.

"And frankly," he went on, "if you are right and, uh, we are wrong—the fastest way you can prove it is to come along." He smiled the smile of reason.

"Yes, true . . ." But for that little matter of a civil war on Barrayar—that tiny stumbling block—that stone—paper wraps stone . . .

"Sorry, Cordelia." He really was.

"It's all right."

"Remarkable ploy of the Barrayarans," Mehta expounded thoughtfully. "Concealing an espionage ring under the cover of a love affair. I might even have bought it, if the principals had been more likely."

"Yes," Cordelia agreed cordially, writhing within. "One doesn't expect a thirty-four-year-old to fall in love like an adolescent. Quite an unexpected—gift, at my age. Even more unexpected at forty-four, I gather."

"Exactly," said Mehta, pleased by Cordelia's ready understanding. "A middle-aged career officer is hardly the stuff of romance."

Tailor, behind her, opened his mouth as if to speak, then shut it again. He stared meditatively at his hands.

"Think you can cure me of it?" asked Cordelia.

"Oh, yes."

"Ah." Sergeant Bothari, where are you now? Too

244

late. "You leave me no choice. Curious." Delay, whispered her mind. Look for an opportunity. If you can't find one, make one. Pretend this is Barrayar, where anything is possible. "Is it all right if I g-get a shower—change clothes, pack? I assume this is going to be a lengthy business."

"Of course." Tailor and Mehta exchanged a relieved look. Cordelia smiled pleasantly.

Dr. Mehta, without the medtech, accompanied her to her bedroom. Opportunity, thought Cordelia dizzily. "Ah, good," she said, closing the door behind the doctor. "We can chat while I pack."

Sergeant Bothari—there is a time for words, and there is a time when even the very best words fail. You were a man of very few words, but you didn't fail. I wish I'd understood you better. Too late . . .

Mehta seated herself on the bed, watching her specimen, perhaps, as it wriggled on its pin. Her triumph of logical deduction. Are you planning to write a paper on me, Mehta? wondered Cordelia dourly. Paper wraps stone . . .

She puttered around the room, opening drawers, slamming cabinets. There was a belt—two belts—and a chain belt. There were her identity cards, bank cards, money. She pretended not to see them. As she moved, she talked. Her brain seethed. Stone smashes scissors . . .

"You know you remind me a bit of the late Admiral Vorrutyer. You both want to take me apart, see what makes me tick. Vorrutyer was more like a little kid, though. Had no intention of picking up his mess afterwards.

"You, on the other hand, will take me apart and not even get a giggle out of it. Of course, you fully intend to put the pieces back together afterwards,

245

but from my point of view that scarcely makes any difference. Aral was right about people in green silk rooms . . ."

Mehta looked puzzled. "You've stopped stuttering," she noted.

"Yes . . ." Cordelia paused before her aquarium, considering it curiously. "So I have. How strange." *Stone smashes scissors . . .*

She removed the top. The old familiar nausea of funk and fear wrung her stomach. She wandered aimlessly behind Mehta, the chain belt and a shirt in her hands. *I must choose now. I must choose now. I choose—now!*

She lunged, wrapping the belt around the doctor's throat, yanking her arms up behind her back, securing them painfully with the other end of the belt. Mehta emitted a strangled squeak.

Cordelia held her from behind, and whispered in her ear.

"In a moment I'll give you your air back. How long depends on you. You're about to get a short course in the real Barrayaran interrogation techniques. I never used to approve of them, but lately I've come to see they have their uses—when you're in a tearing hurry, for instance—" *Can't let her guess I'm play acting. Play acting.* "How many men does Tailor have planted around this building, and what are their positions?"

She loosened the chain slightly. Mehta, eyes stunned with fear, choked, "None!"

"All Cretans are liars," Cordelia muttered. "Bill's not inept either." She dragged the doctor over to the aquarium and pushed her face into the water. She struggled wildly, but Cordelia, larger, stronger, in better training, held her under with a furious strength that astonished herself.

Mehta showed signs of passing out. Cordelia pulled her up and allowed her a couple of breaths.

"Care to revise your estimate yet?" *God help me, what if this doesn't work? They'll never believe I'm not an agent now.*

"Oh, please," Mehta gasped.

"All right, back you go." She held her down again.

The water roiled, splashing over the sides of the aquarium. Cordelia could see Mehta's face through the glass, strangely magnified, deathly yellow in the odd reflected light from the gravel. Silver bubbles broke around her mouth and flowed up over her face. Cordelia was temporarily fascinated by them. *Air flows like water, under water,* she thought; *is there an aesthetic of death?*

"Now. How many? Where?"

"No, really!"

"Have another drink."

At her next breath Mehta gasped, "You wouldn't kill me!"

"Diagnosis, doctor," hissed Cordelia. "Am I a sane woman, pretending to be mad, or a madwoman, pretending to be sane? Grow gills!" Her voice rose uncontrollably. She shoved Mehta back under, and found she was holding her own breath. *And what if she's right and I'm wrong? What if I am an agent, and don't know it? How do you tell a copy from the original? Stone smashes scissors . . .*

She had a vision, trembling to her fingers, of holding the woman's head under, and under, until her resistance drained away, until unconsciousness took her, and a full count beyond that to assure brain death. Power, opportunity, will—she lacked nothing. So this is what Aral felt at Komarr, she thought. Now I understand—no. Now I *know*.

"How many? Where?"

"Four," Mehta croaked. Cordelia melted with relief. "Two outside the foyer. Two in the garage."

"Thank you," said Cordelia, automatically courteous; but her throat was tightened to a slit and squeezed her words to a smear of sound. "I'm sorry . . ." She could not tell if Mehta, livid, heard or understood. Paper wraps stone . . .

She bound and gagged her as she had once seen Vorkosigan do Gottyan. She shoved her down behind the bed, out of sight from the door. She stuffed bank cards, I.D.'s, money, into her pockets. She turned on the shower.

She tiptoed out the bedroom door, breathing raggedly through her mouth. She ached for a minute, just one minute, to collect her shattered balance, but Tailor and the medtech were gone—to the kitchen for coffee, probably. She dared not risk the opening even to pause for boots.

No, God—! Tailor was standing in the archway to the kitchen, just raising a cup of coffee to his lips. She froze, he went still, and they stared at each other.

Her eyes, Cordelia realized, must be huge as some nocturnal animal's. She never could control her eyes.

Tailor's mouth twisted oddly, watching her. Then, slowly, he raised his left hand and saluted her. The incorrect hand, but the other was holding the coffee. He took a sip of his drink, gaze steady over the rim of his cup.

Cordelia came gravely to attention, returned the salute, and slipped quietly out the apartment door.

*   *   *

248

To her temporary terror, she found a journalist and his vidman in the hallway, one of the most persistent and obnoxious, the one she'd had thrown out of the building yesterday. She smiled at him, dizzy with exhilaration, like a sky diver just stepping into air.

"Still want to do that interview?"

He jumped at the bait.

"Slow down, now. Not here. I'm being watched, you know." She dropped her voice conspiratorially. "The government's doing a cover-up. What I know could blow the administration sky-high. Things about the prisoners. You could—make your reputation."

"Where, then?" He was avid.

"How about the shuttleport? Their bar's quiet. I'll buy you a drink, and we can—plan our campaign." Time ticked in her brain. She expected her mother's apartment door to slam open any second. "It's dangerous, though. There are two government agents up in the foyer and two in the garage. I'd have to get past them without being seen. If it were known I was talking to you, you might not get a chance at a second interview. No rough stuff—just a little quiet disappearance in the night, and the ripple of a rumor about 'gone for medical tests.' Know what I mean?" She was fairly sure he didn't—his media service dealt mainly in sex fantasies—but she could see a vision of journalistic glory growing in his face.

He turned to his vidman. "Jon, give her your jacket, your hat, and your holovid."

She tucked her hair up in the broad-brimmed hat, concealed her fatigues under the jacket, and carried the vid ostentatiously. They took the lift tube up to the garage. There were two men in blue uniforms waiting by its exit. She placed the vid casually on her shoulder, her arm half-concealing her face, as they walked past them to the journalist's ground car.

At the shuttleport bar she ordered drinks, and took a large gulp of her own. "I'll be right back," she promised, and left him sitting there with the unpaid-for liquor in front of him.

The next stop was the ticket computer. She punched up the schedule. No passenger ships leaving for Escobar for at least six hours. Far too long. The shuttleport would surely be one of the first places searched. A woman in shuttleport uniform walked past. Cordelia collared her.

"Pardon me. Could you help me find out some-thing about private freighter schedules, or any other private ships leaving soon?"

The woman frowned, then smiled in sudden rec-ognition. "You're Captain Naismith!"

Her heart lurched, and pounded drunkenly. No—steady on . . . "Yes. Um . . . The press have been giving me a rather hard time. I'm sure *you* under-stand," Cordelia gave the woman a look that raised her to an inner circle. "I want to do this quietly. Maybe we could go to an office? I know *you're* not like *them*. You have a respect for privacy. I can see it in your face."

"You can?" The woman was flattered and excited, and led Cordelia away. In her office she had access to the full traffic control schedules, and Cordelia keyed through them rapidly. "Hm. This looks good. Starts for Escobar within the hour. Has the pilot gone up yet, do you know?"

"That freighter isn't certified for passengers."

"That's all right. I just want to talk to the pilot.

Personally. And privately. Can you catch him for me?"

"I'll try." She succeeded. "He'll meet you in Docking Bay 27. But you'll have to hurry."

"Thanks. Um . . . You know, the journalists have been making my life miserable. They'll stop at nothing. There's even a pair who've gone so far as to put on Expeditionary Force uniforms to try and get in. Call themselves Captain Mehta and Commodore Tailor. A real pain. If any of them come sniffing around, do you suppose you could sort of forget you saw me?"

"Why, sure, Captain Naismith."

"Call me Cordelia. You're first-rate! Thanks!"

The pilot was a very young one, getting his first experience on freighters before taking on the larger responsibilities of passenger ships. He too recognized her, and promptly asked for her autograph.

"I suppose you're wondering why you were chosen," she began as she wrote it out for him, without the faintest idea of where she was going, but only with the thought that he looked the sort of person who had never won a contest in his life.

"Me, ma'am?"

"Believe me, the security people went over your life from end to end. You're trustworthy. That's what you are. Really trustworthy."

"Oh—they can't have found out about the cordolite!" Alarm struggled with response to flattery.

"Resourceful, too," Cordelia extemporized, wondering what cordolite was. She'd never heard of it. "Just the man for this mission."

"What mission!"

"Sh, not so loud. I'm on a secret mission for the

President. Personally. It's so delicate, even the Department of War doesn't know about it. There'd be heavy political repercussions if it ever got out. I have to deliver a secret ultimatum to the Emperor of Barrayar. But no one must know I've left Beta Colony."

"Am I supposed to take you there?" he asked, amazed. "My freight run—"

I believe I could talk this kid into running me all the way to Barrayar on his employer's fuel, she thought. But it would be the end of his career. Conscience controlled soaring ambition.

"No, no. Your freight run must appear to be exactly the same as usual. I'm to meet a secret contact on Escobar. You'll simply be carrying one article of freight that isn't on the manifest. Me."

"I'm not cleared for passengers, ma'am."

"Good heavens, don't you think we know that? Why do you suppose you were picked over all the other candidates, by the President himself?"

"Wow. And I didn't even vote for him."

He took her aboard the freighter shuttle, and made her a seat among the last-minute cargo. "You know all the big names in Survey, don't you, ma'am? Lightner, Parnell . . . Do you suppose you could ever introduce me?"

"I don't know. But—you will get to meet a lot of the big names from the Expeditionary Force, and Security, when you get back from Escobar. I promise." Will you ever . . .

"May I ask you a personal question, ma'am?"

"Why not? Everyone else does."

"Why are you wearing slippers?"

She stared down at her feet. "I'm—sorry, Pilot Officer Mayhew. That's classified."

"Oh." He went forward to lift ship.

Alone at last, she leaned her forehead against the cool smooth plastic side of a packing case, and wept silently for herself.

> > **CHAPTER FOURTEEN**

It was about noon, local time, when the lightflyer she had rented in Vorbarr Sultana brought her over the long lake. The shore was bordered by vine-garlanded slopes backed in turn by steep, scrub-covered hills. The population here was scattered thinly, except around the lake, which had a village at its foot. A cliffed headland at the water's edge was crowned by the ruins of an old fortification. She circled it, rechecking her map on which it was a principle landmark. Counting northward from it past three large properties, she brought her flyer down on a driveway that wound up the slope to a fourth.

A rambling old house built of native stone blended with the vegetation into the side of the hill. She retracted the wings, killed the engine, pocketed the keys, and sat staring at its sun-warmed front uncertainly.

A tall figure in a strange brown and silver uniform ambled around the corner. He bore a weapon in a holster on his hip, and his hand rested on it caressingly. She knew then that Vorkosigan must be nearby, for it was Sergeant Bothari. He looked to be in good health, at least physically.

She hopped out of the lightflyer. "Uh, good afternoon, Sergeant. Is Admiral Vorkosigan at home?"

He stared at her, narrow-eyed, then his face seemed to clear, and he saluted her. "Captain Naismith. Ma'am. Yes."

"You're looking a lot better than when we last met."

"Ma'am?"

"On the flagship. At Escobar."

He looked troubled. "I—can't remember Escobar. Admiral Vorkosigan says I was there."

"I see." Took away your memory, did they? Or did you do it yourself? No telling now. "I'm sorry to hear that. You served bravely."

"Did I? I was discharged, after."

"Oh? What's the uniform?"

"Count Vorkosigan's livery, ma'am. He took me into his personal guard."

"I'm—sure you'll serve him well. May I see Admiral Vorkosigan?"

"He's around back, ma'am. You can go up." He wandered away, evidently making some kind of patrol circuit.

She trudged around the house, the sun warm on her back, kicking at the unaccustomed skirts of her dress and making them swirl about her knees. She had bought it yesterday in Vorbarr Sultana, partly for fun, mostly because her old tan Survey fatigues with the insignia taken off collected stares in the streets. Its dark floral pattern pleased her eye. Her hair hung loose, parted in the middle and held back from her face by two enameled combs, also purchased yester-day.

A little farther up the hill was a garden, sur-rounded by a low grey stone wall. No, not a garden, she realized as she approached; a graveyard. An old man in old coveralls was working in it, kneeling in the dirt planting young flowers from a flat. He squinted up at her as she pushed through the little gate. She did not mistake his identity. He was a little taller than his son, and his musculature had gone thin and stringy with age, but she saw Vorkosigan in the bones of his face.

"General Count Vorkosigan, sir?" She saluted him automatically, then realized how peculiar it must look in the dress. He rose stiffly to his feet. "My name is Cap—my name is Cordelia Naismith. I'm a friend of Aral's. I—don't know if he mentioned me to you. Is he here?"

"How do you do, madam." He came more or less to attention, and gave her a courteous half-nod that was achingly familiar. "He said very little, and it did not lead me to think I might meet you." A smile creaked across his face, as if those muscles were stiff from long disuse. "You have no idea how pleased I am to be wrong." He gestured over his shoulder up the hill. "There is a little pavilion at the top of our property, overlooking the lake. He, ah, sits up there most of the time."

"I see." She spotted the path, winding up past the graveyard. "Um. I'm not sure how to put this . . . Is he sober?"

He glanced at the sun, and pursed leathery lips. "Probably not, by this hour. When he first came home he only drank after dinner, but the time has been creeping up, gradually. Very disturbing, but

257

there isn't much I can do about it. Although if that gut of his starts bleeding again I may . . ." he broke off, looking her over with intense, uncertain speculation. "He has taken this Escobar failure unnecessarily personally, I think. His resignation was not in the least called for."

She deduced the old Count was not in the Emperor's confidence on this matter, and thought, it wasn't its failure that slew his spirit, sir; it was its success. Aloud, she said, "Loyalty to your Emperor was a very great point of honor for him, I know." Almost its last bastion, and your Emperor chose to flatten it to its foundations in the service of his great need . . .

"Why don't you go on up," suggested the old man. "Although, this isn't a very good day for him, I—had better warn you."

"Thank you. I understand."

He stood looking after her as she left the walled enclosure and went on up the winding walk. It was shaded by trees, most of them Earth imports, and some other vegetation that had to be local. The hedge of bush-like things with flowers—she assumed they were flowers, Dubauer would have known—that looked like pink ostrich feathers was particularly striking.

The pavilion was a faintly oriental structure of weathered wood, commanding a fine view of the sparkling lake. Vines climbed it, seeming to claim it for the rocky soil. It was open on all four sides, and furnished with a couple of shabby chaises, a large faded armchair and footstool, and a small table holding two decanters, some glasses, and a bottle of a thick white liquid.

Vorkosigan lay back in the chair, eyes closed, bare feet on the stool, a pair of sandals kicked carelessly over the side. Cordelia paused at the pavilion's edge to study him with a sort of delicate enjoyment. He wore an old pair of black uniform trousers and a very civilian shirt, a loud and unexpected floral print. He obviously had not shaved that morning. His toes, she noticed, had a little wiry black hair on them like the backs of his fingers and hands. She decided she definitely liked his feet; indeed could easily become quite foolishly fond of every part of him. His generally seedy air was less amusing. Tired, and more than tired. Ill.

He opened his eyes to slits and reached for a crystal tumbler filled with an amber liquid, then appeared to change his mind and picked up the white bottle instead. A small measuring cup stood beside it, which he ignored, knocking back a slug of the white liquid directly from its source instead. He sneered briefly at the bottle, then traded it for the crystal tumbler and took a drink, rinsing it around in his mouth and swallowing. He hunched back down in the armchair, at a slightly lower level than before.

"Liquid breakfast?" Cordelia inquired. "Is it as tasty as oatmeal and blue cheese dressing?"

His eyes snapped open. "You," he said hoarsely after a moment, "are not a hallucination." He started to get up, then appeared to think better of it and sank back in frozen self-consciousness. "I never wanted you to see . . ."

She mounted the steps to the shade, pushed a chaise closer to him, and seated herself. Blast, she thought, I've embarrassed him, catching him all awry like this. Off balance. How to put him at his ease? I would have him at his ease, always . . . "I tried to call ahead, when I first landed yesterday, but I kept missing you. If hallucinations are what you expect,

259

that must be remarkable stuff. Pour me one too, please."

"I think you'd prefer the other." He poured from the second decanter, looking shaken. Curious, she tasted from his glass.

"Faugh! That's not wine."

"Brandy."

"At this hour?"

"If I start after breakfast," he explained, "I can generally achieve total unconsciousness by lunch."

Pretty close to lunch now, she thought. His speech had misled her at first, being perfectly clear, only slower and more hesitant than usual. "There must be less poisonous general anesthetics." The straw-pale wine he had poured her was excellent, although dry for her taste. "You do this every day?"

"God, no," he shuddered. "Two or three times a week at most. One day drinking, the next day being ill—a hangover is quite as good as being drunk for taking your mind off other things—the next day running errands and such for my father. He's slowed down a great deal in the last few years."

He was gradually pulling himself into better focus, as his initial awkward terror of being repellant to her ebbed. He sat up and rubbed his hand over his face in the familiar gesture, as if to scrub away the numbness, and made a stab at light conversation. "That's a pretty dress. A great improvement over those orange things."

"Thanks," she said, falling in immediately with his lead. "I'm sorry I can't say the same for your shirt—does that represent your own taste, by chance?"

"No, it was a gift."

"I'm relieved."

"Something of a joke. Some of my officers got

together and purchased it on the occassion of my first promotion to Admiral, before Komarr. I always think of them, when I wear it."

"Well, that's nice. In that case I guess I can get used to it."

"Three of the four are dead, now. Two died at Escobar."

"I see." So much for light chit-chat. She swirled her wine around in the bottom of her glass. "You look like hell, you know. Pasty."

"Yes, I stopped exercising. Bothari's quite offended."

"I'm glad Bothari didn't get in too much trouble over Vorrutyer."

"It was touch and go, but I got him off. Illyan's testimony helped."

"Yet they discharged him."

"Honorably. On a medical."

"Did you put your father up to hiring him?"

"Yes. It seemed like the right thing to do. He'll never be normal, as we think of it, but at least he has a uniform, and a weapon, and regulations of a sort to follow. It seems to give him an anchor." He ran a finger slowly around the rim of the brandy tumbler. "He was Vorrutyer's batman for four years, you see. He was not too well, when he was first assigned to the *General Vorkraft*. On the verge of a split personality—separating memories, the works. Rather scary. Being a soldier seems to be about the only human role he can meet the demands of. It allows him a kind of self-respect." He smiled at her. "You, on the other hand, look like heaven. Can you, ah—stay long?"

There was a hesitant hunger in his face, soundless desire suppressed by uncertainty. We have hesitated so long, she thought, it's become a habit. Then it

261

dawned on her that he feared she might only be visiting. Hell of a long trip for a chat, my love. You *are* drunk.

"As long as you like. I discovered, when I went home—it was changed. Or I was changed. Nothing fit anymore. I offended nearly everybody, and left one step ahead of, um, a whole lot of trouble. I can't go back. I resigned my commission—mailed it in from Escobar—and everything I own is in the back of that flyer down there."

She savored the delight that ignited his eyes during this speech, as it finally penetrated that she was here to stay. It contented her.

"I would get up," he said, sliding to the side of his chair, "but for some reason my legs go first and my tongue last. I'd rather fall at your feet in some more controlled fashion. I'll improve shortly. Meantime, will you come sit here?"

"Gladly." She changed chairs. "But won't I squash you? I'm kind of tall."

"Not a bit. I loathe tiny women. Ah, that's better."

"Yes." She nestled down with him, arms around his chest, resting her head on his shoulder, and hooking one leg over him as well, to emphatically complete his capture. The captive emitted something between a sigh and a laugh. She wished they might sit like that forever.

"You'll have to give up this suicide-by-alcohol thing, you know."

He cocked his head. "I thought I was being subtle."

"Not noticeably."

"Well, it suits me. It's extraordinarily uncomfortable."

"Yes, you've worried your father. He gave me the funniest look."

262

"Not his glare, I hope. He has a very withering glare. Perfected over a lifetime."

"Not at all. He smiled."

"Good God." A grin crinkled the corners of his eyes.

She laughed, and craned her neck for a look at his face. That *was* better . . .

"I'll shave, too," he promised in a burst of enthusiasm.

"Don't go overboard on my account. I came to retire, too. A separate peace, as they say."

"Peace, indeed." He nuzzled her hair, breathing its scent. His muscles unwound beneath her like an overtaut bow unstrung.

A few weeks after their marriage they took their first trip together, Cordelia accompanying Vorkosigan on his periodic pilgrimmage to the Imperial Military Hospital in Vorbarr Sultana. They travelled in a ground car borrowed from the Count, Bothari taking what was evidently his usual role as combination driver and bodyguard. To Cordelia, who was just beginning to know him well enough to see through his taciturn facade, he seemed on edge. He glanced uncertainly over her head, seated between him and Vorkosigan.

"Did you tell her, sir?"

"Yes, everything. It's all right, Sergeant."

Cordelia added encouragingly, "I think you're doing the right thing, Sergeant. I'm, um, very pleased."

He relaxed a little, and almost smiled. "Thank you, Milady."

She studied his profile covertly, her mind ranging over the array of difficulties he would be taking back to the hired village woman at Vorkosigan Surleau this day, gravely doubtful of his ability to handle them. She risked probing a little.

"Have you thought about—what you're going to tell her about her mother, as she grows older? She's bound to want to know eventually."

He nodded, was silent, then spoke. "Going to tell her she's dead. Tell her we were married. It's not a good thing to be a bastard here." His hand tightened on the controls. "So she won't be. No one must call her that."

"I see." Good luck, she thought. She turned to a lighter question. "Do you know what you're going to name her?"

"Elena."

"That's pretty. Elena Bothari."

"It was her mother's name."

Cordelia was surprised into an unguarded remark. "I thought you couldn't remember Escobar!"

A little time went by, and he said, "You can beat the memory drugs, some, if you know how."

Vorkosigan raised his eyebrows. Evidently this was new to him, too. "How do you do that, Sergeant?" he asked, carefully neutral.

"Someone I knew once told me . . . You write down what you want to remember, and think about it. Then hide it—the way we used to hide your secret files from Radnov, sir—they never figured it out either. Then first thing when you get back, before your stomach even settles, take it out and look at it. If you can remember one thing on the list, you can usually get the rest, before they come back again. Then do the same thing again. And again. It helps if you have an, an object, too."

"Did you have, ah, an object?" asked Vorkosigan, clearly fascinated.

"Piece of hair." He fell silent again for a long time, then volunteered, "She had long black hair. It smelled nice."

Cordelia, boggled and bemused by the implications of his story, settled back and found something to look at out the canopy. Vorkosigan looked faintly illuminated, like a man who'd found a key piece in a difficult puzzle. She watched the varied scenery, enjoying the clear sunlight, summer air so cool one needed no protective devices, and the little glimpses of green and water in the hollows of the hills. She also noticed something else. Vorkosigan saw the direction of her glance.

"Ah, you spotted them, did you?"

Bothari smiled slightly.

"The flyer that doesn't outpace us?" said Cordelia. "Do you know who it is?"

"Imperial Security."

"Do they always follow you to the capital?"

"They always follow me all the time. It hasn't been easy to convince people I was serious about retiring. Before you came I used to amuse myself flushing them out. Do things like go drunk driving in my flyer in those canyons to the south on the moonlit nights. It's new. Very fast. That used to drive them to distraction."

"Heavens, that sounds positively lethal. Did you really do that?"

He looked mildly ashamed of himself. "I'm afraid so. I didn't think you'd be coming here, then. It was a thrill. I hadn't gone adrenalin-tripping on purpose since I was a teenager. The Service rather supplied that need."

"I'm surprised you didn't have a wreck."

"I did, once," he admitted. "Just a minor crack-up.

That reminds me, I must check on the repairs. They seem to be taking forever at it. The alcohol made me limp as a rag, I suppose, and I never quite had the nerve to do without the shoulder harness. No harm done, except to the flyer and Captain Negri's agent's nerves."

"Twice," commented Bothari unexpectedly.

"I beg your pardon, Sergeant?"

"You wrecked it twice." The Sergeant's lips twitched. "You don't remember the second time. Your father said he wasn't surprised. We helped, um, pour you out of the safety cage. You were unconscious for a day."

Vorkosigan looked startled. "Are you pulling my leg, Sergeant?"

"No, sir. You can go look at the pieces of the flyer. They're scattered for a kilometer and a half down Dendarii Gorge."

Vorkosigan cleared his throat, and shrunk down in his seat. "I see." He was quiet, then added, "How—unpleasant, to have a blank like that in one's memory."

"Yes, sir," agreed Bothari blandly.

Cordelia glanced up at the following flyer through a gap in the hills. "Have they been watching us all this time? Me, too?"

Vorkosigan smiled at the look on her face. "From the moment you set foot in the Vorbarr Sultana shuttleport, I should imagine. I happen to be politically hot, after Escobar. The press, which is Ezar Vorbarra's third hand here, has me set up as a kind of hero-in-retreat, snatching victory spontaneously from the jaws of defeat and so on—absolute tripe. Makes my stomach hurt, even without the brandy. I should have been able to do a better job, knowing what I knew in advance. Sacrificed too many cruisers, covering the troopships—it had to be traded off that way, sheer arithmetic demanded it, though . . ."

She could mark by his face as his thoughts wandered into a well-trodden labyrinth of military might-have-beens. Damn Escobar, she thought, and damn your Emperor, damn Serg Vorbarra and Ges Vorrutyer, damn all the chances of time and place that combined to squeeze a boy's dream of heroism into a man's nightmare of murder, crime, and deceit. Her presence was a great palliative for him, but it was not enough; still something remained unwell in him, out of tune.

As they approached Vorbarr Sultana from the south, the hill country flattened out into a fertile plain, and the population grew more concentrated. The city straddled a broad silver river, with the oldest government buildings, ancient converted fortresses most of them, hugging the bluffs and high points commanding the river's edge. The modern city spilled back from them to the north and south.

The newer government offices, efficient blocky monoliths, were concentrated between. They passed through this complex, making for one of the city's famous bridges to cross the river to the north.

"My God, what happened there?" asked Cordelia, as they passed one whole block of burnt-out buildings, blackened and skeletal.

Vorkosigan smiled sourly. "That *was* the Ministry of Political Education, before the riots two months ago."

"I heard a little about those, at Escobar, on my way here. I had no idea they were so extensive."

"They weren't, really. Quite carefully orchestrated. Personally, I thought it was a damn dangerous way to get the job done. Although I suppose it was a step up in subtlety from Yuri Vorbarra's Defenestration of the Privy Council. A generation of progress, of sorts . . . I didn't think Ezar was going to get that genie back in the bottle, but he seems to have managed it. As soon as Grishnov was killed all the troops they'd called for, which for some reason all seemed to have been diverted to guard the Imperial Residence—" he snorted, "turned up and cleared the streets, and the riot just melted away, except for a few fanatics, and some wounded spirits who'd lost kin at Escobar. That got ugly, but it was suppressed in the news."

They crossed the river and came at length to the large and famous hospital, almost a city within a city, spread out in its walled park. They found Ensign Koudelka alone in his room, lying glumly on his bed in the green uniform pajamas. Cordelia thought at first that he waved to them, but abandoned the idea as his left arm continued to move up and down from the elbow in slow rhythm.

He did sit up and smile as his ex-commander entered, and exchange nods with Bothari. The smile broadened to a grin as he saw her in Vorkosigan's wake. His face was much older than it used to be.

"Captain Naismith, ma'am! Lady Vorkosigan, I should say. I never thought I'd see you again."

"I thought the same. Glad to be mistaken," she smiled back.

"And congratulations, sir. Thanks for sending the note. I sort of missed you the past few weeks, but—I can see you had better things to do." His grin made this comment stingless.

"Thank you, Ensign. Ah—what happened to your arm?"

Koudelka grimaced. "I had a fall this morning. Something's shorted out. Doc should be coming

268

around to fix it in a few minutes. It could have been worse."

The skin on his arms, Cordelia noted, was covered with a network of fine red scars, marking the lines of the prosthetic nerve implants.

"You're walking, then. That's good to hear," Vorkosigan encouraged.

"Yeah, sort of." He brightened. "And at least they've got my guts under control now. I don't care that I can't feel anything from that department, now that I've finally got rid of that damned colostomy."

"Are you in very much pain?" asked Cordelia diffidently.

"Not much," Koudelka tossed off. She felt he was lying. "—but the worst part, besides being so clumsy and out-of-balance, are the sensations. Not pain, but weird things. False intelligence reports. Like tasting colors with your left foot, or feeling things that aren't there, like bugs crawling all over you, or not feeling things that *are* there, like heat . . ." His gaze fell on his bandaged right ankle.

A doctor entered, and conversation stopped while Koudelka removed his shirt. The doctor attached a 'scope to his shoulder, and went fishing for the short circuit with a delicate surgical hand tractor. Koudelka went pale and stared fixedly at his knees, but at last the arm stopped its slow oscillation and lay limply at his side.

"I'm afraid I'm going to have to leave it out of commission for the rest of the day," apologized the doctor. "We'll get it tomorrow when you go in for the work on that adductor group on your right leg."

"Yeah, yeah," Koudelka waved him away with his working right hand, and he gathered his tools and moved on.

"I know it must seem to you to be taking forever," said Vorkosigan, looking at Koudelka's frustrated face, "but it seems to me every time I come in here you've made more progress. You are going to get out of here," he said confidently.

"Yeah, the surgeon says they're going to kick me out in about two months." He smiled. "But they say I'll never be fit for combat again." The smile slid away, and his face crumpled. "Oh, sir! They're going to *discharge* me! All this endless hacking around for *nothing*!" He turned his face away from them, rigid and embarrassed, until his features were under control again.

Vorkosigan too looked away, not inflicting his sympathy, until the ensign looked back again with his smile carefully re-attached. "I can see why," Koudelka said brightly, nodding to the silent Bothari propping up the wall and apparently content just to listen. "A few good body blows like the ones you used to give me in the practice ring, and I'd be flopping around like a fish. *Not* a good example to set my men. I guess I'll just have to find—some kind of desk work." He glanced at Cordelia. "Whatever happened to your ensign, the one that got hit in the head?"

"The last time I saw him, after Escobar—I visited him just two days before I left home, I guess. He's the same. He did get out of the hospital. His mother quit her job, and stays home to take care of him, now."

Koudelka's eyes fell, and Cordelia was wrenched by the shame in his face. "And I bitch my head off about a few twitches. Sorry."

She shook her head, not trusting herself to speak.

Later, alone with Vorkosigan in the corridor a moment, Cordelia leaned her head against his shoulder, and was taken in his arms. "I can see why you started drinking after breakfast, on the days after this. I could use a stiff one myself, just now."

"I'll take you to lunch after the next stop, and we can all have one," he promised.

The research wing was their next destination. The military doctor in charge greeted Vorkosigan cordially, and only looked a little blank when Cordelia was introduced, without explanation, as Lady Vorkosigan.

"I hadn't realized you were married, sir."

"Recently."

"Oh? Congratulations. I'm glad you decided to come see one of these, sir, before they're all done. It's really almost the most interesting part. Would Milady wish to wait here while we take care of this little business?" He looked embarrassed.

"Lady Vorkosigan has been fully briefed."

"Besides," added Cordelia brightly, "I have a personal interest."

The doctor looked puzzled, but led on to the monitoring room. Cordelia stared doubtfully at the half dozen remaining canisters lined up in a row. The technician on duty joined them trundling some equipment obviously borrowed from some other hospital's obstetrics department.

"Good morning, sir," he said cheerfully. "Going to watch us hatch this chick today?"

"I wish you'd find some other term for it," said the doctor.

"Yes, but you can't call it being born," he pointed out reasonably. "Technically, they've all been born once already. You tell me what it is, then."

"They call it cracking the bottle at home," suggested Cordelia helpfully, watching the preparations with interest.

The technician, laying out measuring devices and placing a bassinet under a warming light, shot her a look of great curiosity. "You're Betan, aren't you, Milady? My wife caught the Admiral's marriage announcement in the news, way down in the fine print. I never read the vital statistics section, myself."

The doctor looked up, startled, then returned to his checklist. Bothari pretended to lean against the wall, eyes half closed, concealing his sharp attention. The doctor and the technician finished their preparations and motioned them closer.

"Got the soup ready, sir?" muttered the technician to the doctor.

"Right here. Inject into feed line C . . ."

The correct hormone mixture was inserted into the right aperture, the doctor rechecking the instruction disk on his monitor repeatedly.

"Five minute wait, mark—now." The doctor turned to Vorkosigan. "Fantastic machine, sir. Have you heard any more about getting funding and engineering personnel to try and duplicate them?"

"No," replied Vorkosigan. "I'm out of this project officially as soon as the last live child is—released, finished, whatever you call it. You're going to have to work on your own regular superiors for it, and you'll have to think up a military application to justify it, or at least something that sounds like one, to camouflage it."

The doctor smiled thoughtfully. "It's worth pursuing, I think. It might be a nice change from thinking up novel ways of killing people."

"Time mark, sir," said the technician, and he turned back to the current project.

"Placental separation looks good—tightening up just like it's supposed to. You know, the more I study this, the more impressed I am with the surgeons who did the sections on the mothers. We've got to get more medical students off planet, somehow. Getting those placentas out undamaged must be the most—there. There. And there. Break seal." He completed the adjustments and lifted the top. "Cut the membrane—and out she comes. Suction, quickly, please."

Cordelia realized that Bothari, still pinned to the wall, was holding his breath.

The wet and squirming infant took a breath and coughed as the cold air hit her. Bothari breathed too. She looked rather pretty to Cordelia, unbloodied, and much less red and squashed-looking than the vids of ordinary newborns she had seen. The infant cried, loud and strong. Vorkosigan jumped, and Cordelia laughed out loud.

"Why, she looks quite perfect." Cordelia hovered at the shoulders of the two medical men, who were making their measurements and taking their samples from their tiny, astonished, bewildered and blinking charge.

"Why is she crying so loudly?" asked Vorkosigan nervously, like Bothari still in his original spot.

Because she knows she's been born on Barrayar, was the comment Cordelia suppressed on her lips. Instead she said, "What, you'd cry too if a bunch of giants hooked you out of a nice warm doze and tossed you around like a bag of beans." Cordelia and the technician exchanged a look half-amused, half-glowering.

"All *right*, Milady," surrendered the technician, as the doctor turned back to his precious machine.

"My sister-in-law says you're supposed to hold them close, like this. Not out at arm's length. I'd squall too if I thought I was being held over a pit about to be dropped. There, baby. Smile or something for Auntie Cordelia. That's it, nice and calm. Were you old enough to remember your mother's heartbeat, I wonder?" She hummed at the infant, who smacked her lips and yawned, and tucked the receiving blanket around her more firmly. "What a long, strange journey you've had."

"Want a look at the inside of this, sir?" the doctor went on. "You, too, Sergeant—you were asking so many questions the last time you were here . . ."

Bothari shook his head, but Vorkosigan went over for the technical exposition the doctor was obviously itching to supply. Cordelia carried the baby over to the Sergeant.

"Want to hold her?"

"Is it all right, Milady?"

"Heavens, you don't have to ask me for permission. If anything, the other way around."

Bothari picked her up gingerly, his large hands seeming almost to engulf her, and stared into her face. "Are they sure it's the right one? I thought she'd have a bigger nose."

"They've been checked and rechecked," Cordelia reassured him, hoping he wouldn't ask her how she knew. But it seemed a safe assumption. "All babies have little noses. You don't know what kids are going to look like till they're eighteen."

"Maybe she'll look like her mother," he said hopefully. Cordelia seconded the hope, silently.

The doctor finished dragging Vorkosigan through the guts of his dream machine, Vorkosigan politely managing to look only a little unsettled.

"Want to hold her too, Aral?" Cordelia offered.

"Quite all right," he excused himself hastily.

"Get some practice. Maybe you'll need it some-day." They exchanged a look of their private hope, and he loosened up and permitted himself to be talked into it.

"Hm. I've held cats with more heft. This isn't really my line." He looked relieved when the medical men repossessed her to complete their technical log.

"Um, let's see," said the doctor. "This is the one we don't take to the Imperial Orphanage, right? Where do we take her, after the observation period?"

"I've been asked to take care of that personally," said Vorkosigan smoothly. "For the sake of her family's privacy. I—Lady Vorkosigan and I, will be delivering her to her legal guardian."

The doctor looked extremely thoughtful. "Oh. I see, sir." He didn't look at Cordelia. "You're the man in charge of the project. You can do what you like with them. No one will ask any questions, I—I assure you, sir," he said earnestly.

"Fine, fine. How long is the observation period?"

"Four hours, sir."

"Good, we can go to lunch. Cordelia, Sergeant?"

"Uh, may I stay here, sir? I'm—not hungry."

Vorkosigan smiled. "Certainly, Sergeant. Captain Negri's men can use the exercise."

On the way to the ground car, Vorkosigan asked her, "What are you laughing about?"

"I'm not laughing."

"Your eyes are laughing. Twinkling madly, in fact."

"It was the doctor. I'm afraid we combined to mislead him, quite unintentionally. Didn't you catch it?"

"Apparently not."

"He thinks that kid we uncorked today is mine. Or maybe yours. Or perhaps both. I could practically see the wheels turning. He thinks he's finally figured out why you didn't open the stopcocks."

"Good God." He almost turned around.

"No, no, let it go," said Cordelia. "You'll only make it worse if you try to deny it. I know. I've been blamed for Bothari's sins before. Just let him go on wondering." She fell silent. Vorkosigan studied her profile.

"Now what are you thinking? You've lost your twinkle."

"Just wondering what happened to her mother. I'm certain I met her. Long black hair, named Elena, on the flagship—there could only have been one. Incredibly beautiful. I can see how she caught Vorrutyer's eye. But so young, to deal with that sort of horror . . ."

"Women shouldn't be in combat," said Vorkosigan, grimly glum.

"Neither should men, in my opinion. Why did your people try to cover up her memories? Did you order it?"

"No, it was the surgeon's idea. He felt sorry for her." His face was tense and his eyes, distant.

"It was the damndest thing. I didn't understand it at the time. I do now, I think. When Vorrutyer was done with her—and he outdid himself on her, even by his standards—she was catatonic. I—it was too late for her, but that's when I decided to kill him, if it happened again, and to hell with the Emperor's script. First Vorrutyer, then the Prince, then myself. Should have left Vorhalas in the clear . . .

"Anyway, Bothari—begged the body from him, so

to speak. Took her off to his own cabin. Vorrutyer assumed, to continue torturing her, presumably in imitation of his sweet self. He was flattered, and left them alone. Bothari fuzzed his monitors, somehow. Nobody had the foggiest idea what he was doing in there, every minute of his off duty time. But he came to me with this list of medical supplies he wanted me to sneak to him. Anesthetic salves, some things for treatment of shock, really a well-thought-out list. He was good at first aid, from his combat experience. It occurred to me then that he wasn't torturing her, he just wanted Vorrutyer to think so. He was insane, not stupid. He was in love, in some weird way, and had the mother-wit not to let Vorrutyer guess."

"That doesn't sound altogether insane, under the circumstances," she commented, remembering the plans Vorrutyer had had for Vorkosigan.

"No, but the way he went about it—I caught a glimpse or two." Vorkosigan blew out his breath. "He took care of her in his cabin—fed her, dressed her, washed her—all the while keeping up this whispered dialogue. He supplied both halves. He had apparently worked out this elaborate fantasy in which she was in love with him, married in fact—a normal sane happy couple. Why shouldn't a madman dream of being sane? It must have terrified the hell out of her during her periods of consciousness."

"Lord. I feel almost as sorry for him as I do for her."

"Not quite. He slept with her, too, and I have every reason to believe he didn't limit that marriage fantasy thing to just words. I can see why, I suppose. Can you imagine Bothari getting within a hundred

277

kilometers of such a girl under any normal circumstances?"

"Mm, hardly. The Escobarans fielded their best
against you."

"But that, I believe, is what he chose to try and
remember from Escobar. It must have taken incredible
strength of will. He was in therapy for months."

"Whew," breathed Cordelia, haunted by the vi-
sions his words conjured. She was glad she would
have a few hours to settle before seeing Bothari
again. "Let's go get that drink now, all right?"

———

▶ ▶ CHAPTER FIFTEEN

Summer was waning when Vorkosigan proposed a trip to Bonsanklar. They were about half packed on the morning selected when Cordelia looked out of their front bedroom window, and said in a constricted voice, "Aral? A flyer just landed out front and there are six armed men getting out of it. They're spreading out all over your property."

Vorkosigan, instantly alert, came to her side to look, then relaxed. "It's all right. Those are Count Vortala's men. He must be coming to visit my father. I'm surprised he found time to break away from the capital just now. I heard the Emperor's been keeping him jumping."

A few minutes later a second flyer landed beside the first, and Cordelia had her first view of Barrayar's new Prime Minister. Prince Serg's description of him as a wrinkled clown was an exaggeration, but a just one; he was a lean man, shrunken with age but still moving briskly. He carried a stick, but from the way he swung it around Cordelia guessed it was an affectation. Clipped white hair fringed a bald and liver-spotted head that shone in the sunshine as he and a pair of aides, or bodyguards, Cordelia was not sure which, passed under her line of sight to the front door.

The two Counts were standing chatting in the front hall as Cordelia and Vorkosigan came down the stairs, the General saying, "Ah, here he comes now."

Vortala looked them over with a bright and penetrating twinkle. "Aral, my boy. Good to see you looking so well. And is this your Betan Penthesileia? Congratulations on a remarkable capture. Milady." He bent over her hand and kissed it with a sort of manic savoir faire.

Cordelia blinked at this description of herself, but managed a "How do you do, sir?" in return. Vortala met her eyes calculatingly.

"Nice that you could get away for a visit, sir," said Vorkosigan. "My wife and I," the phrase was emphasized in his mouth, like a sip of wine with a superior bouquet, "very nearly missed you. I'm promised to take her to the ocean today."

"Just so . . . This isn't a social call, as it happens. I'm playing messenger boy for my master. And my time is unfortunately tight."

Vorkosigan gave a nod. "I'll leave you gentlemen to it, then."

"Ha. Don't try to weasel off on me, boy. The message is for you."

Vorkosigan looked wary. "I didn't think the Emperor and I had anything further to say to each other. I thought I made that clear when I resigned."

"Yes, well, he was perfectly content to have you out of the capital while that dirty work on the Ministry of Political Education was in progress. But I am charged to inform you," he gave a little bow, "that you are requested and required to attend him. This afternoon. Your wife, too," he added as an afterthought.

"Why?" asked Vorkosigan bluntly. "Frankly, Ezar Vorbarra was not in my plans for the day—or any other day."

Vortala grew serious. "He's run out of time to wait for you to get bored in the country. He's dying, Aral."

Vorkosigan blew out his breath. "He's been dying for the last eleven months. Can't he die a little longer?"

Vortala chuckled. "Five months," he corrected absently, then frowned speculation at Vorkosigan. "Hm. Well, it has been very convenient for him. He's flushed more rats out of the wainscotting in the last five months than the past twenty years. You could practically mark the shake-down in the Ministries by his medical bulletins. One week; condition very grave. Next week; another deputy minister caught out on charges of peculation, or whatever." He became serious again. "But it's the real thing, this time. You must see him today. Tomorrow could be too late. Two weeks from now will definitely be too late."

Vorkosigan's lips tightened. "What does he want me for? Did he say?"

"Ah . . . I believe he has a post in mind for you in the upcoming Regency government. The one you didn't want to hear about at your last meeting."

Vorkosigan shook his head. "I don't think there's a post in the government that would tempt me to step back into that arena. Well, maybe—no. Not even the Ministry of War. It's too damn dangerous. I have a nice quiet life here." His arm circled Cordelia's waist protectively. "We're going to have a family. I'll not risk them in those gladiator politics."

"Yes, I can just picture you, whiling away your twilight years—at age forty-four. Ha! Picking grapes, sailing your boat—your father told me about your sailboat. I hear they're going to rename the village Vorkosigan Sousleau in your honor, by the way—"

Vorkosigan snorted, and they exchanged an ironic bow.

"Anyway, you will have to tell him so yourself."

"I'd be—curious, to see the man," murmured Cordelia. "If it's really the last chance."

Vortala smiled at her, and Vorkosigan yielded, reluctantly. They returned to his bedroom to dress, Cordelia in her most formal afternoon wear, Vorkosigan in the dress greens he had not worn since their wedding.

"Why so jumpy?" asked Cordelia. "Maybe he just wants to bid you farewell or something."

"We're talking about a man who can make even his own death serve his political purposes, remember? And if there's some way to govern Barrayar from beyond the grave, you can bet he's figured it out. I've never come out ahead on any dealing I've ever had with him."

On that ambiguous note they joined the Prime Minister for the flight back to Vorbarr Sultana.

The Imperial Residence was an old building, almost a museum piece, thought Cordelia, as they climbed the worn granite steps to its east portico. The long facade was heavy with stone carving, each figure an individual work of art, the aesthetic opposite of the modern, faceless Ministry buildings rising a kilometer or two to the east.

They were ushered into a room half hospital, half antique display. Tall windows looked out on the formal gardens and lawns to the north of the Residence. The room's principal inhabitant lay in a huge carved bed inherited from some splendor-minded ancestor, his body pierced in a dozen places by the utilitarian plastic tubes that kept him alive this day.

Ezar Vorbarra was the whitest man Cordelia had ever seen, as white as his sheets, as white as his hair. His skin was white and wrinkled over his sunken cheeks. His eyelids were white, heavy and hooded over hazel eyes whose like she had seen once before, dimly in a mirror. His hands were white, with blue veins standing up on their backs. His teeth, when he spoke, were ivory yellow against their bloodless backdrop.

Vortala and Vorkosigan, and after an uncertain beat Cordelia, went down on one knee beside the bed. The Emperor waved his attendant physician out of the room with a little effortful jerk of one finger. The man bowed and left. They stood, Vortala rather stiffly.

"So, Aral," said the Emperor. "Tell me how I look."

"Very ill, sir."

Vorbarra chuckled, and coughed. "You refresh me. First honest opinion I've heard from anyone in weeks. Even Vortala beats around the bush." His voice cracked, and he cleared his throat of phlegm. "Pissed away the last of my melanin last week. That damned doctor won't let me out into my garden any more during daylight." He snorted, for disapproval or breath. "So this is your Betan, eh? Come here, girl."

Cordelia approached the bed, and the white old man stared into her face, hazel eyes intent. "Commander Illyan has told me of you. Captain Negri, too. I've seen all your Survey records, you know. And that astonishing flight of fancy of your psychiatrist's. Negri wanted to hire her, just to generate ideas for his section. Vorkosigan, being Vorkosigan, has told me much less." He paused, as if for breath. "Tell me quite truly, now—what do you see in him, a broken down, ah, what was that phrase? hired killer?"

"Aral has told you something, it seems," she said, startled to hear her own words in his mouth. She stared back at him with equal curiosity. The question seemed to demand an honest answer, and she struggled to frame it.

"I suppose—I see myself. Or someone like myself. We're both looking for the same thing. We call it by different names, and look in different places. I believe he calls it honor. I guess I'd call it the grace of God. We both come up empty, mostly."

"Ah, yes. I recall from your file that you are some sort of theist," said the Emperor. "I am an atheist, myself. A simple faith, but a great comfort to me, in these last days."

"Yes, I have often felt the pull of it myself."

"Hm." He smiled at that. "A very interesting answer, in light of what Vorkosigan said about you."

"What was that, sir?" asked Cordelia, her curiosity piqued.

"You must get him to tell you. It was in confidence. Very poetic, too. I was surprised." He waved her away, as if satisfied, and motioned Vorkosigan closer. Vorkosigan stood in a kind of aggressive parade rest. His mouth was sardonic but his eyes, Cordelia saw, were moved.

284

"How long have you served me, Aral?" asked the Emperor.

"Since my commission, twenty-six years. Or do you mean body and blood?"

"Body and blood. I always counted it from the day old Yuri's death squad slew your mother and uncle. The night your father and Prince Xav came to me at Green Army Headquarters with their peculiar proposition. Day One of Yuri Vorbarra's Civil War. Why is it never called Piotr Vorkosigan's Civil War, I wonder? Ah, well. How old were you?"

"Eleven, sir."

"Eleven. I was just the age you are now. Strange. So body and blood you have served me—damn, you know this thing is starting to affect my brain, now . . ."

"Thirty-three years, sir."

"God. Thank you. Not much time left."

From the cynical expression on his face Cordelia gathered that Vorkosigan was not in the least convinced of the Emperor's self-proclaimed senility.

The old man cleared his throat again. "I always meant to ask what you and old Yuri said to each other, that day two years later when we finally butchered him in that old castle. I've developed a particular interest in Emperors' last words, lately. Count Vorhalas thought you were playing with him."

Vorkosigan's eyes closed briefly, in pain or memory. "Hardly. Oh, I thought I was eager for the first cut, until he was stripped and held before me. Then—I had this impulse to strike suddenly at his throat, and end it cleanly, just be done with it."

The Emperor smiled sourly, eyes closed. "What a riot that would have started."

"Mm. I think he knew by my face I was funking

out. He leered at me. 'Strike, little boy. If you dare while you wear *my* uniform. My uniform on a child.' That was all he said. I said, 'You killed all the children in that room,' which was fatuous, but it was the best I could come up with at the time, then took my cut out of his stomach. I often wished I'd said—said something else, later. But mostly I wished I'd had the guts to follow my first impulse."

"You looked pretty green, out on the parapet in the rain."

"He'd started screaming by then. I was sorry my hearing had come back."

The Emperor sighed. "Yes, I remember."

"You stage-managed it."

"Somebody had to." He paused, resting, then added, "Well, I didn't call you here to chat over old times. Did my Prime Minister tell you my purpose?"

"Something about a post. I told him I wasn't interested, but he refused to convey the message."

Vorbarra closed his eyes wearily and addressed, apparently, the ceiling. "Tell me—Lord Vorkosigan—who should be Regent of Barrayar?"

Vorkosigan looked as if he'd just bitten into something vile, but was too polite to spit it out. "Vortala."

"Too old. He'd never last sixteen years."

"The Princess, then."

"The General Staff would eat her alive."

"Vordarian?"

The Emperor's eyes snapped open. "Oh, for God's sake! Gather your wits, boy."

"He does have some military background."

"We will discuss his drawbacks at length—if the doctors give me another week to live. Have you any other jokes, before we get down to business?"

"Quintillian of the Interior. And that is not a joke."

The Emperor grinned yellowly. "So you do have something good to say for my Ministers after all. I may die now; I've heard everything."

"You'd never get a vote of consent out of the Counts for anyone without a Vor in front of his name," said Vortala. "Not even if he walked on water."

"So, make him one. Give him a rank to go with the job."

"Vorkosigan," said Vortala, aghast, "he's not of the warrior caste!"

"Neither are many of our best soldiers. We're only Vor because some dead Emperor declared one of our dead ancestors so. Why not start the custom up again, as a reward for merit? Better yet, declare everybody a Vor and be done with the whole bloody nonsense forever."

The Emperor laughed, then choked and coughed, sputtering. "Wouldn't that pull the rug out from under the People's Defense League? What an attractive counter-proposal to assassinating the aristocracy! I don't believe the most wild-eyed of them could come up with a more radical proposal. You're a dangerous man, Lord Vorkosigan."

"You asked for my opinion."

"Yes, indeed. And you always give it to me. Strange." The Emperor sighed. "You can quit wriggling, Aral. You shall not wriggle out of this.

"Allow me to put it in a capsule. What the Regency requires is a man of impeccable rank, no more than middle-aged, with a strong military background. He should be popular with his officers and men, well-known to the public, and above all respected by the General Staff. Ruthless enough to hold near-absolute power in this madhouse for sixteen years, and honest enough to hand over that power at the

287

end of those sixteen years to a boy who will no doubt be an idiot—I was, at that age, and as I recall, so were you—and, oh yes, happily married. Reduces the temptation of becoming bedroom Emperor via the Princess. In short, yourself."

Vortala grinned. Vorkosigan frowned. Cordelia's stomach sank.

"Oh, no," said Vorkosigan whitely. "You're not going to lay that thing on me. It's grotesque. Me, of all men, to step into his father's shoes, speak to him with his father's voice, become his mother's advisor— it's worse than grotesque. It's obscene. No."

Vortala looked puzzled at his vehemence. "A little decent reticence is one thing, Aral, but let's not go overboard. If you're worried about the vote, it's already bagged. Everyone can see you're the man of the hour."

"Everyone most certainly will not. Vordarian will become my instant enemy, and so will the Minister of the West. And as for absolute power, you sir, know what a false chimera that notion is. A shaky illusion, based on—God knows what. Magic. Sleight of hand. Believing your own propaganda."

The Emperor shrugged, carefully, cautious of dislodging his tubing. "Well, it won't be my problem. It will be Prince Gregor's, and his mother's. And that of—whatever individual can be persuaded to stand by them, in their hour of need. How long do you think they could last, without help? One year? Two?"

"Six months," muttered Vortala.

Vorkosigan shook his head. "You pinned me with that 'what if' argument before Escobar. It was false then—although it took me some time to realize it— and it's false now."

"Not false," the Emperor denied. "Either then or now. I must so believe."

Vorkosigan yielded a little. "Yes. I can see that you must." His face tensed in frustration, as he contemplated the man in the bed. "Why must it be me? Vortala has more political acuity. The Princess has a better right. Quintillian has a better grasp of internal affairs. You even have better military strategists. Vorlakial. Or Kanzian."

"You can't name a third, though," murmured the Emperor.

"Well—perhaps not. But you must see my point. I am not the irreplaceable man which for some reason you choose to imagine me."

"On the contrary. You have two unique advantages, from my point of view. I have kept them in mind from the day we killed old Yuri. I always knew I wouldn't live forever—too many latent poisons in my chromosomes, absorbed when I was fighting the Cetagandans as your father's military apprentice, and careless about my clean techniques, not expecting to live to grow old." The Emperor smiled again, and focused on Cordelia's intent, uncertain face. "Of the five men with a better right by blood and law to the Imperium of Barrayar than mine, your name heads the list. Ha—" he added, "I was right. Didn't think you'd told her that. Tricky, Aral."

Cordelia, faint, turned wide grey eyes to Vorkosigan. He shook his head irritably. "Not true. Salic descent."

"A debate we shall not continue here. Be that as it may, anyone who wishes to dislodge Prince Gregor using argument based on blood and law must first either get rid of you, or offer you the Imperium. We all know how hard you are to kill. And you are the one man—the only man on that list who I am absolutely certain, by the scattered remains of Yuri Vorbarra, *truly* does not wish to be Emperor. Others may believe you coy. I know better."

"Thank you for that, sir." Vorkosigan looked extremely saturnine.

"As an inducement, I point out that you can be no better placed to prevent that eventuality than as Regent. Gregor is your lifeline, boy. Gregor is all that stands between you, and being targeted. Your hope of heaven."

Count Vortala turned to Cordelia. "Lady Vorkosigan. Won't you lend us your vote? You seem to have come to know him very well. Tell him he's the man for the job."

"When we came up here," said Cordelia slowly, "with this vague talk of a post, I thought I might urge him to take it up. He needs work. He's made for it. I confess I wasn't anticipating that offer." She stared at the Emperor's embroidered bedspread, caught by its intricate patterns and colors. "But I've always thought—tests are a gift. And great tests are a great gift. To fail the test is a misfortune. But to refuse the test is to refuse the gift, and something worse, more irrevocable, than misfortune. Do you understand what I'm saying?"

"No," said Vortala.

"Yes," said Vorkosigan.

"I've always felt that theists were more ruthless than atheists," said Ezar Vorbarra.

"If you think it's really wrong," said Cordelia to Vorkosigan, "that's one thing. Maybe that's the test. But if it's only fear of failure—you have not the right to refuse the gift for that."

"It's an impossible job."

"That happens, sometimes."

He took her aside, quietly, to the tall windows. "Cordelia—you have not the first conception of what kind of life it would be. Did you think our public men surrounded themselves with liveried retainers for decoration? If they have a moment's ease, it is at the cost of twenty men's vigilance. No separate peace permitted. Three generations of Emperors have spent themselves trying to untangle the violence in our affairs, and we're still not come to the end of it. I haven't the hubris to think I can succeed where *he* failed." His eyes flicked in the direction of the great bed.

Cordelia shook her head. "Failure doesn't frighten me as much as it used to. But I'll quote you a quote, if you like. 'Exile, for no other motive than ease, would be the last defeat, with no seed of future victory in it.' I thought the man who said that was on to something."

Vorkosigan turned his head, to some unfocused distance. "It's not the desire for ease I'm talking about now. It's fear. Simple, squalid terror." He smiled ruefully at her. "You know, I fancied myself quite a bravo once, until I met you and rediscovered funk. I'd forgotten what it was to have your heart in the future."

"Yeah, me too."

"I don't have to take it. I can turn it down."

"Can you?" Their eyes met.

"It's not the life you were anticipating, when you left Beta Colony."

"I didn't come for a life. I came for you. Do you want it?"

He laughed, shakily. "God, what a question. It's the chance of a lifetime. Yes. I want it. But it's poison, Cordelia. Power is a bad drug. Look what it did

291

to *him*. He was sane too, once, and happy. I think I could turn down almost any other offer without a blink."

Vortala leaned on his stick ostentatiously, and called across the room, "Make up your mind, Aral. My legs are beginning to ache. But for your delicacy—it's a job any number of men I know would kill for. And you're getting it offered free and clear."

Only Cordelia and the Emperor knew why Vorkosigan barked a short laugh at this. He sighed, gazed at his master, and nodded.

"Well, old man. I thought you might find a way to rule from your grave."

"Yes. I propose to haunt you continually." A little silence fell while the Emperor digested his victory. "You'll need to start assembling your personal staff immediately. I'm willing Captain Negri to my grandson and the Princess, for Security. But I thought perhaps you might like to have Commander Illyan, for yourself."

"Yes. I think he and I might deal very well together." A pleasant thought seemed to strike a light in Vorkosigan's dark face. "And I know just the man for the job of personal secretary. He'll need a promotion for it—a lieutenancy."

"Vortala will take care of it for you." The Emperor lay back wearily, and cleared his throat of phlegm again, lips leaden. "Take care of it all. I suppose you'd better send that doctor back in." He waved them out with a tired twitch of one hand.

Vorkosigan and Cordelia emerged from the Imperial Residence into the warm air of the late summer evening, soft and grey with humidity from the nearby river. They were trailed by their new bodyguards, trim in the familiar black uniforms. There had been a lengthy conference with Vortala, Negri, and Illyan. Cordelia's head swam with the number and detail of subjects covered. Vorkosigan, she'd noticed enviously, seemed to have no trouble keeping up; indeed, he'd set the pace.

His face seemed focused, more electric than she'd seen it since she'd come to Barrayar, filled with an eager tension. He's alive again, she thought. Looking out, not in; forward, not back. Like when I first met him. I'm glad. Whatever the risks.

Vorkosigan snapped his fingers and said "Tabs," out loud, cryptically. "First stop Vorkosigan House."

They had driven past the Count's official residence on their last trip to Vorbarr Sultana, but this was the first time Cordelia had been in it. Vorkosigan took the wide circular staircase two steps at a time to his own room. It was a large chamber, simply furnished, overlooking the back garden. It had the same feel as Cordelia's own room in her mother's apartment, of frequent and prolonged disoccupation, with archeological layers of past passions stuffed into drawers and closets.

Not surprisingly, there was evidence of interest in all kinds of strategy games, and civil and military history. More surprising was a portfolio of yellowing pen and ink drawings, run across as he sorted through a drawer full of medals, mementos, and pure junk.

"Did you do these?" Cordelia asked curiously. "They're pretty good."

"When I was a teenager," he explained, still sorting. "Some later. I gave it up in my twenties. Too busy."

His medal and campaign ribbon collection showed a peculiar history. The early, lesser ones were carefully arranged and displayed on velvet-covered cards, with notes attached. The later, greater ones were piled haphazardly in a jar. One, which Cordelia recognized as a high Barrayaran award for valor, was shoved loose in the back of the drawer, its ribbon crumpled and tangled.

She sat on his bed and sorted through the portfolio. They were mostly meticulous architectural studies, but also a few figure studies and portraits done in a less certain style. There were several of a striking young woman with short dark curls, both clothed and nude, and Cordelia realized with a shock from the notes on them that she was looking at Vorkosigan's first wife. She had seen no other pictures of her anywhere in his things. There were also three studies of a laughing young man labeled "Ges" that seemed hauntingly familiar. She mentally added forty pounds and twenty years to him, and the room seemed to tilt as she recognized Admiral Vorrutyer. She closed the portfolio back up quietly.

Vorkosigan finally found what he was looking for; a couple of sets of old red lieutenant's tabs. "Good. It was quicker than going by headquarters."

At the Imperial Military Hospital they were stopped by a male nurse. "Sir? Visiting hours are over, sir."

"Did no one call from headquarters? Where's that surgeon?"

Koudelka's surgeon, the man who had worked on, or over, him with the hand tractor during Cordelia's first visit, was routed out at last.

"Admiral Vorkosigan, sir. No, of course visiting hours don't apply to him. Thank you, corpsman, dismissed."

"I'm not visiting this time, doctor. Official business. I mean to relieve you of your patient tonight, if it's physically possible. Koudelka's been reassigned."

"Reassigned? He was to be discharged in a week! Reassigned to what? Hasn't anybody read my reports? He can barely walk.'"

"He won't need to. His new assignment is all desk work. I trust you have his hands working?"

"Pretty well."

"Any medical work left to be done?"

"Nothing important. A few last tests. I was just holding him to the end of the month, so he would have completed his fourth year. Thought it would help his pension a bit, such as it is."

Vorkosigan sorted through the papers and disks, and handed the pertinent ones to the doctor. "Here. Cram this in your computer and get his release signed. Come on, Cordelia, let's go surprise him." He looked happier than he had all day.

They entered Koudelka's room to find him still dressed for the day in black fatigues, struggling with a therapeutic hand coordination exercise and cursing under his breath.

"Hello, sir," he greeted Vorkosigan absently. "The trouble with this damn tin-foil nervous system is that you can't *teach* it anything. Practice only helps the organic parts. I swear some days I could beat my head on the wall." He gave up the exercise with a sigh.

"Don't do that. You're going to need it in the days to come."

"I suppose so. It was never the best part, though." He stared, abstracted and downcast, at the board, then remembered to be cheerful for his commander. Looking up, he noticed the time. "What are you doing here at this hour, sir?"

"Business. Just what are your plans for the next few weeks, Ensign?"

"Well, they're discharging me next week, you know. I'll go home for a while. Then start looking for work, I guess. I don't know what kind."

"Too bad," said Vorkosigan, keeping his face straight. "I hate to make you alter your plans, Lieutenant Koudelka, but you've been reassigned." And laid on his bedside tray, in order, like a fine hand of cards, Koudelka's newly cut orders, his promotion, and a pair of red collar tabs.

Cordelia had never enjoyed Koudelka's expressive face more. It was a study in bewilderment and rising hope. He picked up the orders carefully and read them through.

"Oh, sir! I know this isn't a joke, but it's got to be a mistake! Personal secretary to the Regent-elect—I don't know anything about the work. It's an impossible job."

"Do you know, that's almost exactly what the Regent-elect said about his job, when he was first offered it," said Cordelia. "I guess you'll both have to learn them together."

"How did he come to pick me? Did you recommend me, sir? Come to think of it . . ." He turned the orders over, reading them through again, "who is the Regent going to be, anyway?" He raised his eyes to Vorkosigan, and made the connection at last. "My God," he whispered. He did not, as Cordelia thought he might, grin and congratulate, but instead looked quite serious. "It's—a hell of a job, sir. But I think the government's finally done something right. I'd be proud to serve you again. Thank you."

Vorkosigan nodded, in agreement and acceptance.

Koudelka did grin, when he picked up the promotion order. "Thanks for this, too, sir."

"Don't thank me too soon. I intend to sweat blood out of you in return."

Koudelka's grin widened. "Nothing new about that." He fumbled clumsily with the collar tabs.

"May I do that, Lieutenant?" asked Cordelia. He looked up defensively. "For my pleasure," she added.

"It would be an honor, Milady."

Cordelia fastened them to his collar straightly, with the greatest care, and stepped back to admire her work. "Congratulations, Lieutenant."

"You can get shiny new ones tomorrow," Vorkosigan said. "But I thought these would do for tonight. I'm springing you out of here now. We'll put you up at the Count, my father's, Residence tonight, because work starts tomorrow at dawn."

Koudelka fingered the red rectangles. "Were they yours, sir?"

"Once. I hope they don't bring you my luck, which was always vile, but—wear them in good health."

Koudelka gave him a nod, and a smile. He clearly found Vorkosigan's gesture profoundly meaningful, exceeding his capacity for words. But the two men understood each other perfectly well without them. "Don't think I want new ones, sir. People would just think I'd been an ensign yesterday."

Later, lying warm in the darkness in Vorkosigan's room in the Count's townhouse, Cordelia remembered a curiosity. "What did you say to the Emperor, about me?"

He stirred beside her, and pulled the sheet tenderly up over her bare shoulder, tenting them together. "Hm? Oh, that." He hesitated. "Ezar had been questioning me about you, in our argument about Escobar. Implied that you had affected my nerve, for the worse. I didn't know then if I'd ever see you again. He wanted to know what I saw in you. I told him . . ." he paused again, and then continued almost shyly, "that you poured out honor like a fountain, all around you."

"That's weird. I don't feel full of honor, or anything else, except maybe confusion."

"Naturally not. Fountains keep nothing for themselves."

THE END

Postlude

>> AFTERMATHS

The shattered ship hung in space, a black bulk in
the darkness. It still turned, imperceptibly slowly;
one edge eclipsed and swallowed the bright point of
a star. The lights of the salvage crew arced over the
skeleton. *Ants, ripping up a dead moth,* Ferrell
thought. *Scavengers . . .*

He sighed dismay into his forward observation
screen, and pictured the ship as it had been, scant
weeks before. The wreckage untwisted in his mind—a
cruiser, alive with patterns of gaudy lights that always made him think of a party seen across night
waters. Responsive as a mirror to the mind under its
Pilot's headset, where man and machine penetrated
the interface and became one. Swift, gleaming, func-
tional . . . No more. He glanced to his right, and
cleared his throat self-consciously.

"Well, Medtech," he spoke to the woman who
stood beside his station, staring into the screen as
silently and long as he had. "There's our starting

point. Might as well go ahead and begin the pattern sweep now, I suppose."

"Yes, please do, Pilot Officer." She had a gravelly alto voice, suitable for her age, which Ferrell judged to be about forty-five. The collection of thin silver five-year service chevrons on her left sleeve made an impressive glitter against the dark red uniform of the Escobaran military medical service. Dark hair shot with grey, cut short for ease of maintenance, not style; a matronly heaviness to her hips. A veteran, it appeared. Ferrell's sleeve had yet to sprout even his first-year stripe, and his hips, and the rest of his body, still maintained an unfilled adolescent stringiness.

But she was only a tech, he reminded himself, not even a physician. He was a full-fledged Pilot Officer. His neurological implants and biofeedback training were all complete. He was certified, licensed, and graduated—just three frustrating days too late to participate in what was now being dubbed the 120 Day War. Although in fact it had only been 118 days and part of an hour between the time the spearhead of the Barrayaran invasion fleet penetrated Escobaran local space, and the time the last survivors fled the counterattack, piling through the wormhole exit for home as though scuttling for a burrow.

"Do you wish to stand by?" he asked her.

She shook her head. "Not yet. This inner area has been pretty well worked over in the last three weeks. I wouldn't expect to find anything on the first four turns, although it's good to be thorough. I've a few things to arrange yet in my work area, and then I think I'll get a catnap. My department has been awfully busy the last few months," she added apologetically. "Understaffed, you know. Please call me if

300

you do spot anything, though—I prefer to handle the tractor myself, whenever possible."

"Fine by me." He swung about in his chair to his comconsole "What minimum mass do you want a bleep for? About forty kilos, say?"

"One kilo is the standard I prefer."

"One kilo!" He stared. "Are you joking?"

"Joking?" She stared back, then seemed to arrive at enlightenment. "Oh, I see. You were thinking in terms of whole—I can make positive identification with quite small pieces, you see. I wouldn't even mind picking up smaller bits than that, but if you go much under a kilo you spend too much time on false alarms from micrometeors and other rubbish. One kilo seems to be the best practical compromise."

"Bleh." But he obediently set his probes for a mass of one kilo, minimum, and finished programming the search sweep.

She gave him a brief nod and withdrew from the closet-sized Navigation and Control Room. The obsolete courier ship had been pulled from junkyard orbit and hastily overhauled with some notion first of converting it into a personnel carrier for middle brass—top brass in a hurry having a monopoly on the new ships—but like Ferrell himself, it had graduated too late to participate. So they both had been re-routed together, he and his first command, to the dull duties he privately thought on a par with sanitation engineering, or worse.

He gazed one last moment at the relic of battle in the forward screen, its structural girdering poking up like bones through sloughing skin, and shook his head at the waste of it all. Then, with a little sigh of pleasure, he pulled his headset down into contact with the silvery circles on his temples and midforehead, closed his eyes, and slid into control of his own ship.

Space seemed to spread itself all around him, buoyant as a sea. He was the ship, he was a fish, he was a merman; unbreathing, limitless, and without pain. He fired his engines as though flame leapt from his fingertips, and began the slow rolling spiral of the search pattern.

"Medtech Boni?" he keyed the intercom to her cabin. "I believe I have something for you here."

She rubbed sleep from her face, framed in the intercom screen. "Already? What time—oh. I must have been tireder than I realized. I'll be right up, Pilot Officer."

Ferrell stretched, and began an automatic series of isometrics in his chair. It had been a long and uneventful watch. He would have been hungry, but what he contemplated now through the viewscreens subdued his appetite.

Boni appeared promptly, and slid into the seat beside him. "Oh, quite right, Pilot Officer." She unshipped the controls to the exterior tractor beam, and flexed her fingers before taking a delicate hold.

"Yeah, there wasn't much doubt about that one," he agreed, leaning back and watching her work. "Why so tender with the tractors?" he asked curiously, noting the low power level she was using.

"Well, they're frozen right through, you know," she replied, not taking her eyes from her readouts. "Brittle. If you play hot-shot and bang them around, they can shatter. Let's stop that nasty spin, first," she added, half to herself. "A slow spin is all right. Seemly. But that fast spinning you get sometimes—it must be very unrestful for them, don't you think?"

302

His attention was pulled from the thing in the screen, and he stared at her. "They're *dead*, lady!"

She smiled slowly as the corpse, bloated from decompression, limbs twisted as though frozen in a strobe-flash of convulsion, was drawn gently toward the cargo bay. "Well, that's not their fault, is it? —one of our fellows, I see by the uniform."

"Bleh!" he repeated himself, then gave vent to an embarrassed laugh. "You act like you enjoy it."

"Enjoy? No . . . But I've been in Personnel Retrieval and Identification for nine years, now. I don't mind. And of course, vacuum work is always a little nicer than planetary work."

"Nicer? With that godawful decompression?"

"Yes, but there are the temperature effects to consider. No decomposition."

He took a breath, and let it out carefully. "I see. I guess you would get—pretty hardened, after a while. Is it true you guys call them corpse-sicles?"

"Some do," she admitted. "I don't."

She maneuvered the twisted thing carefully through the cargo bay doors and keyed them shut. "Temperature set for a slow thaw and he'll be ready to handle in a few hours," she murmured.

"What do you call them?" he asked as she rose.

"People."

She awarded his bewilderment a small smile, like a salute, and withdrew to the temporary mortuary set up next to the cargo bay.

On his next scheduled break he went down himself, drawn by morbid curiosity. He poked his nose around the doorframe. She was seated at her desk. The table in the center of the room was yet unoccupied.

"Uh—hello."

303

She looked up with her quick smile. "Hello, Pilot Officer. Come on in."

"Uh, thank you. You know, you don't really have to be so formal. Call me Falco, if you want," he said, entering.

"Certainly, if you wish. My first name is Tersa."

"Oh, yeah? I have a cousin named Tersa."

"It's a popular name. There were always at least three in my classes at school." She rose, and checked a gauge by the door to the cargo bay. "He should be just about ready to take care of, now. Pulled to shore, so to speak."

Ferrell sniffed, and cleared his throat, wondering whether to stay or excuse himself. "Grotesque sort of fishing." *Excuse myself, I think.*

She picked up the control lead to the float pallet, and trailed it after her into the cargo bay. There were some thumping noises, and she returned, the pallet drifting behind her. The corpse was in the dark blue of a deck officer, and covered thickly with frost, which flaked and dripped upon the floor as the medtech slid it onto the examining table. Ferrell shivered with disgust.

Definitely excuse myself. But he lingered, leaning against the doorframe at a safe distance.

She pulled an instrument, trailing its lead to the computers, from the crowded rack above the table. It was the size of a pencil, and emitted a thin blue beam of light when aligned with the corpse's eyes.

"Retinal identification," Tersa explained. She pulled down a pad-like object, similarly connected, and pressed it to each of the monstrosity's hands. "And fingerprints," she went on. "I always do both, and cross-match. The eyes can get awfully distorted. Errors in identification can be brutal for the families.

Hm. Hm." She checked her readout screen. "Lieutenant Marco Deleo. Age twenty-nine. Well, Lieutenant," she went on chattily, "let's see what I can do for you."

She applied an instrument to its joints, which loosened them, and began removing its clothes.

"Do you often talk to—them?" inquired Ferrell, unnerved.

"Always. It's a courtesy, you see. Some of the things I have to do for them are rather undignified, but they can still be done with courtesy."

Ferrell shook his head. "I think it's obscene, myself."

"Obscene?"

"All this horsing around with dead bodies. All the trouble and expense we go to collecting them. I mean, what do they care? Fifty or a hundred kilos of rotting meat. It'd be cleaner to leave them in space."

She shrugged, unoffended, undiverted from her task. She folded the clothes and inventoried the pockets, laying out their contents in a row.

"I rather like going through the pockets," she remarked. "It reminds me of when I was a little girl, visiting in someone else's home. When I went upstairs by myself, to go to the bathroom or whatever, it was always a kind of pleasure to peek into the other rooms, and see what kind of things they had, and how they kept them. If they were very neat, I was always very impressed—I've never been able to keep my own things neat. If it was a mess, I felt I'd found a secret kindred spirit. A person's things can be a kind of exterior morphology of their mind—like a snail's shell, or something. I like to imagine what kind of person they were, from what's in the pockets. Neat, or messy. Very regulation, or full of personal things . . . Take Lieutenant Deleo, here. He must have been very conscientious. Everything regulation, except this little vid disc from home. From his wife, I'd imagine. I think he must have been a very nice person to know."

She placed the collection of objects carefully into its labeled bag.

"Aren't you going to listen to it?" asked Ferrell.

"Oh, no. That would be prying."

He barked a laugh. "I fail to see the distinction."

"Ah." She completed the medical examination, readied the plastic body bag, and began to wash the corpse. When she worked her way down to the careful cleaning around the genital area, necessary because of sphincter relaxation, Ferrell fled at last.

That woman is nuts, he thought. I wonder if it's the cause of her choice of work, or the effect?

It was another full day before they hooked their next fish. Ferrell had a dream, during his sleep cycle, about being on a deep-sea boat, and hauling up nets full of corpses to be dumped, wet and shining as though with iridescent scales, in a huge pile in the hold. He awoke from it sweating, but with very cold feet. It was with profound relief that he returned to the pilot's station, and slid into the skin of his ship. The ship was clean, mechanical and pure, immortal as a god; one could forget one had ever owned a sphincter muscle.

"Odd trajectory," he remarked, as the medtech again took her place at the tractor controls.

"Yes . . . Oh, I see. He's a Barrayaran. He's a long way from home."

"Oh, bleh. Throw him back."

"Oh, no. We have identification files for all their

missing. Part of the peace settlement, you know, along with prisoner exchange."

"Considering what they did to our people as prisoners, I don't think we owe them a thing."

She shrugged.

The Barrayaran officer had been a tall, broad-shouldered man, a commander by the rank on his collar tabs. The medtech treated him with the same care she had expended on Lieutenant Deleo, and more. She went to considerable trouble to smooth and straighten him, and massage the mottled face back into some semblance of manhood with her fingertips, a process Ferrell watched with a rising gorge.

"I wish his lips wouldn't curl back *quite* so much," she remarked, while at this task. "Gives him what I imagine to be an uncharacteristically snarly look. I think he must have been rather handsome."

One of the objects in his pockets was a little locket. It held a tiny glass bubble filled with a clear liquid. The inside of its gold cover was densely engraved with the elaborate curlicues of the Barrayaran alphabet.

"What is it?" asked Ferrell curiously.

She held it pensively to the light. "It's a sort of charm, or memento. I've learned a lot about the Barrayarans in the last three months. Turn ten of them upside down and you'll find some kind of good luck charm or amulet or medallion or something in the pockets of nine of them. The high-ranking officers are just as bad as the enlisted people."

"Silly superstition."

"I'm not sure if it's superstition or just custom. We treated an injured prisoner once—he claimed it was just custom. People gave them to the soldiers as presents, and that nobody really believes in them.

307

But when we took his away from him, when we were undressing him for surgery, he tried to fight us for it. It took three of us to hold him down for the anesthetic. I thought it a rather remarkable performance for a man whose legs had been blown away. He wept . . . Of course, he was in shock."

Ferrell dangled the locket on the end of its short chain, intrigued in spite of himself. It hung with a companion piece, a curl of hair embedded in a plastic pendant.

"Some sort of holy water, is it?" he inquired.

"Almost. It's a very common design. It's called a mother's tears charm. Let me see if I can make out—he's had it a while, it seems. From the inscription—I think that says 'ensign,' and the date—it must have been given him on the occasion of his commission."

"It's not really his mother's tears, is it?"

"Oh, yes. That's what's supposed to make it work, as a protection."

"Doesn't seem to be very effective."

"No, well . . . No."

Ferrell snorted ironically. "I hate those guys—but I do guess I feel sort of sorry for his mother."

Boni retrieved the chain and its pendants, holding the curl in plastic to the light and reading its inscription. "No, not at all. She's a fortunate woman."

"How so?"

"This is her death lock. She died three years ago, by this."

"Is that supposed to be lucky, too?"

"No, not necessarily. Just a remembrance, as far as I know. Kind of a nice one, really. The nastiest charm I ever ran across, and the most unique, was this little leather bag hung around a fellow's neck. It was filled with dirt and leaves, and what I took at first to be some sort of little frog-like animal skeleton, about ten centimeters long. But when I looked at it more closely, it turned out to be the skeleton of a human fetus. Very strange. I suppose it was some sort of black magic. Seemed an odd thing to find on an engineering officer."

"Doesn't seem to work for any of them, does it?"

She smiled wryly. "Well, if there are any that work, I wouldn't see them, would I?"

She took the processing one step further, by cleaning the Barrayaran's clothes and carefully re-dressing him, before bagging him and returning him to the freeze.

"The Barrayarans are all so army-mad," she explained. "I always like to put them back in their uniforms. They mean so much to them, I'm sure they're more comfortable with them on."

Ferrell frowned uneasily. "I still think he ought to be dumped with the rest of the garbage."

"Not at all," said the medtech. "Think of all the work he represents on somebody's part. Nine months of pregnancy, childbirth, two years of diapering, and that's just the beginning. Tens of thousands of meals, thousands of bedtime stories, years of school. Dozens of teachers. And all that military training, too. A lot of people went into making him."

She smoothed a strand of the corpse's hair into place. "That head held the universe, once. He had a good rank for his age," she added, rechecking her monitor. "Thirty-two. Commander Aristede Vorkalloner. It has a kind of nice ethnic ring. Very Barrayaranish, that name. Vor, too, one of those warrior-class fellows."

"Homicidal-class loonies. Or worse," Ferrell said

automatically. But his vehemence had lost momentum, somehow.

Boni shrugged. "Well, he's joined the great de-
mocracy now. And he had nice pockets."

Three full days went by with no further alarms but
a rare scattering of mechanical debris. Ferrell began
to hope the Barrayaran was the last pick-up they
would have to make. They were nearing the end of
their search pattern. Besides, he thought resentfully,
this duty was sabotaging the efficiency of his sleep
cycle. But the medtech made a request.

"If you don't mind, Falco," she said, "I'd greatly
appreciate it if we could run the pattern out just a
few extra turns. The original orders are based on this
average estimated trajectory speed, you see, and if
someone just happened to get a bit of extra kick
when the ship split, they could well be beyond it by
now."

Ferrell was less than thrilled, but the prospect of
an extra day of piloting had its attractions, and he gave
a grudging consent. Her reasoning proved itself; before the day was half done, they turned up another
gruesome relic.

"Oh," muttered Ferrell, when they got a close
look. It had been a female officer. Boni reeled her in
with enormous tenderness. He didn't really want to
go watch, this time, but the medtech seemed to have
come to expect him.

"I—don't really want to look at a woman blown
up," he tried to excuse himself.

"Mm," said Tersa. "Is it fair, though, to reject a
person just because they're dead? You wouldn't have
minded her body a bit when she was alive."

310

He laughed a little, macabrely. "Equal rights for the dead?"

Her smile twisted. "Why not? Some of my best friends are corpses."

He snorted.

She grew more serious. "I'd—sort of like the company, on this one." So he took up his usual station by the door.

The medtech laid out the thing that had been a woman upon her table, undressed, inventoried, washed, and straightened it. When she finished, she kissed the dead lips.

"Oh, God," cried Ferrell, shocked and nauseated. "You *are* crazy! You're a damn, damn necrophiliac! A *lesbian* necrophiliac, at that!" He turned to go.

"Is that what it looks like, to you?" Her voice was soft, and still unoffended. It stopped him, and he looked over his shoulder. She was looking at him as gently as if he had been one of her precious corpses. "What a strange world you must live in, inside your head."

She opened a suitcase, and shook out a dress, fine underwear, and a pair of white embroidered slippers. A wedding dress, Ferrell realized. This woman is a bona fide *psychopath* . . .

She dressed the corpse, and arranged its soft dark hair with great delicacy, before bagging it.

"I believe I shall place her next to that nice tall Barrayaran," she said. "I think they would have liked each other very well, if they could have met in another place and time. And Lieutenant Deleo was married, after all."

She completed the label. Ferrell's battered mind was sending him little subliminal messages; he struggled to overcome his shock and bemusement, and pay attention. It tumbled into the open day of his consciousness with a start.

She had not run an identification check on this one.

Out the door, he told himself, is the way you want to walk. I guarantee it. Instead, timorously, he went over to the corpse and checked its label.

Ensign Sylva Boni, it said. *Age twenty*. His own age . . .

He was trembling, as if with cold. It *was* cold, in that room. Tersa Boni finished packing up the suitcase, and turned back with the float pallet.

"Daughter?" he asked. It was all he could ask.

She pursed her lips, and nodded.

"It's—a helluva coincidence."

"No coincidence at all. I asked for this sector."

"Oh." He swallowed, turned away, turned back, face flaming. "I'm sorry I said—"

She smiled her slow sad smile. "Never mind."

They found yet one more bit of mechanical debris, so agreed to run another cycle of the search spiral, to be sure that all possible trajectories had been outdistanced. And yes, they found another; a nasty one, spinning fiercely, guts split open from some great blow and hanging out in a frozen cascade.

The acolyte of death did her dirty work without once so much as wrinkling her nose. When it came to the washing, the least technical of the tasks, Ferrell said suddenly, "May I help?"

"Certainly," said the medtech, moving aside. "An honor is not diminished for being shared."

And so he did, as shy as an apprentice saint washing his first leper.

"Don't be afraid," she said. "The dead cannot hurt

you. They give you no pain, except that of seeing your own death in their faces. And one can face that, I find."

Yes, he thought, the good face pain. But the great— they embrace it.

Headline books are available at your book-shop or newsagent, or can be ordered from the following address:

Headline Book Publishing PLC
Cash Sales Department
PO Box 11
Falmouth
Cornwall
TR10 9EN
England

UK customers please send cheque or postal order (no currency), allowing 60p for postage and packing for the first book, plus 25p for the second book and 15p for each additional book ordered up to a maximum charge of £1.90 in UK.

BFPO customers please allow 60p for postage and packing for the first book, plus 25p for the second book and 15p per copy for the next seven books, thereafter 9p per book.

Overseas and Eire customers please allow £1.25 for postage and packing for the first book, plus 75p for the second book and 28p for each subsequent book.